"I love you, Marge," Nate murmured. "Tell me what's wrong. Maybe I can help."

For long moments she pressed her face tightly to his shoulder. "You can't help," she said finally. "There's nothing anyone can do."

"Then tell me. It helps to talk."

"You'd never understand. Never. I don't want to lose you, Nate. I'd die if I lost you...."

"Why do you think you'd lose me?" It was amazingly difficult to ask that question. He couldn't imagine what was so awful that she'd fear such a thing, but the fact that she did was enough to clamp a vise on his chest and make it almost impossible to breathe.

And it got even worse when she didn't answer but instead burst into fresh tears. All he could do was hold her and wait for this storm to pass.

And hope that it wasn't about to tear his life to shreds.

Dear Reader,

I just have to start telling you about this month's books with Dallas Schulze's *Michael's Father,* our American Hero title. For Kel Bryan, Megan Roarke was the answer to a heartfelt prayer—until she left him alone on the ranch, taking with her a secret that could change his life. Then it's back to Conard County with Rachel Lee's *Point of No Return,* a look inside the marriage of Nate and Marge Tate as the past returns to haunt them. Doreen Roberts sets your soul on fire in *Where There's Smoke,* while Maggie Shayne throws off enough heat to melt... Well, see for yourself in *Miranda's Viking.* Jo Leigh's *Suspect* matches a by-the-book cop with the most beautiful suspected murderess ever to cross his path. Finally, in *True Blue,* new author Ingrid Weaver puts her own spin on the classic tale of a good girl falling for an oh-so-bad boy.

In months to come, more excitement will be coming your way in books by authors such as Kathleen Korbel, Linda Turner, Judith Duncan and Marilyn Pappano, to name only a few of the favorite writers entertaining you every month—here in Silhouette Intimate Moments.

Enjoy!

Leslie Wainger
Senior Editor and Editorial Coordinator

Please address questions and book requests to:
Reader Service
U.S.: P.O. Box 1325, Buffalo, NY 14269
Canadian: P.O. Box 1050, Niagara Falls, Ont. L2E 7G7

POINT OF NO RETURN

Rachel Lee

Silhouette® ™
INTIMATE MOMENTS®

Published by Silhouette Books

America's Publisher of Contemporary Romance

SILHOUETTE BOOKS

ISBN 0-373-07566-9

POINT OF NO RETURN

Copyright © 1994 by Susan Civil

Books by Rachel Lee

Silhouette Intimate Moments

An Officer and a Gentleman #370
Serious Risks #394
Defying Gravity #430
*Exile's End #449
*Cherokee Thunder #463
*Miss Emmaline and the Archangel #482
*Ironheart #494
*Lost Warriors #535
*Point of No Return #566

*Conard County series

Silhouette Shadows

Imminent Thunder #10

RACHEL LEE

wrote her first play in the third grade for a school assembly, and by the age of twelve she was hooked on writing. She's lived all over the United States, on both the East and West coasts, and now resides in Florida.

Having held jobs as a security officer, real estate agent and optician, she uses these, as well as her natural flair for creativity, to write stories that are undeniably romantic. "After all, life is the biggest romantic adventure of all—and if you're open and aware, the most marvelous things are just waiting to be discovered."

To Cris Brown—
Sometimes only the heart can see.

ACKNOWLEDGMENTS

My deepest thanks to Nathaniel Brown for invaluable law research, for unstinting help and advice in the murky mires of divorce and adoption.

Thanks to dear friend Judy Newton for directing me to LCDR John Wrenn, SEAL Team 2, Little Creek NS, VA. LCDR Wrenn was kind enough to share his insights and answer questions.

Many thanks also to Tom Smith, a former SEAL who served in Vietnam. Tom shared some truly invaluable insights.

And, of course, any errors are mine.

Prologue

There was a strange truck parked out front, with a man sitting in it.

Marge Tate paused by the bay window in the living room and looked out through the sheers at the summer day. The light had the flat look of noon, and even though it wasn't too hot, heat shimmered up off the paved street.

Salesman? she wondered. But no, a salesman would be knocking on doors, not sitting in a truck looking as if he had nowhere to go. Or as if he had arrived and now didn't know what to do about it.

She didn't recognize the truck, or the driver's silhouette, and the longer she watched him sit there, the more she thought perhaps she ought to call her husband and ask him to send a deputy around to check it out. But even as she started to turn away from the window to go to the phone, she hesitated. If she called, Nate would come himself, and she hated to drag him away from his work.

Just then, the man in the truck climbed out. Standing on the far side, he was visible from the waist up. Marge relaxed as soon as she recognized the khaki shirt and garrison cap of a military uniform. Some friend of Nate's, certainly. She was used to unexpected visits from people Nate had met on his travels over the years, good people whom he always invited to drop by if they were in the area. And a surprising number of them did just that, lured by Nate's personality and glowing tales of the peace and beauty to be found in Conard County, Wyoming.

Smiling at her own thoughts, at thoughts of her husband, Marge went to the door to open it. Usually visitors hunted Nate up at the sheriff's office, but perhaps this one had been given his home address for some reason. It never occurred to her she might have anything to fear.

As she opened the door, she saw the man striding up the sidewalk toward her. Something familiar about him struck a chord within her, and another smile curved her mouth as she tried to remember where they had met.

But as he walked closer, the smile on her face began to fade, and her hands clasped over her stomach, a woman's instinctive protective gesture. She knew that walk. She knew the set of those shoulders.

She almost knew the face. It was as if she looked at a familiar photograph that had blurred somehow, sharpening some features, softening others. Erasing years. Erasing twenty-seven years.

In an instant, with gut-searing certainty, she knew her worst nightmare and her best dream were coming to pass. A buzzing filled her ears, and her vision narrowed to a small tunnel, at the end of which stood a tall young man in the uniform of a naval petty officer. A man who would be twenty-six, almost twenty-seven now. A man she had thought she would never see and had always hoped she would.

Reaching out, she braced herself against the doorjamb, battling weakness and fear and joy and terror. Battling shock. It couldn't be. It couldn't be.

"Mrs. Tate?" The voice came from far away.

She stiffened, straightening, locking her hands together across her waist, determined to face these moments. Determined to handle the next few minutes with all the dignity and composure she could muster. She had always known this moment would come. Somehow she had always known.

But for one wild instant as she looked up into a face that was too familiar, she tried to deny what her heart told her. Surely there were other men in the world who resembled Nathan Tate as much... or more. Surely.

But surely none of them would be walking up to her on a fine August afternoon in Conard County, Wyoming. The beautiful ends of the earth, Nate always called it. No, none of his look-alikes could be here by accident, could they?

The man stopped five or six feet away, giving her space she needed as the afternoon became ominous, and the air became too thick to breathe.

"Mrs. Tate, I'm Seth Hardin. I'm the child you gave up for adoption twenty-seven years ago."

It was as if the world spiraled away. Everything ceased to exist save her and Seth Hardin. In an endless instant of shocked acceptance of what her heart had already realized and her mind had tried to deny, everything else vanished. Going wonderfully, blessedly numb, she stepped back, opening the door wide.

"Come in."

She led the way to the kitchen. She didn't even think about it; in the Tate household all major matters were discussed around the large, round oak pedestal table that had come down to Marge from her great-grandmother. Motioning Seth to a seat, she asked if he'd like coffee. The request was automatic, and it hung awkwardly in the air, as if they both realized at the same instant that the simple courtesy hardly fit the moment.

"Thank you," Seth said. "Black, if it's no trouble."

It was no trouble. In the Tate household, there was always a pot of fresh coffee for drop-in visitors. It gave her another few moments, but finally there was no longer any way to avoid looking at him. No longer any way to pretend this wasn't actually happening. The muffling numbness of shock was just beginning to wear off.

She couldn't sit. She couldn't make herself adopt a relaxed posture, or, in fact, even stay that close. On the far side of the kitchen, she leaned back against the counter and folded her arms beneath her breasts.

He was an attractive young man, she thought. As handsome as Nate had been at that age. Very like Nate, with his dark eyes, dark hair and weather-tanned skin. Early crow's-feet at his eyes proclaimed him a man who lived largely outdoors. She wondered if anyone but her would notice the resemblance. Probably not. Nate's features were more rugged, more bluntly shaped. This young man had the look of her grandfather... hawkish.

She suddenly drew a shaky breath as she realized that she had recognized him at least as much because of that resemblance as any resemblance to Nate. No, only she would have recognized him, but having recognized him there was no doubt at all in her mind that this tall, competent stranger in a naval uniform was her son. Knife-edged pain gripped her as she faced the absolute, stark reality of the connection, of what was happening.

Seth rose abruptly, a tall, lean specimen of physical conditioning. A SEAL, she realized with some corner of her mind as she noticed for the first time the trident insignia he wore on his left breast, above rows of ribbons. A SEAL. Her son had become a SEAL, and his father had been a Green Beret....

Circles, she thought. Circles ever spiraling, and closing no matter what....

"Mrs. Tate? Mrs. Tate, are you all right?"

All right? *All right?* She stared at him as he stood on the other side of the table, looking ready to fly to her aid, and wondered how he could even ask such a question.

"Why didn't you call first?" The question burst from her with anguished force as the full impact hit her. The girls could have been home. Nate could have been here. She needed time to deal with this, time to explain to Nate, time to explain to herself why a young frightened girl had given up her child under pressure from every quarter, some way

to make Nate understand that when he didn't reply to her letters she had thought . . . had thought . . .

"Oh, my God," she whispered. "Oh, my God."

Whirling, she turned her back to him and hugged herself as she stared blindly down at the counter. The girls. How would she ever explain to their daughters... "Oh, my God!"

Long minutes ticked by in utter silence, but finally Seth spoke. "I didn't intend to introduce myself to you," he said finally. "I just came because I had to see . . ."

"Just had to see?" Marge turned again, facing him. "Had to see *what?*"

"You," he said simply. "You're my mother."

The simple statement was breathtaking in its impact. Seth Hardin spoke the words unflinchingly, but they didn't strike Marge Tate that way. With a trembling hand, she pushed her fiery hair back from her forehead and closed her eyes. For twenty-seven years she had grieved for her lost child, had felt guilty for giving him up, guilty for not telling her husband he had a son. For all those years she had wondered if her child was all right, whether he was still alive, whether her son had grown up to be a man to be proud of. No, there was nothing simple about any of this.

"Just to see," she said, opening her eyes and staring into a strange but familiar face. "Just to see. The way people come to look at animals in the zoo?"

"No! Mrs. Tate . . . look." He spread his hands. "Curiosity was driving me mad. Plus, my adoptive parents died while I was in Iraq during Desert Storm. They were the only family I had. And then . . . well, I decided to look for my birth parents. But I don't want to disrupt your life. I'm quite serious about that. I intended to come, knock on your door and give you some excuse about needing directions, and then I was going to look around town a little and leave."

He shook his head. "In all honesty, ma'am, I don't know why I told you the truth. It was never my intention to cause you any trouble."

She looked away a moment, hardly able to absorb what he was saying as she battled the shock of his presence. She knew why he had told her the truth, though. He had seen the recognition on her face. The knowledge.

She had once been a scared child who had, under pressure and believing her boyfriend to have lost interest, given up a child for adoption. But she was no longer a child, and years of raising six daughters and loving a man who was sheriff had given her backbone. Seth Hardin's presence must be dealt with.

"I . . . need time," she said. "I need time to prepare my husband. My daughters. I can't just spring you on them...." Looking at him again, she saw him shake his head.

"You don't need to prepare anyone for me. I told you, I don't want to disrupt your life. I wanted a look at you. A look at my father. Maybe figure out a way to speak to you both for a few minutes without telling you who I was. I'm serious, Mrs. Tate. I just wanted to know my roots."

He still stood on the far side of the table, so proud and serious, so tall and straight. Enough to make any mother's heart swell with pride. Enough to make young women swoon, as once Nate had done.

"You can't be serious," she heard herself say. "You can't possibly be serious."

One corner of his mouth lifted in a charming half smile. "I know it's hard to believe after the way I introduced myself, but I really am serious. If you can spare a few minutes to speak with me, and tell me how I might find my biological father so I can perhaps pass a few words with him, I'd be grateful. But I have no desire to wreck your marriage or upset your children."

He didn't know, she realized. He had no idea who his father was. And when he found out, he was going to be unable to understand why she had given him up. Just as Nate could never possibly understand. She had to tell him. Had to tell Nate. He'd always wanted a son. . . .

"I'll tell him," she heard herself say. "I'll tell him."

Seth Hardin shook his head. "Absolutely not. Look. I'm the one who was given up, and I'm the one who was adopted, and I think I should be the one to decide who I tell who I am. I don't want my father to know. Absolutely not."

"But . . ." Now she was truly confused. "Why not? And why did you come if you don't want anyone to know?"

And suddenly Seth Hardin's face was sculpted stone. "It's really quite simple, Mrs. Tate. Family isn't a matter of biology, it's a matter of love. There's no love here, only a small curiosity on my part. Quite frankly, I'm not sure I want to share my life with either of you."

There was nothing insulting in the way he spoke, merely a matter-of-fact recognition that they were strangers. Intellectually, she understood what he was saying, but emotionally it felt like a slap in the face.

Seth seemed to realize that. While his face never softened, he spoke more kindly. "I don't know you, you see. And you don't know me. And we might not like each other at all. There's no obligation between us of any kind, and I don't want anyone to think there is. I'd like to meet my father, but I want the absolute freedom to walk away if I don't care to know him. And I think you *owe* me that much."

"Owe you?" Suddenly she was fighting mad. "I owed you life, once you were conceived, and I gave it to you. I owed you a good home, and since I couldn't provide it myself at the time, I gave you to an agency that promised you would have one. Whatever I owed you, I gave you! Now you want me to lie to my husband—"

She broke off in horror, realizing what she had just revealed—that her husband, who didn't know of Seth's existence, was his father.

"Isn't that what you've been doing all along?"

Seth's words fell like heavy stones into her heart, each one striking as a painful blow. *Isn't that what you've been doing all along?* Lying to her husband. Protecting him, but lying all the same. Anguish paralyzed her. From eyes that were filling with tears, she stared at this stranger who was her son, and wondered if anything at all could be salvaged from this terrible, terrible mess.

After a moment, Seth sighed. "Look, just come over here and sit down, okay? I want to hear whatever you've got to say about what happened all those years ago. I'm not here to play hanging judge. I'd just like to *know*."

She glanced at the clock and saw she had hours yet before the youngest girls would be home from school. Before Nate would come home for the day. Hours. And if somebody dropped in...

She looked back at Seth. "How do you want to be explained?"

"Say I'm a distant cousin's kid. An old friend's kid. Surely there's something that'll fit. I'll be gone in an hour or so, anyway. I've got a flight to catch this afternoon."

So she came to the table, a little warily, and sat facing him. "What do you want to know?"

He shook his head. "What happened. A little about you. About the man who fathered me. Just an outline to fill in the biggest blanks."

Tell me why you gave me away. For twenty-seven years she had had a recurrent dream in which a child's piping voice recited that demand. And always, always, she awoke with her face wet with tears to wonder how she could reply. And now she had to reply. This was one more thing she owed her stranger-son.

"My husband is your father," she said finally, her voice scratchy. "Nathan Tate. We...weren't married when you were conceived. I was still in high school, as a matter of fact. Nate and I had dated for two years over my parents objections...." She shook her head. "This is all so hard to explain simply. It was all so complicated! My parents hated Nate. He was a hell-raiser, a troublemaker, a good-for-nothing, going-to-hell kid in their eyes. Of course he wasn't. But they thought he was, because he was a little wild, because his mother was divorced... Lord, that was a major crime back then! Anyway, I used to have to meet him in secret."

Seth nodded encouragingly, and there was no mistaking his interest.

"Then he enlisted in the army and volunteered for the Special Forces. When next I saw him, he had finished his training and was getting ready to ship out to Vietnam. And he wasn't a boy any longer. He was a man."

She lifted her eyes to Seth, and saw understanding. He had probably become a man in the same way, she realized. In the SEALs.

"At that point, we had never been together. Never. Nate was always so careful of me. More than I was of myself, I think." She had to close her eyes to continue, and on her knees her hands turned into fists. "Just before he had to leave... I think both of us kind of lost our heads because he was going and might never return. I know... I know I wanted to give him...myself. Because it was all I could give. Because..."

A broken breath, almost a sob, silenced her for a moment as she remembered. Nearly forgetting Seth, she returned to the past.

"Anyway, when he'd been gone for two months, I knew for sure I was pregnant. I hadn't heard from him in all that time, but I assumed he was somewhere he couldn't write from. He'd warned me that might happen sometimes, and I wasn't to worry. I worried, anyway. And then I was pregnant. I wrote him, and he didn't answer. I wrote again and still no answer. And then I was four months along and there was no way of hiding the truth anymore."

She drew a long, shaky sigh. "There was no question at the time. Unwed mothers didn't keep their babies. It wasn't done. Reverend Castille told me I had to give you up, that it wouldn't be fair to you to keep you, to have you raised a bastard child whose father hadn't wanted him.... And I didn't dare tell anyone else.

"And then Nate's mother was told that he was missing in action and presumed dead. Somebody had seen him fall in a firefight, they said. Later it turned out not to be true, of course, but...I was wrecked. I would have told his mother about you, for comfort, I guess, except that she left town. Just packed and left, nobody knew where to. By the time they sent me off to my cousin Lou in Colorado to have the baby... Well, giving you up seemed like the only thing to do."

She looked at him with sudden intensity from eyes that seemed to burn. "The only part of this I'm proud of is that

I refused to abort you. I didn't show a whole lot of back-bone, I admit, but on that subject I didn't let my father push me. I couldn't let him. I thought you were the last living part of Nate left in the world.''

Drawing a shuddery breath, she covered her mouth with her hand and closed her eyes, aching with remembered pain, aching with the pain of now. Silently, she shook her head.

"Anyhow, Nate came home on leave when his first tour was up. By then we knew he was alive. Even I knew he was alive. You see—" she opened her eyes "—my father was intercepting all the mail. My letters never went out, and the letters Nate wrote to me were destroyed as soon as my father removed them from the post office box. So... Nate didn't know about you. And I thought he didn't want me, and..." Biting her lip, she looked away.

"It sounds incredible now, doesn't it? But that's what happened. Nate came back, hopping mad because I hadn't written, and once we straightened everything out between us we eloped. And I never mentioned you because it was too late. It was too late, and I just couldn't bring myself to tell him something that would cause him so much pain. Something he couldn't fix. Something beyond fixing.''

Drawing a shaky breath, she closed her eyes against the threatening tears. "I made a kind of peace with myself over the years, Seth," she said unsteadily. "I never forgot about you, but I believed I had done the best I could, under the circumstances. And I believed that protecting Nate from the hurt was good, too. We have six daughters now. He would have loved a son. Not that he doesn't love his daughters, but he would have loved a son. And between us, my parents and I deprived him of that.

"But I did the best I could at the time. Hindsight always shows things in a different light, but when I remember who I was, what I believed, what I thought, the options available to me... I did the best I could. And when I knew it had been the wrong thing, it was too late to change anything.''

Seth didn't say a word. She suspected he was absorbing all that she told him, and that he was allowing her time to deal with her anguish. He seemed not to have any anguish at all about this—although there was no reason he should, if he had a good adoptive home.

But there was one more thing she wanted him to know. "I dream about you. Never a month goes by that I don't dream of a little boy who asks me, 'Why did you give me away?'"

At that confession, she heard him draw a long breath. "I'm sorry, Mrs. Tate," he said. "Truly sorry. I had no intention of stirring things up for you."

She looked at him then from eyes that brimmed with tears. "I recognized you. I didn't expect to, you know. I told myself for years that I could pass you on the street and never know you. But I never stopped looking, either. I looked for Nate in every face, especially when we went to Denver, because Denver was where I gave you up."

He nodded slowly. "I was raised in Denver."

"I . . . thought so. So I looked. But I was sure I'd never recognize you. And then when you came up the driveway. . . You walk just like Nate. You hold yourself the same way. And you look like him. And like my grandfather. And I knew you."

"I thought so. I think that's why I couldn't pretend. You looked so shocked." He shook his head. "Look. I'm not going to shake things up for you. There's really no point, is there? I'll just be going. . . ."

"No." Her insides twisted at what she was about to say, but she couldn't let this young man go. Not like this. "Nate . . . Nate would want to know you. And I think he should."

"And I told you, I'm not sure I want to know you. Or him. Look, Mrs. Tate, let's be honest here. Our connection is purely biological. I don't know you. We're strangers. He might not like me. I might not like him. It might get really uncomfortable or painful for one of us."

"You'll like him. Everybody likes Nate. Everybody. And he'd be so proud to know his son is a SEAL." Reaching out impulsively, she touched his arm. "He was so like you at your age. The same arrogance."

"Arrogance?" For a moment, he looked almost as if he might smile, but then he shook his head. "The arrogance, as you call it, is a Special Forces trait, not a genetic one."

"He's a good man, Seth. Folks around here don't keep reelecting him sheriff for any other reason. There's not a doubt in my mind you'd be glad to know him."

He opened his mouth, as if about to argue, then closed it and looked away. Marge had the definite feeling he wasn't accustomed to indecisiveness, or rethinking his decisions.

She also couldn't believe she was pressing for this. Nate's reaction when he learned about Seth was going to be explosive. She couldn't be sure he would ever be able to stand looking at her again.

And yet, it was suddenly impossible to continue to live this lie. Seth was no longer a child she had heard squawling as it was carried away, a dim memory of loss. He was now a real, living, breathing man who was her husband's son. A son she suspected Nate would be very proud of.

And Nate had always wanted a son, though he had never actually said so. She had known for years that, much as he loved his six daughters, he'd felt the lack of a boy. It had been evident to her the last few times she gave birth, the minute moment of adjustment he had made when the doctor announced another girl. An adjustment so minute that it was undetectable to anyone but his wife. She had seen it, though, and carried the ache in her heart, an ache all the worse for knowing he really did have a son. The son she had given away.

Seth suddenly impaled her with dark brown eyes. This was the stare of a man who knew all that he was capable of, and was not afraid to use it. A man who expected no arguments because he could win them all. "You absolutely will not tell him who I am."

"But..."

Seth silenced her with a sharp shake of his head. "This is my condition, Mrs. Tate. If I choose to walk, I want to be able to walk away without worrying about the impact on others. Otherwise, I'll leave right now and that will be the end of this."

"But..." But it would mean continuing the lie. She'd lost count of the nights she'd lain awake, smothering in guilt because she lived a lie. Smothering a need to confess, to ease her guilt, knowing confession could only inflict pain on the man she loved above life.

Seth's arrival had presented a reason to confess, she realized now. Her weary conscience had seized on him as a reason to alleviate her guilt, as a justification for the pain the truth would inflict on Nate. Realizing that, realizing that her silence now might get Nate a son while it could hardly make matters much worse, she nodded.

"All right," she said. "I won't tell him who you are."

Seth nodded. "Fine, then. I have to leave today. Very shortly, as a matter of fact. But I'll let you know when I can come back for a few days or a week. It probably won't be for months yet. If you need to explain me, say I'm the son of a friend you haven't seen in years."

"Candy Walker," Marge said after a moment. "We were best of friends in high school. Nate would remember her. She moved away right after graduation and doesn't have any family here now."

Suddenly Marge rose. "I want to show you something before you go. I'll be right back."

In a box on the closet shelf in the bedroom were Nate's mementos from his seven years in the Special Forces. Marge pulled the box down and lifted away the green beret, the boxes of medals, the packets of letters he had written her after their marriage, all tied up in a red ribbon.

And when she reached the bottom, she lifted out a photo album. This album was not kept with the others, because it contained the photographic history of Nate's military years. The pictures of friends he had fought beside, many dead. The young men he had considered to be sons. The places where they had shed their blood.

And pictures of Nate. She wanted Seth to see those. She very much wanted Seth to see those.

She expected a questioning look, or perhaps reluctance when she placed the album before him. Instead, without hesitation, he simply opened it.

The first photo was a black-and-white portrait of Nate in his army greens, with his green beret perched jauntily on his head. He had given that to her before he went on his first tour to Nam. Right there, Seth seemed to freeze. After a full minute, he lifted his gaze to Marge's face. It was evident to her he had seen the strong resemblance.

"I'll be back. Probably around Christmas."

With that, he stood, reached for his hat and walked out of the house. Marge stood at the living room window and watched him walk away. It seemed she hadn't been the only one to get a shock this afternoon. Seth Hardin had looked into the face of his father. He *would* return. There was not a doubt in her mind.

Chapter 1

From the window of the front office at the sheriff's department, the day looked uninviting. Winter had once again settled over Conard County, Wyoming, and had brought leaden skies, a layer of snow that had begun to look grimy alongside the streets and colder-than-usual temperatures.

Sheriff Nathan Tate stood with his hands on his hips and stared out across the street at the Courthouse Square, where wrought-iron-and-wood benches sat unoccupied and the sidewalks were gritty with sand. From between rows of leafless trees, the Victorian Gothic horror of the courthouse rose in somebody's idea of splendor. Nate always figured somebody from back East had been responsible for that architecture, but he'd never bothered to check it out.

Sighing, he looked past the courthouse to the shops on the other side of the square. It was a quiet day in Conard County. Behind him, Velma Jansen, the dispatcher, puffed on a cigarette and waited for the radio to squawk. At the duty desk, Dave Winters read a girlie magazine that was discreetly tucked inside a newsmagazine. Dave would probably have flushed bright red if he realized that his boss had long since figured out he wasn't *that* fascinated with news.

And this morning Nate didn't give a damn what Dave was reading, anyway. This morning all he could think about was his wife of twenty-six years and the strange way she was acting. Something was definitely wrong, had been wrong for a couple of months now, and Nate had a hole growing in his gut from worrying about it. More than once he'd asked her what was bothering her, but every time Marge just shook her head. "Nothing, I'm just thinking" was the most she would say.

Smothering another sigh, aware that Velma would start asking him what the hell was wrong if he sighed too many times, he turned around and went back to his office. Stacks of paperwork were awaiting his attention as always, but he ignored them.

Four months ago he'd started a diet-and-exercise regimen that had put him back in a physical condition almost as good as the one he'd enjoyed so long ago when he'd been in the Special Forces. Now that he was lean and fit again, it was harder than ever to sit still and shuffle papers. And it was driving him crazy that he had his thirty-four-inch waist back and his wife didn't even notice.

There had been a time when Marge Whelan had thought that Nathan Tate was the handsomest man who ever walked the face of the earth. They had become sweethearts during high school, had dated exclusively, even though Marge's parents didn't approve of Nate, whom they classified as a hellion.

And at the end of Marge's junior year, just after Nate finished his Special Forces training and was on leave before shipping out to Vietnam, they became lovers. Even now, all these years later, his heart leapt as he remembered those stolen times, those wonderful, unforgettable moments of their first lovemaking.

But he had left for Vietnam without making any promises or demanding any, because he knew there was a high likelihood he would never return. Special Forces A-Teams worked behind enemy lines.

But he *had* returned, a year later, and the first thing he had done was ask Marge to marry him. And she had. Even though at that time he had intended to make the army a career. Even though he would be going back to Nam. Marge had loved him so much, she said, that she would take each moment life gave them and be grateful even if there was never to be another one.

Now, out of the clear blue, she wasn't interested in his touch. Forty times a day he wondered if she was having an affair with someone . . . only he was sure she wasn't. He would know. That he believed. In his heart he would know.

So what the hell was wrong?

Something was eating the woman alive. She'd lost weight, dropped those few extra pounds the years had given her . . . pounds which he had been quite fond of, actually. Now she was as lean as she had been in high school. Too thin, in his opinion.

And lately it seemed every time he looked at her, he became freshly aware of the passing years. It wasn't that Marge looked old. Hell, to his way of thinking she could put to shame a lot of women fifteen, even twenty, years younger. But all of a sudden he was noticing those silver threads in her fiery hair. Noticing the faint little crow's-feet by her green eyes. Noticing the laugh lines were etched a teeny bit deeper.

Mortality was looking him in the eyes . . . and he was scared to death he was losing her.

It was a terrible thing to face, a possibility awful to contemplate. He found himself remembering every single occasion when he had failed her somehow. The emergency calls that had dragged him out of bed in the dead of night. The missed dinners, the forgotten anniversaries. Hell, he was no saint, and he knew it. But up until just lately, he had never wondered if that had bothered Marge. She had always been so understanding. Had always laughed off his apologies and kissed him into silence. Marge had been the saint in their marriage.

Oh, there had been plenty of times she had blown her stack. She was a redhead, after all. He smiled faintly at the old joke that always ruffled Marge's feathers. She had no more temper than anyone else in the world, not really, and she *hated* it when people implied she had a worse temper because of her coloring. He could always get a rise out of her with that one.

But that wasn't the point. The point was that she was not being herself. The point was that he was remembering every time he had failed as a husband and a father, and was wondering if they had somehow all accumulated until at last she could barely tolerate him.

Or what if she felt unfulfilled? What if she felt she had wasted the last twenty-five years? What if she was thinking that being a wife and mother and all-around volunteer had left her unsatisfied? What if she was thinking it was time she had a life of her own? For herself?

He'd heard that happened with women when the kids started growing up and leaving. Marge had done what was expected of a woman of her generation ... and maybe now she was regretting it.

Maybe after all these years she looked at her husband and realized the love had died somewhere along the way and that now there was nothing left.

Aw, hell, this wasn't helping a thing. He snatched up his hat and jacket, put them on and headed out.

He didn't quite make it. Just as he stomped into the front office, the outside door opened, and a man in a blue wool naval uniform stepped inside. The sight was so unusual in Wyoming that activity came to a complete halt.

Nate's first reaction was one of irritation that someone was getting between him and the door. His next realization was that he knew this guy. Somehow, from somewhere, he knew him. There was something too familiar about the face, about the stance....

A SEAL. He recognized the "budweiser," the brass insignia with its oversize trident, the arrogant badge of a greater pride. But the man was too young to be a Special Forces contemporary. Far too young. Under thirty for all the elements had left a mark on him.

Dave Winters was the first to move. Slapping his magazines shut, he shoved them into a drawer while rising to his feet. "Can I help you?"

"I'm Seth Hardin," the SEAL replied. "I'm looking for Sheriff Tate."

Oh, hell, Nate thought with an inward sigh. Oh, hell. Stepping forward, he offered his hand and glanced quickly at the rank insignia. "I'm Nathan Tate. What can I do for you, Chief?"

The younger man's handclasp was firm, brief, business-like. "My mother was raised here years ago, Sheriff. Since I happened to be visiting her old haunts, I thought I'd stop and introduce myself."

Well, that explained the familiarity, Nate thought. "Who was she?"

"Candy Walker."

Nate gave a quick shake of his head; then he remembered. "She was my wife's friend in high school. Marge is the one you want to talk to." But not now, he thought. Not now. Not when he needed to talk to Marge himself.

"Actually," Seth Hardin said, "I was hoping for a word with *you*. I'm giving some thought to resigning and settling in this area. I wondered if there were any opportunities for a man with my skills."

That insignia on Seth's chest told Nate all he needed to know in that regard. A look at the steadiness of the younger man's eyes was enough. He turned to Dave.

"Dave, Micah's on a close patrol today, isn't he?"

"Yep."

"Radio him to come on in and have him take Hardin here out with him." He turned back to Seth. "The question, Chief, is not what you can do, but whether it'll bore you to death. Micah put in better than twenty years in special warfare. Ride shotgun with him for a few days. He'll give you the dope. And if you're still interested, we'll talk."

Hardin nodded. "Thanks. Appreciate it."

That out of the way, Nate turned to the dispatcher. "I'm going to be at home," he told Velma, not caring what she or Dave might think. Sheriff Nathan Tate never just went home during the duty day, not unless something serious had happened. They'd be wondering what was eating him, what was making him act out of character.

But he didn't care. Let the whole damn county wonder. The only thing that mattered was that he was losing his wife and he didn't know why.

She was home. Her cherry red Pontiac Fiero was sitting in the driveway beside the family van, looking as if it hadn't moved in days. Maybe it hadn't. He didn't think she was going out as often as she used to. With six daughters, she had once complained that God should have just put the wheels on her feet so she could cart them everywhere....

He pulled into the driveway and parked his Blazer. Just last week she had asked him if he regretted that they had never had a son. Periodically over the years she had asked him that, as if it troubled her. He always assured her that it had never bothered him at all.

But it had, once or twice, given him a little twinge. Just a small one. Nothing even worth mentioning. He wondered if she'd picked up on that and was now stewing about it.

And this wasn't accomplishing a thing. Muttering an oath, he climbed out of the Blazer, determined that once and for all he was going to find out what was going on with her. *Something* was wrong, and he couldn't continue like this, wondering endlessly if his life was blowing up in his face. He had to *know*.

And all that stuff about opening Pandora's box wasn't going to stop him. He couldn't live like this, wondering when the ax was going to fall.

Inside, the house was quiet. Perhaps Marge was taking a nap, he thought. She hadn't been sleeping well at all lately. Walking quietly, he headed down the hallway to the master bedroom. The door was closed, but even before he opened it he knew she was there. And she was crying.

He froze where he was, squeezing his eyes closed and absorbing the sounds of her sobs as if each one were a blow to his soul, to his heart. He had known she was unhappy, worried . . . but not like this. Not this bad.

For a moment he stood there, wondering what it was that made her hurt so badly, wondering if he had inside him whatever she needed . . . or if he was the problem. Then, without knocking, he entered the room he had shared with her for almost their entire marriage.

She lay facedown on the quilt, her fist pressed to her mouth as if to smother the sobs, her eyes swollen and red, her face wet and chapped from tears. She appeared not to hear him as he entered the room. He paused just long enough to remove his hat, jacket and Sam Browne belt, listening to her sobs as he did so. Each wrenching, gulping sound tore at him.

Then, sitting on the bed, he drew her up into his arms and hugged her tightly to his chest.

"God, baby, don't cry like this. We'll make it better. Somehow we'll make it better...."

Empty words. Over her head, he saw his reflection in the mirror and nearly grimaced. He looked every one of his forty-seven years, he thought. Every single one of them. The sun and wind and the years had carved his face deeply and burned it permanently. His hair, once dark, was now flecked with gray. He'd whipped his body back into some kind of shape, but that didn't erase the fact that he was getting on in years.

"Marge...sugar, tell me what to do. Tell me what you need."

But her tears came as if there were no end to them, and the front of his khaki uniform shirt grew soaked. Later, much, much later, exhaustion quieted her. Her sobs turned into erratic sniffles and shaky breaths. Tears still flowed, but only occasionally.

Reaching behind him, he piled the pillows for a backrest and then lay back with her on his chest.

"God, baby," he whispered roughly. "Tell me. Are you sick?"

She shook her head against his chest and sniffled. "No," she said thickly. "No. I'm fine."

"Fine? Damn it, Marge, who do you think you're kidding? You're losing weight, you haven't been interested in making love for months, sometimes I get the feeling you can hardly stand to look at me.... Are you thinking about leaving me?"

Her head jerked up at that, and she looked at him from horrified, swollen eyes. "No! Oh, no! Nate I'd never, ever..."

The fist gripping his heart eased, but only a little. There was still something seriously wrong, and in all the years of their marriage, he couldn't remember *ever* having seen Marge this distraught, except when her parents had died. Looking down at her, he shook his head. "You're scaring me to death."

She caught her breath and then flung her arms around his neck in that way he so dearly loved, the way that made him feel big and strong and loved, that made him feel as if she were flinging herself into his love and his care. "I love you, Nate. I love you with all my heart."

Gently, he rubbed her slender back with one of his big hands, feeling anew how much weight she'd lost. Suddenly conscious of how fragile she was. "I love you, too, Marge. So tell me what's wrong. Maybe I can help."

She caught her breath, and for long moments pressed her face tightly to his shoulder, as if she wanted to burrow inside of him. "You can't help," she said finally, her voice muffled against his shirt. "There's nothing anyone in the world can do."

The fist took a fresh grip on his heart. "Then tell me," he said. "It helps to talk."

"You'd never understand. Never. I don't want to lose you, Nate. I couldn't stand it. I'd die if I lost you."

The fist squeezed his heart even tighter. He didn't like the sound of this at all. Not at all.

"Why do you think you'd lose me, sugar?" It was amazingly difficult to ask that question. He couldn't begin to imagine what could be so awful that she'd fear such a thing, but the fact that she feared it was enough to clamp a vise on his chest and make it almost impossible to breathe.

And it got even worse when she didn't answer, but instead burst into fresh tears. All he could do was hold her shaking body and wait for the storm to pass.

And hope that it wasn't a tornado that was about to tear his life to shreds.

* * *

The girls had choir practice that evening. Nate insisted Marge stay in, and he drove them himself through the frozen streets of Conard City to Good Shepherd Church.

When he got back from dropping them off, Marge was waiting with hot brandy-laced coffee. She had always done that when he had to go out at night in the winter... but not for the last several months. He didn't know whether to be relieved or even more worried.

She had lit a fire in the fireplace, and he found himself remembering nights last winter, nights just like this, when the girls had Christmas choir practice nearly every night for three hours. Nights when he had come home from dropping them off and they had sat before the fire, sipping brandy and coffee... and finally making love.

Turning from the fire, he looked down into Marge's face and saw a kind of nervous expectancy there. A look he hadn't seen since the first few times they had made love. When she had still been unsure of herself, her charms, whether he would want her.

It pierced him that after all this time she should be feeling that way. After all these good years of marriage, she should know how attractive he always found her. She shouldn't ever be wondering whether he wanted her.

He set his mug down on the table and reached out for her, drawing her close, whispering how much he loved her. Yet he was afraid to make promises, afraid to swear that everything would be all right simply because she was so frightened herself. Her fear deprived him of surety.

She melted against him with the soft sigh that always tightened his throat and linked her arms around his waist.

"I love this time of year," he said quietly, rubbing her back from shoulder to hip. "The girls are so busy we have all these quiet evenings together."

"Mmm..." The sound of agreement trailed away into a sigh he felt in his groin. It had been a long dry spell, and the woman of his fantasies was at last melting into him in a way he well knew. Relief, almost as strong as the growing passion, filled him.

She snuggled a little closer and rubbed her cheek against his chest. "I bet you could get into your army uniform again."

He smiled and bent his head until his mouth rested against her soft, silky hair. "So you noticed."

"Of course I noticed. Nate, I . . . I'm just really confused right now. I just . . . need time to think, okay? But I promise I'm not sick, and I'm not thinking of leaving. I'd *never* leave you. Never."

That he was able to believe right now, and it was an added dimension of relief that whispered through him like a soothing breeze. And for now, it was enough. His wife wanted him again, was holding on to him and promising she would never leave him.

Tilting her face up, he took her mouth in a kiss intended to make up for all the long-lost weeks behind them. He kissed her gently, coaxing her into passion as he had not needed to do in many years. It was terribly, terribly important to him that she want this as much as he did. Over the years, from time to time, spouses gave each other the gift of lovemaking even when they were not especially aroused, simply because they loved. This time he did not want that. He did not want Marge to love him simply out of love. He wanted her to love him out of passion.

A sweep of his tongue opened her mouth for him, and he was further inflamed by the shy little quiver he felt in her, a quiver he had not felt since their first few times, but had never, ever forgotten.

"You feel so hard," she whispered, and he chuckled throatily. She knew he liked her to say things like that, liked to hear what she was experiencing. That was another thing they hadn't done in a long time.

"You feel so good to me, sugar," he murmured, though in fact she felt too thin. He could feel each rib in painstaking detail and her shoulder blades were frighteningly prominent. "You're sure you're not sick?"

"I'm perfectly healthy. I just haven't been hungry. . . ."

The sentence trailed off as he tilted her head farther back and then plunged his tongue deeply into her. Ah, she tasted so good, like cool water on a parching day. She bowed into him, like a young willow, and her hands slipped up his back, clinging tightly as she invited him deeper, deeper. Then, in the most tantalizing way, she stroked her tongue along his and joined the play.

There was something, he found himself thinking as his body began to throb in earnest, something truly seductive about a familiar partner. The years guided the dance with a surety, giving pleasure a steady, certain rising crescendo that no two first-time lovers could ever hope to find. The thrill of newness and adventure gave way to the magic of knowledge, comfort and confidence. What they brought each other was years of caring, learning and growing that made their mating an exquisite ballet.

And then he stopped thinking about it. Abstinence had added a reckless impatience to his need, and soon he was gasping for air and reaching for zippers and buttons as if he were twenty, not forty-seven. And Marge was right there with him, gasping and giggling and as eager as she had ever been.

It would be all right, he thought. It was going to be all right. Whatever was happening would mend....

And then the phone rang.

"Ignore it," he said through gritted teeth.

"I can't...Nate, the girls are out...."

He knew she was right. Something might have happened to one of their daughters. He let go of her, and she hurried across the room to pick up the phone. Moments later she held the receiver out to him.

"It's Ed Dewhurst," she said. "There's been a train derailment."

He swore a word then that had left his vocabulary the day he left the army. Snatching the phone from Marge, he barked questions at Ed, then snapped, "I'll be there when you see me." After he slammed the receiver down, he picked it up out of the cradle and left it off the hook. They were cut off now. Completely.

Marge drew a sharp breath as he turned to face her. A breath of astonishment and disbelief. He knew what caused her shock. Not once in all these years had he put his job second to anything except a family emergency. But tonight...tonight this was an emergency, not just of his body, but of his heart. He held out his arms.

And with a soft, soft cry of joy, Marge threw herself into his arms.

The derailed train was not a passenger train, thank God. But it was potentially worse for the people of Conard City. Right at the edge of town, near the stockyards, fourteen cars had jumped the tracks. Two of the cars carried lashed barrels, contents unknown.

"I thought all this stuff was supposed to be identified," Ed said to him.

Nate shook his head. "I would think so. Warning labels. Contents labels. Has anybody called the railroad for a manifest?"

"Yeah. They're checking."

With his hand-held floodlight, Nate walked around the wreckage, taking in the size of the disaster. Whatever was in those barrels, it was going to take some time to clean up the mess. A few barrels, he noted, were beneath the tipped car, dangerously crushed, but not yet leaking anything, as far as he could see. It wouldn't take much, though.

"We'd better clear the area," Nate said to Ed. "Move everybody back to a good distance, until we find out what's in those barrels."

"It's probably nothing," said one of the volunteer firemen who was standing nearby. "They're pretty strict about labeling dangerous cargoes."

"They're pretty strict about labeling *everything,*" Nate pointed out. "Right now I'm not willing to bet this isn't hazardous."

Ed nodded. "An ounce of prevention..."

"Exactly," agreed the fireman.

"So let's move everybody away," Nate said with a touch of impatience. Damn, standing here jawing like idiots when just about *anything* could be in those barrels....

They moved the emergency crews back a quarter mile, then Nate had his deputies go to all the dwellings and businesses within a mile and tell occupants that they might have to be evacuated if the situation changed in any way. As a precaution, the high school was opened as an emergency shelter.

A half hour later, the railroad radioed back: dry-cleaning fluid.

Nate nearly sighed with relief. "Okay, ask the folks in the evacuation area to keep their doors and windows closed tightly," he told his deputies. "The stuff isn't that toxic, but..."

"But," said a strange voice behind him, "dry-cleaning fluid is seldom transported in drums like this on a train."

Nate swung around and stared at the stranger, a tall, dark, powerfully built man. "Who are you?"

"Peter Little. I work for the railroad." He handed Nate an identification card. "We usually ship dry-cleaning fluid in a tank car. This doesn't look right at all."

"Hell," Nate said, turning to look at the brightly spotlighted jumble of derailed cars. "What *do* you ship in drums?"

"Toxic waste, liquid chlorine..."

"Liquid chlorine!"

"We don't do it often because it's so highly toxic, but sometimes..." Little shrugged. "And we always ship it in small barrels to limit the damage if something develops a leak."

"And you always label it?"

"Always."

"These aren't labeled."

"So the head office tells me. And that makes me uneasy as hell. As a carrier, we're required to know what we're shipping. Anything remotely dangerous has to be precisely labeled, according to federal regulation. Sheriff, we *never* should have loaded those barrels without labeling of some kind on each and every one of them."

Nate swore and looked at the jumbled heap of cars. He spared one last thought for Marge waiting at home for him, and then banished it. They were facing a potential catastrophe here, and there was no time for thoughts of personal matters.

"Okay, Little. How do we determine what we're facing here?"

"The head office has dispatched a team. I guess the EPA has been notified, too, of a potential hazardous spill. At this point, Sheriff, I'm supposed to suggest to you that you evacuate everyone except emergency personnel who is within a one-mile radius."

Nate looked over at Little. "Suggest?"

The man smiled faintly. "I can't very well order you to."

"But you would if you could."

"Exactly. I don't like the looks of this at all."

It was one week before Christmas and bitterly cold. The only blessing Nate could perceive was that the high school was well out of the danger zone, so they had somewhere warm to put the hundreds of evacuees. His own house was not in the danger zone, but he had to end choir practice at Good Shepherd and send his daughters home.

He could just imagine Marge's face when the girls burst through the door early, followed by one of his deputies. She would immediately imagine the worst, before Deputy Charlie Huskins even had a chance to reassure her....

Shaking his head, he put the thoughts aside. Right now he had the welfare of most of the county to worry about.

Peter Little had some knowledge of the potential dangers involved in the derailment. The fire chief, Roger Armitage, and Nate himself, had taken training in disaster management. Between the three of them, they did what they could to minimize any danger of fire.

A couple of tank cars were carrying anhydrous ammonia. It wasn't particularly toxic, but if it started to burn it might be days before they could put it out. The rest of the manifest was checked for other items of concern, but nothing more turned up.

Nate was not a man who was built to wait. He was a man who preferred action, and had learned patience only through long experience. When things could not be hurried, he restrained himself and popped antacids to ease the burning in his stomach.

He waited now. Waited for the experts and emergency disposal teams from the railroad. He waited for certain knowledge of the danger his community faced ... or for certain assurance that there was none.

And he was angry. Angry that someone had defied interstate regulations and had loaded those unlabeled barrels. It might well be nothing, but folks weren't going to be much appeased to learn they had been hauled out of their warm homes on a cold December night over barrels full of tar or some such thing. Any way you looked at it, people were going to be upset, with justification.

From his point of view, it was a glum prospect. He and the mayor and the commissioners—just about everybody in the county in an elected post—were going to get hell over this. It wouldn't matter that there was nothing that could have been done to prevent it. Nope, it wouldn't matter at all.

He would have laughed aloud except that he kept thinking of Marge, thinking of the all-too-brief hour they had shared, wondering if they might share another one later.

And wondering what the hell was eating her alive.

Dawn arrived with a gray overcast, cold and gloomy. As the morning brightened, the floodlights looked weaker and weaker, until at last they were shut off. The team from the railroad had cautiously unhitched the front end of the train and had driven it from the area. Then they had brought in an engine and had taken out the undamaged cars from the rear end. That left the fourteen cars that had derailed, and there was a great deal of argument and low-voiced discussion about those unlabeled barrels. The head office was trying to get someone from the shipper to identify the contents, but the shipper turned out to be a freight-forwarding company, so the search continued for the originator.

"It's not good," Peter Little admitted to Nate. "It sounds more and more suspicious all the time."

Nate nodded. Somebody was clearly trying to hide something. "What worries me is why it's unlabeled. Somebody must be transporting something illegal, or something that requires such expensive measures for shipping that they wanted to avoid it."

"Exactly." Little nodded. "I hope we open those drums and find marijuana."

Nate looked at him and gave a weary chuckle. "Yeah. I could handle that. What's the worst case?"

The other man shook his head. "There's a whole lot of worst cases. Everything from deadly poison to radioactive materials. The problem is, legitimate users of these items turn them over for disposal to firms they assume will handle them legitimately. Somewhere along the way, though, somebody gets greedy . . ." He left the sentence incomplete. Nate knew all that, anyway.

"And Conard County winds up facing an unknown threat," Nate completed. "I want that stuff out of here. I think the least you guys can do is transport it away from town before you fool around with it in any way. Get it far enough out into the countryside that the folks here can get on with their lives while you figure out what kind of mess this is."

"We don't want to move anything before we're sure it's safe to move it."

"Great." Nate settled his hands on his hips and watched a gust of his breath turn into a white cloud of ice crystals.

"Things should start happening fast now that it's daylight. We should be able to roust someone at the freight forwarder."

That was the other thing that was troubling Nate—the fact that they couldn't get ahold of anyone at the freight forwarder. Most businesses had an emergency phone number posted somewhere, an after-hours number that could be found by law enforcement personnel. A freight forwarder would certainly have an emergency number available for the shippers it contracted with. Wouldn't it?

This one evidently didn't, and it made him uneasy as hell.

The day lightened further. He sent one of his deputies out for breakfast for everyone. An hour later he was sipping hot coffee and eating cold eggs. Velma patched through a call from Marge on his car radio, and he talked to her for several minutes, noting unhappily that she once again sounded strained. He might have sworn a savage oath, except that there were too many curious ears around.

But he was furious. After months of worrying, after months of tiptoeing around waiting for the ax, after months of trying to appease a mood he didn't understand, he was mad enough to tear steel with his bare hands. How *dare* she treat him like this? How dare she ignore his questions and refuse to tell him what was bothering her? Damn it, he had a *right* to know because he was her husband. Because he loved her. Because she was tearing him to shreds with her silence.

But getting mad wasn't likely to mend matters, so he swallowed the fury and paced back and forth like a big caged cat. There had to be an answer. There had to be a solution. To Marge's problem. To the railroad problem. To *all* the problems. He was a man who needed to fix things, to mend them and make them all better. He was not a passive victim of life, but a leading actor on life's stage. That was his temperament and inclination.

And Marge had his hands as good as tied.

By ten, the freight forwarder, a California firm, had answered their phone. They had been told the barrels contained dry-cleaning fluid, which was little to worry about. Except that the consignee was merely the name of someone who would accept the shipment in Conard City.

"Who'd need that much dry-cleaning fluid around here?" Little asked.

"Beats me. Who is it consigned to?" Little spoke into his radio phone. A moment later he looked at Nate. "Someone named Westin Weatherill."

Nate stiffened and stared off into space for a long moment. "Well, Little, I hate to say this, but there isn't anyone in the county by that name. Unless someone just got here and I haven't heard about it yet."

He and Little exchanged long looks. "I think," Nate said, "we'd better locate the consignee before we do another thing."

Little nodded. "That would be wise."

While Nate's deputies searched for any information about a Westin Weatherill, the railroad pursued the matter from the other end, trying to locate the original shipper of the drums. The freight forwarder had a number and a name, but neither one matched up. When it was learned that the shipping had been paid for with a bank money order, purchased in cash, hopes of an easy solution grew dim. By late afternoon, the only clue they had was that one of the deputies—Fred—seemed to remember that one of the ranchers had hired a down-at-the-heels cowpoke named Westy Weatherill last summer.

The news immediately heightened concern. If that was true, then Weatherill could have had no legitimate reason to receive such shipments. None at all.

Emergency teams were tapped to move in under the assumption that the contents were extremely hazardous. Everyone was removed from the area, and roadblocks set up a half mile from the wreck. Even Nate had to stand back at this point and let the trained personnel handle matters.

The team cautiously tapped into one of the barrels and extracted samples. An hour later, the worst was known.

"PCBs," said the voice on the radio. "Appears to be toxic waste. No guarantee that the contents of all the barrels are the same."

Nate looked at Little. "Get it the hell out of my county. All of it."

Little nodded. "We need to find out where it was going to be dumped."

"You think I don't realize that?" Only by a vast exercise of will did Nate hang on to his temper. Toxic waste in unlabeled barrels that had been headed for Conard City. That were going to be off-loaded at the docks just up the track. That some person was going to pick up and put only God knew where, endangering the county's residents, endangering the future of the county's children. . . .

He was spitting mad. "Tell 'em to clear it out. I'll get to the bottom of my end. You just get that filth out of my county!"

He stalked away toward his car, but before he had walked two steps, he looked back. "The diner's closed, thanks to the evacuation. When you get done here, ask one of the deputies how to find my place. I'll feed you."

Little looked surprised. "It really isn't—"

"It really *is,*" Nate growled. "Just come. You need to eat sometime, and from the look of it, you're going to be at this for a while." Then he turned away before Little could argue any more about it. He hesitated a moment when he saw Micah Parish, one of his deputies, pointing out something to Seth Hardin about the train. He really should go over and say something, he told himself. Make a gesture to see if Hardin was finding out what he wanted. Candy Somebody's kid.

Oh, to hell with it, he thought. To hell with it. He had more important things on his mind than entertaining passers-through.

Damn and double damn, Nate thought as he put the Blazer in gear and headed home. *Damn!* Now the question was whether he had an illegal toxic waste dump somewhere in his county. Had this been going on for some time? Or was this the first shipment? And who was behind it? Where was it supposed to go from the loading docks?

He pounded his fist on the steering wheel and detoured by the office. Sara Ironheart was at the duty desk, and Nate explained what he suspected and what he wanted Sara to do about it. Assured his deputy would handle things and let him know if anything happened, Nate started home yet again.

And arrived to find Marge had gone to help at the high school with all the evacuees. Well, of course she would, he told himself, restraining his temper. She was always the first to volunteer when help was needed, and he had always admired her for that. He was just irritable from lack of sleep, he told himself. Lack of sleep and worry beyond description....

Oh, hell! He told his youngest daughter, Krissie, to put together some kind of dinner that could be eaten cold and to let him know when Mr. Little showed up.

And then Nate Tate went to take a hot shower and collapse on his bed for a nap. He'd learned a long time ago that matters had a way of coming to a head in their own good time. He could worry all he wanted, but he wouldn't learn a damn thing until it was time.

But what the hell could be eating Marge alive?

Chapter 2

Late that night, Nate put Peter Little up in the guest room and then settled down to wait for Marge. Tired from a sleepless night, and hardly caught up from his nap, he dozed a little on the couch while he waited. She'd be back soon, he told himself. She'd stay until everyone at the shelter was settled, and then she'd be home to check on her own family.

Marge, he found himself thinking, was one of the constants in his life. Maybe she was the single most important constant of all. She was...what was that word? Yes, she was his touchstone. Except for those rare occasions when he had to be out of town, and emergencies like the derailment, they had breakfasted together every morning of their marriage. That time of day was sacred to them, and nothing ever disrupted it. Not even Marge's worries of the past few months.

Every morning, long before the girls were up, they had coffee and toast together. Often they talked quietly and lazily about the events of the day before, or their plans for the day ahead. They were not important conversations, but the fact that they shared those moments *was* important.

Even these past few months they had continued their breakfast ritual, though Marge had said little. And before he left for work, she still kissed him goodbye. But he doubted he had been imagining the hint of desperation in her kiss these past few weeks. And the more he thought about that, the more uneasy he grew.

Why should she be so concerned that he would leave her? He couldn't imagine a thing in the world that she could have done that would make him feel that way.

Rubbing his eyes wearily, he settled lower on the couch so that he could rest his head against the back. The hell of it was, he found himself thinking, that by temperament he wanted to confront her and demand explanations, but through experience he knew how hopeless that would be. Marge had a stubborn streak as big as his own, which was probably the only reason their marriage had lasted these many years. She gave as good as she got, and couldn't be pushed into anything.

Even now, worried as he was, he smiled at the thought. God, how he loved that woman. Loved her enough to recognize that he had to give her the space and time she was demanding right now, even if it killed him. He owed her that, at the very least.

It was shortly before midnight when she at last returned, looking tired and concerned. She bent over the couch and kissed Nate on the cheek.

"I need some decaf," she said, and turned away toward the kitchen.

Shoving himself up, he followed her. "How's it going at the school?"

"About like you'd expect. We got most of the kids quieted down, and hot food into everybody." She shoved a cup of water into the microwave and set the timer. "Nate, they're talking about toxic waste."

He sighed, thinking he should have guessed word would get out. "Sit down. I'll make your coffee. By the way, I gave the guest room to an investigator the railroad sent out. His name is Peter Little."

As she slipped onto a stool at the counter, she merely nodded. "Fine. Now, what about the spill?"

"There hasn't been one. But until that stuff is cleared out of there, it's best to keep folks safely away. They checked out one barrel and found PCBs."

Marge shook her head. "Is that what's in all of them?"

"They don't know. At this point, the priority is going to be getting that stuff away from here and out somewhere it doesn't pose a public threat. Then they'll look into what's in all those barrels. But until that stuff is moved, I don't want anyone close enough to get hurt if something goes wrong."

"How long will that take?"

Nate shook his head. "Little said they should be done sometime tomorrow, if everything goes all right. They're bringing up another flatbed car and some equipment to load the barrels." He placed Marge's coffee in front of her and slid onto the stool beside her. "You look beat, sugar."

She glanced at him with a wan smile. "No more than you, Nate. Did you get a nap, at least?"

"A short one. Look, why don't you hurry and drink that coffee and come lie down. I'll give you a nice, easy back rub."

She caught her breath. He heard the sound and felt a small leap of jubilation. She wasn't indifferent to him. Despite everything, she wasn't indifferent. Last night hadn't been something she had given him out of obligation.

But she shook her head. "Too tired," she said. "I just want to crash as soon as I wind down." Leaning forward, she rested her elbows on the counter and stared into her coffee cup. "Why don't they know what's in those barrels, Nate? Shouldn't they know what they're dealing with?"

"They should. They don't. Heads are gonna roll." He didn't say anything about the fact that the shipment had been destined for here. No point upsetting her any more than she was already upset. "Well, it'll be cleared out by tomorrow, I reckon, and things can get back to normal."

Except for his life, he thought, watching Marge sip her coffee. He was beginning to wonder if that would ever get back to normal again.

In the morning, Peter Little ate breakfast with Nate and Marge, thanked them profusely for their hospitality, and departed on the promise that all the toxic substances would be out of harm's way before nightfall.

Nate watched Marge blush as Little complimented her, and felt his stomach turn sour. He hadn't been able to make her blush in years.

Back in the bedroom, he pulled on a freshly pressed uniform and buckled his gun belt with a grim feeling that he was going to have to force a showdown. He couldn't let this go on much longer. Sooner or later she was going to have to come clean with him or the marriage was going to fall apart simply from stress. Both of them were so obviously unhappy right now that even their youngest daughter was looking at them with evident worry.

His mind made up, he headed for the kitchen, determined that he was going to get to the bottom of this before he set foot out the front door. Of course, nothing was ever that easy. First they had to get Krissie, Patti and Carol off to school. Then the phone rang; it was for Marge. She talked PTA business for ten or fifteen minutes while Nate drank two cups of coffee and pretended it wasn't unusual for him to dawdle around the kitchen when he should already be at work.

When she at last hung up the phone, she glanced at him, clearly preoccupied with whatever she had just been discussing. "Is something wrong?" she asked.

"Yes."

He said the word flatly, in a steely voice. There was no mistaking the tone, and Marge immediately paled. "What happened?"

"That's what I want *you* to tell me," he said in the same uncompromising tone. "I've had enough of this, whatever it is. I think you'd better explain why you're so on edge, why you can hardly stand to have me touch you, why you're losing weight.... Marge, I'm not blind and I'm not a fool. What the hell is going on?''

Just then the phone rang again. Nate swore savagely and snatched at the receiver, prepared to give short shrift to whoever it was.

He couldn't. It was one of his deputies. There were sixteen sick cattle over at Hamilton's ranch, and the vet was saying it was poison. Combined with the railroad accident, trouble was brewing.

Nate slammed the receiver down and glared at his wife. "Tonight," he said. "Tonight we *will* finish this discussion."

Grabbing his hat and coat, he turned to go, but Marge suddenly stopped him. When he looked down into her green eyes, he saw they were tear filled.

"Nathan Tate," she whispered, "just remember, I love you."

With a groan, he hauled her to him in a bear hug and kissed her hard and fast. Then he walked away.

Somehow, he thought as he climbed into his Blazer, somehow he had the feeling that remembering she loved him just wasn't going to be enough.

Gage Dalton, the department's investigator, was waiting for him at the veterinary clinic, along with Jake Llewellyn, the county's only vet. Jake was a lean, rangy man near Nate's age, a widower with two children in college. Since his wife's death from cancer several years ago, he had stopped talking about getting an assistant to share the work load, and was steadily wearing himself out.

"They're sick, all right," he told Nate and Gage. "But it's no illness I'm familiar with. I'm sending blood samples for toxicology workups, but I'm willing to stick my neck out right now, Nate. Those steers were *poisoned.*"

"So let me ask you to stick your neck out a little farther," Nate said. "Do you think it was deliberate?"

Jake leaned back against a steel examining table and cocked his head as he considered the question. After a few moments, he shook his head. "I can't exactly say why, but

I don't think so. My guess would be something got spilled that shouldn't have got spilled. You might want to take a look at the area, but it's open range out there, Nate. Anybody could have come through and dropped something off the back of a truck."

"Well, that sure as hell was helpful," Nate grumbled as he and Gage walked out to their vehicles.

Gage glanced at him, his eyes a stormy gray green in his scarred face. "I thought it was real helpful. What's eating you lately, Nate?"

"You don't want to know. And even if you did, I wouldn't tell you!"

He was aware that he left a grinning Gage behind him as he climbed into his Blazer and wheeled out onto the road. The whole damn county was going to be wondering what the hell had gotten into Nate Tate at this rate, he thought sourly as he turned onto the road that would eventually take him to the Hamilton place. In his rearview mirror, he could see Gage's Suburban following closely. And Micah Parish was already out there, Velma had said when she had called him this morning. Checking for any clue to what had happened. If men had deliberately poisoned those steers, Micah would find some sign of it.

They halted where Micah's Blazer was pulled over alongside the road, but Micah was nowhere to be seen on the barren, wintry landscape. He had probably walked into a dip or a ravine and would suddenly reappear, Nate thought. There was plenty of trampling beside the road where the vet and the rancher and the cattle had evidently gotten together. The cattle were gone, though. Phil Hamilton might have taken them into his barns to look after them ... or maybe he had put them down. He'd have to look into that.

Gage joined him a few moments later, and the two stood staring out over the snowy fields to the mountains beyond.

"Poison," Nate said. "Of all the damn things."

"Jake could be wrong. Those cattle *could* be sick."

Nate looked over at him. "Son, you haven't been in this county long enough to know, but I'd hang my badge on Jake Llewellyn's veterinary instincts any day."

Gage nodded. "Good enough for me. That leaves poison. And a train that was bringing a load of toxic waste to Conard County."

Nate scowled. "Damn it, son, don't say that to anyone else."

Gage suddenly smiled. He smiled a lot since he married the librarian, Miss Emma. "Aha! So the thought has crossed your mind."

"I may look like a two-bit, penny-ante backwoods sheriff, scout, but I've got a brain between my ears!"

At that Gage laughed. Actually roared with laughter. And in spite of himself, Nate felt his own lips twitching. Finally he, too, laughed, and felt his mood lighten considerably.

There was hardly a thing, he told himself, that couldn't be cured once you knew what you were up against. He'd get to the bottom with the cattle, he'd get to the bottom with the toxic waste shipment, and he'd get to the bottom with Marge. Come hell or high water.

That satisfied in his own mind, he scanned the cold countryside again and saw Micah suddenly appear out of a hidden draw, with Seth Hardin beside him.

"There he is," Gage remarked.

Nate gave a short nod. "See the way Micah's walking? I know that walk. He used to come out of the jungle moving just that way when he'd located the enemy."

Gage looked at him. "What do you mean?"

"See how he's almost slinking? Damn Injun walks like a big cat when he's on the scent. He used to do it in Nam, and he's still doing it today. He found something."

Slogging through deep snow, it took Micah and Seth nearly fifteen minutes to reach them. When they did Micah looked at Nate and shook his head. "You're not going to like this."

"I knew I wasn't going to like it the minute I heard Hamilton's cattle had been poisoned. What did you find?"

"A dozen barrels just like the ones that spilled off the train the night before last."

For a moment, Nate didn't say a word. He tilted his head back, looking up at the gray sky. He settled his hands on his hips and blew air between his lips.

"You're right," he said. "I didn't like it. Gage, radio for that railroad guy to get out here."

"Little?"

"Yeah, him. Tell him to bring his experts with him, and tell him I want to know if there was an earlier shipment of similar description through the same freight forwarder as the one he's cleaning up. And ask him anything else you think might be useful while you're at it." He trusted Gage's nose as an investigator. He looked at Micah. "Take me out there. Show me what you found."

Without a word, his long black hair blowing in the chilly wind, Micah turned and led the way. Seth followed, and Nate didn't object.

Long before they reached the draw, Nate had cause to give thanks for the dieting and exercise he'd been doing the last four months. He doubted that he'd previously been in the condition this trek demanded. The snow was hip deep in places where the wind had drifted it, and it was as fatiguing as walking in sand. The draw was nearly three-quarters of a mile from the road, and his legs were aching by the time he could see it.

"I take it," he said to Micah, "that none of these barrels are labeled?"

"Nope. A little rusty, so they've been here a while, but I wouldn't venture to say how long. Not too long, probably. But they're jumbled every which way, and I'd bet some of them are leaking."

"There's water in the draw now?"

Micah nodded. "Melted snow. Reckon the cattle have been drinking from it. Stock pond's frozen over, but this is running water, so it doesn't freeze as easy."

"It wouldn't freeze as easy if there's something in it, either."

Micah's dark eyes met his. "That thought crossed my mind."

Like antifreeze. Chemicals in that water would lower the freezing temperature, maybe enough to keep it from icing over. And the cattle would be drawn to the running water for drinking.

They stood at the edge of the draw, looking down the slope at the jumbled barrels which were partly concealed by snow.

"Looks like somebody just backed up and dumped 'em from a truck," Nate remarked.

"Yep. Nothing careful about it."

"Could you smell anything?"

"Nothing I could identify, except maybe a little ammonia odor... but that could be from urine." Micah looked at Seth, who shook his head.

"Me neither," Seth said. "A little ammonia is all."

Nate nodded. "Damn and double damn. Okay. I guess we need to get water samples, snow samples. Dirt samples. I guess we ought to get somebody out here who knows how to do this crap. Somebody who doesn't belong to anybody. Somebody who'll tell the damn truth about what the hell is going on in my county."

Turning, he started slogging back through the snow, propelled by an anger he seldom felt. Somebody was risking the lives and livelihood of the people of his county, and there was little guaranteed to make Nathan Tate as angry as that.

Except possibly what was going on with his wife, he thought as he forged forward, heedless of his soaking pants and the cold that bit through the damp cloth. He was beginning to get downright angry at her.

By the time he got back to his Blazer, Gage had finished his calls.

"Little said he'll set the ball in motion," he told Nate. "They'll check shipments for the last year, to see if there've been any similar ones, either from the same forwarding company or to the same consignee. He's also going to send the toxicology team out, but he recommended we get in touch with the proper state and federal agencies, because the railroad isn't responsible once that stuff is off-loaded."

Nate nodded irritably. "I can almost guarantee *nobody's* gonna be responsible for this one." Pulling open the door of his Blazer, he looked at Gage and Micah. "I wonder how many other barrels are tucked in draws, arroyos and ditches around this county?"

Neither man even attempted to answer him.

Ignoring his soaked pants, he waited for Little and his team to show up. With the Blazer's engine running, and the heater blowing full-bore, it wasn't too uncomfortable. Micah and Gage joined him. None of them were given to speculating, but none of them felt it was speculation to conclude that someone in the county was accepting shipments of toxic waste and disposing of them in out-of-the-way places, like that draw. The questions were, how many shipments, how many stashes, what kinds of waste. They could only hope the problem was still small, that they wouldn't spend the next decade discovering dump after dump after dump.

The ramifications hardly bore thinking about. Nate's stomach clenched uneasily when he thought of all the ranch kids who considered the wide open spaces to be their God-given playground. Kids who rode out on horses to the farthest places, and splashed in the stock ponds, and waded in the draws when they were full of spring runoff. Kids who explored from natural curiosity, and feared little because they were children and therefore indestructible. Kids who wouldn't hesitate to open a steel drum to find out what was inside of it.

Nate swore on a sigh and drummed his fingers on the steering wheel. Damn pants felt clammy, and his feet felt frozen. What was taking Little so long?

"We need to see if we can get copies of the manifests on earlier shipments through this forwarder," Gage remarked.

"Maybe we need to check out *all* the shipments that have been delivered to the county," Nate said. "There's no reason to believe the original shipper always uses the same forwarder. Or that whoever is receiving on this end receives only from one forwarder."

"My inclination," Gage said after a moment, "is to assume one forwarder at the outset. First, whoever used them this time would probably use them repeatedly. It can't be the *easiest* thing in the world to find a forwarder who won't worry about federal regulations. I mean, wouldn't it have been simpler to slap phony labels on the stuff? That would have covered the forwarder's butt, anyway. But they didn't even do that."

"So it's a fly-by-night outfit."

"And probably planning to be off the face of the earth in a short period of time. If the train hadn't derailed, they'd probably have been gone long before anyone started asking any questions. Then there's got to be an accomplice within the railroad."

Nate nodded. "Little said they should never have accepted an unlabeled shipment."

"Certainly not for interstate traffic. ICC regulations are stiff. Either the whole original shipping yard is on the take, or they've got an in with someone high enough to order the loading and silence the questions. I imagine the FBI will look into that."

Nate tapped a rapid tattoo on the steering wheel. "At our end, we have to find out how much of this stuff got into the county and where it's at. And that isn't going to be any easy task."

Hundreds and hundreds of square miles, he thought. Most of it unoccupied by anything save brush and cattle. Plenty of hiding places everywhere—draws, gullies, ditches, ponds, gorges. . . . And snow. With all the recent snowfall, aerial searches probably wouldn't be all that useful, either.

"We need to find the receiver," he said heavily. "The most important thing is to get our hands on the person who stashed the stuff. Otherwise we could spend years trying to find it all."

"We need more than a name," Gage said. "A signature. A fingerprint. How about a description from someone at the station who talked to the consignee?"

Micah snorted softly from the back seat. "You sure don't want much, do you?"

"Just a miracle, old son," Nate replied before Gage could. "Just a miracle. I don't like this at all."

And he wasn't liking it much better a couple of hours later when Peter Little and his team agreed that it looked like more of the same.

By midafternoon, an environmental emergency team had shown up and was taking samples of everything in sight. The cattle hadn't been killed, but on Jake Llewellyn's recommendation had been penned in sight of the Hamilton house until toxicology studies could be completed.

When Nate was satisfied that matters at the dump site were under control, he headed on up to the house to question Hamilton about anything he might know, and to take a look at the steers himself. Gage, Micah and Seth accompanied him.

Phil Hamilton was a ruddy-complected, hardworking rancher in his late fifties. He'd seen his share of troubles, everything from drought to fire, but this problem was manmade, if Llewellyn was right, and it had Hamilton hopping mad.

"No, I *don't* know who might have dumped anything out there," Hamilton growled at the sheriff. "Damn it, Nate, do you think if I knew I'd be standing here talking to you about it? Hell, man, I'd be looking for the bastard!"

"I understand how you feel, Phil, but it'll be best for you and everybody else if you let me handle this," Nate warned him. "Your steers are sick. The question is how many other places some of this crap may have been dumped. Vigilantism isn't going to get the answer to that."

Phil's scowl darkened, but he nodded. "And what's to be done in the meantime?"

"Get everybody in the county to be on the lookout for sick cattle and steel drums."

And that wasn't a whole hell of a lot to do, he thought as he drove home that night. Not a whole hell of a lot.

The next few days did nothing to improve the picture. Manifests on file with the railroad showed three other such shipments had been received in Conard County during the past year, all purporting to be dry-cleaning fluid. Nate figured that if all the people in his county dry-cleaned everything they owned daily for the next hundred years, they still wouldn't need anywhere near that quantity of fluid.

Tests on the barrels from the wreck and from the draw showed that a wide variety of toxic waste was involved, which meant it was likely that someone was acting as a receiver for wastes from a wide variety of industries, then shipping through various dummy forwarding companies... because it appeared the earlier freight-forwarding companies, as listed on the earlier manifests, had vanished.

"Well," said Nate to the FBI agent who called to tell him all this, "I'd bet my badge the company that ships the stuff sets up the freight forwarders."

"That's what we think, too," the agent agreed. "We're looking into it. Any luck on finding the Weatherill character on your end?"

"None at all. None of the ranchers we've talked to so far remembers a cowpoke named Westy or Weatherill. The people at the depot have only a vague memory of a guy in a Stetson, boots and jeans... and we got a couple of thousand people by that description around here."

The agent chuckled. "I imagine you do. Well, maybe we'll turn up something with lab analysis of those manifests he signed. Let us know if you find any more waste, Sheriff. And I'll keep you posted on what happens on this end."

Which was really more than he had expected from the FBI, Nate thought. This was an interstate problem. He'd expected to be bumped right off the case.

Instead, he was still square in the middle of it... which suited his nature, but was going to make his chair awfully hot if any more cattle got sick.

Any one of a dozen ranchers or ranch hands could have managed this, he found himself thinking as he settled back in his chair. Any one. There were enough big trucks on most ranches to haul the stuff easily. And there were tens of thousands of places to hide it in all these wide-open spaces.

And nobody at the railroad probably thought a darn thing about it. Big shipments arrived all the time, from feed to fertilizer. It was unlikely anyone would have gotten at all inquisitive as long as the stuff was promptly picked up.

And it was Christmas Eve, he realized suddenly. Rising from his chair, he grabbed his hat and jacket and headed out front. Velma was already gone; the deputy on duty was sitting in Velma's chair.

Nate had worked his share of holidays to give his deputies time with their families. This year, he was leaving it to others. This year he apparently had fences to mend, and he didn't want to give Marge one other blessed thing to be mad about.

"'Night, Lew," he said to the deputy. "I'm going home. Holler if you need me."

Lew shook his head. "Won't need you. Other than an accident or two from too much good cheer, I expect it'll be a quiet night."

It usually was, on Christmas Eve. For him, too. The candlelight service at the church, followed by Marge's special Christmas supper. Yeah, it was always a good time.

But this year he wasn't counting on it.

When he got home, all his girls were there, every blessed one of them, including Wendy, who had married last month. Billy Joe Yuma, her husband, stood beside her, beaming with a pride that made Nate's heart ache for his own losses.

God, how his throat tightened as he looked at them, from littlest Krissie at twelve, to oldest Wendy at twenty-four. They were all dressed in holiday velvet, green and red, as was their family tradition. Each year, Marge had sewn the dresses for them, with the girls' help.

And then, turning, he saw Marge. Unlike her daughters, she wore a full-skirted black velvet dress that made her skin look like cream and ignited her beautiful hair to fiery life. On her shoulder, she wore the poinsettia corsage he always sent to her.

He couldn't even speak. All he could do was open his arms in invitation and then sigh with vast relief when she walked straight into them. He hugged her close and prayed with all his heart that he was not losing her.

"Now go change," she said, drawing back with a smile. "The eggnog is all ready."

Christmas, at least, was apparently going to be unshadowed.

He changed into slacks and the Icelandic sweater Marge had given him last Christmas and joined the family around the wood stove for eggnog and appetizers. The addition of Wendy's husband to the family circle was proving to be a good one. Yuma was nearly Nate's age, and they had both served in Vietnam together. Now they worked together, Yuma as the county medevac pilot. For the first time in many Christmases, Nate had something to listen to besides his daughter's girlish chatter... and while he didn't mind their chatter, it was nice to be able to speak of other things.

It was nice to forget, for a little while, all the things that worried him, and to pretend that for now all was normal.

And then the doorbell rang.

"Must be carolers," Marge said. "I'll get it."

"No, stay," Nate said. "Nobody was planning to carol tonight. It's probably one of my men."

Rising, he went to the small foyer and opened the door expecting to see a familiar face.

It was a familiar face; Seth Hardin stood there, crisply dressed in his navy uniform, ribbons and insignia gleaming on his chest.

"Sorry to disturb you, Sheriff," he said. "I wanted to thank you for allowing me to ride shotgun with Micah the last few days. I'll be leaving...."

Behind him, Nate heard Marge's gasp, and then heard the punch bowl shatter when she dropped it.

They'd received that punch bowl for a wedding present, he found himself thinking vaguely as he looked over his shoulder at the mess, at his wife, who was whiter than the snow outside.

And somehow he felt as if his life had just shattered with it.

An endless eternity passed in silence, then Nate stepped slowly back and opened the door wide. "Come in," he said. "I have the feeling you know my wife, Marge."

Behind Marge, the doorway of the living room filled with the curious faces of his daughters. Yuma immediately stepped forward and lifted Marge out of the puddle of broken glass and eggnog.

"Wendy," Yuma said, "let's see if your mother is hurt. That glass practically exploded."

Normal things, Nate thought as he watched the tall, strong young man enter his house and close the door. As he watched, Yuma and Wendy took care of Marge, setting her on the hall bench and examining her legs.

"Just some small scratches," he heard Wendy say.

The young man looked at him out of dark brown eyes. They were of a height, Nate found himself thinking. And the fellow was familiar, so damn familiar. It was like looking at someone he had known all his life. Uneasiness crawled along his spine as something stirred deep inside. A recognition he'd been too busy to pay attention to for days suddenly seemed almost within his grasp.

Before Nate could speak, before he could ask the question that was now uppermost in his mind, Marge spoke from behind him, sounding ghastly. "You weren't supposed to be here. Not yet. Not until after New Year."

Nate looked at her, and then at the tall young man. The fist squeezing his heart tightened. "What the hell is going on?"

"I apologize," Seth said, looking at Marge. "I have orders to ship out. It's now or never. I couldn't leave you to face this alone."

Marge paled even more and bit her lips.

"Will somebody please tell me what in the hell is going on?" Nate said again. "Now or never for what?"

"Nate..." Her voice, so whispery and anguished, silenced him. "Nate, I'll explain...."

"I'll explain," Seth said. "I made the decision to bring this out in the open. *I'll* explain."

"No, I will," Marge said. "I will. It's my mess."

A silence filled the house in the aftermath of her words. Nate felt as if everyone around him had frozen into a tableau, and he alone was left able to move, think, react.... He looked around him, from the young man who looked too familiar, to the wife who looked completely stricken, to his daughters who were now as pale and worried looking as he had ever seen them.

It was the sight of those young, worried faces that galvanized him. He had always protected his daughters come hell or high water, and right now they apparently needed some kind of protection from whatever bomb was exploding in this house. Or was about to explode.

"Yuma. You and Wendy take the girls to church now. Marge and I ... Marge and I will be along later."

As clear as crystal, as clear as if it were etched in the air before him, he saw the rebellious looks on the girls' faces, saw Wendy and Yuma take over and get everyone into coats and boots. Get everyone shooed out to the van. Nate gave the keys to Yuma, felt Wendy touch his arm as if she somehow knew what he was only guessing.

Then there were just the three of them. Marge, sitting on the bench, looking as if she were on the edge of collapse. The young man, looking as if he had committed a terrible, terrible transgression. And Nate himself, who figured he must look like a man on the way to the gallows.

Surely Marge wasn't leaving him for a younger man?

The possibility was too terrible. He could hardly grasp it. Nor could he just stand there and do nothing. He took control.

"Lay your coat over that chair, Hardin," he said to the young man. "Marge, is there any coffee?"

She nodded automatically, but seconds ticked by before she stirred herself into action.

"Yes. But the mess..." Her voice trailed off as she looked at the shattered glass and eggnog on the tile floor of the entryway.

"I'll take care of it later," Nate said gruffly. "We've apparently got some talking to do, haven't we?"

Marge slowly raised her green eyes and looked at him with an anguish that tore at his soul. "Oh, yes," she whispered.

"Well, I've been waiting for months to find out what's ripping you up. I'm not waiting another minute. Let's just go into the kitchen and have it out."

Without another word, he turned and stomped toward the kitchen. Behind him he heard the dragging steps of his wife and the brisker ones of the young sailor.

And deep inside, somehow, he knew that everything he had believed in, everything he had thought was true, was going to be smashed. That he would never be the same man again. That he would never see anything in exactly the same way.

Lips compressed, he filled coffee mugs and joined his wife and Hardin at the round breakfast table. No one spoke. He looked at Marge, looked at Seth Hardin and then looked at his wife again. Neither of them would look at him.

"So," he said heavily, "who's gonna tell me?"

Hardin stirred and opened his mouth, a man with guts and courage, as befitted a SEAL, Nate thought sourly. Not one to let a lady do the hard thing.

But then, to his surprise, Marge reached out and laid a hand on Hardin's arm, silencing him. Then she turned to look at Nate. Straight in the eye. Huge tears sparkling on her lower eyelashes.

"Nate, Seth is . . . Seth is my son. He's *your* son."

Chapter 3

There was suddenly no air in the universe. The room seemed to have been bled dry of the last drop of oxygen, and his chest heaved uselessly. For a long, terrible moment, he was sure he was having a heart attack, and that his last moment of life was going to be this one, staring at a wife he didn't know and a son he'd never met.

But then the suffocating feeling let go, and blessed air flowed into his lungs, and he was up from the table, uncaring that he knocked the chair over. How *could* he care about something so paltry?

He walked out of the house. Without coat, hat or gloves, he walked out into the icy December night and strode away from the house, feeling as if he left his life behind.

Nothing would ever be the same again. That was the first realization to truly penetrate his numbness. Nothing would ever be the same again. He would never see his daughters quite the same way, would never see his wife quite the same way... and would never see himself the same way.

A son.

A son he had never known about.

Right now he didn't even want to know why that was. He wasn't ready to hear any explanations, any excuses. First he had to cope with the idea that a truth had been withheld from him. That the wife, in whose honesty he had believed implicitly for more than a quarter century, had been dishonest. That he had ached for a son he had thought he never had, and had convinced himself he was an ingrate to even wish he could have fathered a boy. That the yearning he had buried so deep had never needed to be buried.

That he had a son, and that his son had been stolen from him. Somehow. Someway. Some why.

And he didn't dare go back to that house until he could hear the truth without killing someone or smashing something.

Because suddenly, through the shock, he felt anger. Anger of such white heat that he doubted he had felt a fury so strong since Vietnam.

He had been cheated. Lied to. Betrayed. By the wife he had loved with all his heart. The woman to whom he had devoted his entire life. The lady he had worshiped and loved and would have died for.

She had lied to him.

Not about some little thing, like a dent in the car or the cost of a dress. No, Marge had always been scrupulously honest, even when she had known he would be displeased or upset.

Until this.

Except for this.

She had been guilty of a lie so big that . . .

There weren't even words for it.

He found himself standing on the corner across from the sheriff's office, and out of habit more than anything, and needing to be warm now that he was nearing frostbite, he crossed the street and went inside.

He was surprised to find Micah behind the desk.

"I thought Lew was on tonight?"

Micah shook his head. "Baby got sick, so I told him I'd take over."

"But what about your holiday?"

Again Micah shook his head. "Faith understands. Somebody has to work. We'll have Christmas tomorrow night, and Sally's too young to know the difference."

"I guess."

Micah cocked a brow at him. "What the hell are *you* doing here? I thought you had to be at church to hear your girls sing."

"I do."

"Then you'd better get going."

Instead, Nate pulled back one of the chairs across from Micah and sat. "I need to warm up. I need to think."

Micah stared at him for a long moment, in the way he had back in their Vietnam days when he knew Nate was disturbed but wasn't going to admit it. And just as he had all those years ago, Micah didn't question him now. After a moment, he merely nodded and returned his attention to the report he was working on.

For which Nate was grateful. He wasn't anywhere near ready to put words to what he was feeling. Hell, his feelings were so tangled up he couldn't even name them. Except for the anger. It was there with a white heat. He had no trouble picking that feeling out.

But the rest . . . Dazed, upset, hurt, he simply stared out the window at the lighted, decorated street and watched the snow fall gently.

At some point, he realized that for the first time since his eldest daughter had started singing in the choir, he had missed the candlelight service . . . well, except for the time there was that terrible accident.

And then he realized that he was sitting in the office on Christmas Eve, hiding. Hiding from his wife, from a son he might never seen again . . . might never have known.

Hiding from reality.

And he had never done that in his life. Not once, not even in Vietnam. He had always faced the hard stuff straight on.

A fist that seemed to grip his mind let go, and he began to think again. It was Christmas. He would go home and put a good face on it for the girls. What he was going to do about Marge... Well, that could wait. What he was going to do about lies and deceptions and betrayals...could wait.

He had six daughters at home who deserved a good Christmas.

And a son. God, that was going to take getting used to. But he *would* get used to it.

Rising, he headed for the door.

"Let me drive you," Micah said. "The county will keep for ten minutes, but your feet and pants are soaked."

He didn't argue. There didn't seem any point in it. The county would survive.

He wasn't at all sure *he* would.

The house was empty when he stepped inside. Evidently Marge had gone to the church and had taken Seth Hardin with her.

Seth Hardin. Should have been Seth Tate.

Why hadn't she told him?

The question whirled around in his head almost dervish-like as he took a quick hot shower and changed into fresh clothes. He ought to go over to the church and catch the last few minutes of the service, he thought.

And then he rebelled. He had been doing what had been expected of him for years now. He'd been a good sheriff, a good father, a good husband, a good citizen...

And this was what he got for it? A gut punch of such proportions he didn't know how he would ever deal with it? A wound to the heart and soul that was a gaping chasm seeming to widen with each breath he took?

He could, in fact, cling only to the belief that time would help him cope with this. That as the shock wore off he would come to some kind of understanding.

The sound of an engine alerted him to the fact that the van was pulling into the driveway. The girls and Yuma were back. Going to the kitchen, he started the fresh pot of coffee that was a requisite. The girls would come in, gifts would be exchanged....

He wondered if Marge had taken Seth to the motel, or if she was planning to put him up in the guest room. God! He needed to talk to her before he tried to talk to the young man. Not that Seth could be considered even remotely responsible for any of this, but Nate felt a need to understand at least something of how this had come about. Good Lord, he didn't even know for sure how old the boy was!

The girls burst into the kitchen with a blast of cold air and laughter, and he found himself surrounded by his daughters.

With cold noses and reddened cheeks, they hugged him and kissed him . . . and he realized at once they were offering comfort, though they didn't yet know why he needed it. They just knew something was wrong, and all six of them were there to circle him with their love and hold him tight.

And over their heads he saw his son-in-law, Yuma, standing there with a cockeyed, almost sad, smile, watching. As if he, too, understood that something earth-shattering had happened.

Then Marge stepped into the kitchen. And behind her came Seth. There was a moment of silence, then Wendy, his eldest, leapt into the breach.

"Girls, let's get the coffee cake served so we can open presents."

Another bustle of activity filled the tense moment, and throughout it he was aware of Marge's eyes on him. He couldn't bring himself to look at her yet, though. Not yet. He wasn't ready to face a plea for understanding when he wasn't sure he was ever going to be able to understand this.

Seth joined them in the living room, sitting in a chair back from the tree, from which he could observe everything without being obvious. Unasked questions were as much a part of the atmosphere as the scent of pine and coffee.

But at last, at long last, the gifts were opened, the paper and mess were disposed of, the girls headed off to bed, Wendy and Yuma said good-night and left. . . .

And that left Nate, Marge and Seth in the living room, with the winking colored lights on the tree causing the shadows to shift constantly.

Nate looked at the strong, clean lines of Seth's face and thought how very much the young man looked like a photo he had of himself, years ago. In his Special Forces uniform. In his own heart there was no doubt that Seth was his son.

Slowly, he turned his head and looked at Marge.

"Why?" he asked. "Why did you give my son away?"

She drew a short, sharp breath, as if he had struck her. Closing her eyes, she breathed raggedly for a few moments, as if she had to fight for control. Which, he thought detachedly, she probably did. This had to be difficult for her, too. But at the moment he didn't give a damn.

"When you...when you left for Vietnam the first time," she said, her voice breaking repeatedly, "I was barely seventeen. And I was pregnant. You hadn't said anything about marriage. About coming back to me.... You didn't write...." Her voice wavered and trailed off. He gave her no help, and after a bit, she continued.

"When I discovered I was pregnant, my parents wanted to send me to New York for an abortion. The shame...they couldn't handle the shame. I absolutely refused. So they sent me to my cousin Lou's in Colorado, and...I gave Seth up for adoption. It was...the only thing to do."

Nate rose from his chair and strode to the window that looked out across the front yard to the snowy street. "It wasn't the only thing to do," he said quietly. "You could have called the Red Cross. They'd have brought me home. I would have married you. We could have kept...could have kept our child."

Marge drew an audible, shuddery breath. "I was young, scared.... I didn't know what to do. My parents were pushing.... I didn't have anyone to turn to, Nate. I couldn't bring myself to tell anyone else. I was so *ashamed!*"

Slowly Nate turned to face her. "Why didn't you write to me? Why didn't you call the Red Cross? Damn it, Marge, why didn't you once in twenty-seven years just tell me the truth?"

He roared the last words, and she flinched but continued to meet his angry gaze bravely. Tears welled in her eyes and rolled down her cheeks. "I *did* write to you! You know I did! My father was stealing all our letters.... Oh, Nate, how could you think I never tried to tell you I was carrying your child?

"And when you didn't answer any of my letters, I thought you didn't care. Then we heard you were missing in action, and I thought for months that you were dead. By the time you came home, it was done, Nate. It was finished. What good would it have done to tell you back then? The adoption was sealed, you could never have gotten to him.... It would simply have caused you pain...."

He tilted his head back and looked away, seeking calm. Seeking control and patience. "It's causing me pain now, Marge," he said finally. "How the hell can I ever trust you again?"

She didn't answer. He didn't expect her to. He stood there, drawing one breath after another because he had to. There was simply no way he could just cease to exist, no way he could evade the pain to come. And it was only just beginning, he realized. Even as he was handed a son, the very heart and soul of his marriage was going up in flames of betrayal.

Presently—he was never afterward sure how long he stood there trying to absorb the impact of the blow—he shook himself and faced Seth. "Let me show you the guest room, son. It's better if we get to know each other when we've had some rest." He hesitated. "You *can* stay? Or did you have to leave right away?"

"No, sir. I called in earlier and extended my leave by a few days. I can stay." The young man stood, straight and tall, the spitting image of his father.

Twenty-seven years, Nate thought as he led the way down the hall to the guest room. Twenty-seven years. And every one of them had been a living lie.

He slept on a cot in the den, the first time in his entire marriage that he did not share the big bed with Marge when they were together. He was exhausted, and slept despite a mind that wouldn't slow down, but when he woke in the late morning, he felt as if he had never slept at all...and his mind was still worrying the problem.

First, he thought as he shaved, he had to get through Christmas Day. For the sake of the girls, today would be what Christmas should be. For the sake of the girls, he was going to act as if a nuclear bomb hadn't just been dropped in the center of his existence. Seth would be welcomed as the son he was, and nothing would be said about it. Marge could tell the girls whatever she saw fit for the moment. For the moment he wasn't going to comment on the situation to anyone.

As usual, the dining room table was set for the traditional Christmas brunch. A red-and-green tablecloth had almost vanished beneath the special dishes with a holly-and-berry design that were used only for this occasion. The table groaned beneath ham and eggs and coffee cakes. The girls were bustling around making everything perfect. And Seth, this morning in jeans and a pressed dress shirt, helped as much as they would let him.

His daughters, he realized, were making a valiant effort to act as if Seth's arrival was a perfectly normal, perfectly welcome event. Marge looked pale and determined. He figured he didn't look much better.

During brunch, Marge coaxed Seth to speak a little about his career. He regaled them all with tales that were carefully chosen to entertain without shocking, and soon had all the girls hanging on his every word.

Only a few days, Nate thought with a sudden sense of discomfort. Only a few days. They might be the only days he ever had with his son. The only chance he would ever have to know him. His marital problems suddenly seemed less significant than that one appalling fact. He'd already been cheated of twenty-seven years. Was he going to cheat himself of these few days, too?

The girls shooed Seth and him away from the table after brunch, and he took the opportunity to speak directly to the young man for the first time that morning. "Let's go for a walk."

Seth nodded. "I'll get my jacket."

The day was overcast and cold, and last night's fresh snowfall, though pristine, looked dull. Excited shrieks came from the end of the street where kids played with sleds on a small hill, and near it, skaters whirled and glided on the small rink the local homeowners created on a vacant lot each year. Nate purposefully turned away from the children and led the way toward quieter avenues.

In the end, he was the one who broke the silence.

"How do you feel about all of this, son?"

Seth turned his head and looked at him. A faint smile creased the corners of his dark eyes—Nate's eyes. "I've had a lot longer to get used to the idea, sir. I probably feel a lot better about it than you do."

Nate nodded, liking the cut of the young man. "Well, you've gathered it was a hell of a shock for me."

"I apologize for that. I insisted Marge not tell you about me until I was sure it would be right. I never thought that stopping by the house to tell you I was leaving town would let the cat out of the bag this way. Stupid, I guess."

Nate shrugged. "It doesn't make a damn bit of difference. It was going to be a shock any way you slice it. I never had even a whisper of a suspicion. Well, that's not your fault. And stand down, son. I don't bite, and I haven't been in the military for twenty years."

"Marge says you were Special Forces A-Team."

Nate nodded. He looked at his son. The realization still struck him like a punch. "Guess we have something else in common . . . besides genes, I mean."

"Looks that way. My family—my adoptive family—didn't quite know what to make of me. Going into the SEALs, I mean." He glanced at Nate again and grinned. "They weren't very adventurous people, and I think I spent most of my childhood scaring them to death. It's actually rather nice to know where it came from."

Nate felt his face cracking into a smile for the first time in what felt like forever. He hadn't thought of any of this from Seth's perspective yet, and he had to admit it wasn't likely he would ever fully understand what it must be like to grow up without knowing such things about yourself. "Well, I guess you can blame me for that. And Marge, too. I can remember when she was pretty damn adventurous herself."

Climbing out of her second-floor bedroom window and down a tree to be with him in the evenings while they were still in high school. Her parents would have killed her, but she crept out, anyway, to spend relatively innocent hours with him, just walking, or hiding in the barn loft, keeping warm under blankets and hay while they talked.

Like that country song, they'd often set out to meet in the middle on slow summer afternoons when they could get away from their chores. Countless hours spent lazing in open fields beneath clear summer skies, watching clouds or counting stars and talking in the aimless easy way of the young.

But not adventurous enough in the end, Nate thought now. Not adventurous enough to insist on keeping their child. To stand up against her parents and call the Red Cross. No. Instead she had allowed herself to be pushed into giving up her child, and then for the next twenty-seven years she had kept her lie.

The taste was bitter on his tongue. But he would deal with Marge and her lies later. For now he had a son to get to know, and very little time in which to do it. "Did you know you were adopted all along?"

Seth nodded. "The Hardins never made a secret of it. They were good people."

"Were?"

"They died in an auto accident."

"I'm sorry."

Seth nodded. "I sure was. They were good parents. Then I shipped out on a mission, and we were too busy to think much about it. Anyhow, afterwards . . . well, I got to thinking that I had real parents somewhere. A real mother. And I didn't have anyone else. The Hardins had only me, and no family themselves. So . . ."

"You started searching."

"That's right. It took a long time and was expensive, and I finally had to hire a private investigator. And then when I located Mrs. Tate, I had to decide whether I was going to do anything about it." He glanced at Nate and found the sheriff listening intently. "I'm not ordinarily indecisive, but this time I was. I thought long and hard before I even came up here to scout. And even then, I didn't intend to make myself known to Mrs. Tate. But when she opened the door, I—'' Seth looked away a moment, then shook his head. "I'm still not sure what happened. I saw something like recognition on her face, and I told her."

Which brought Nate around to another question that had been stewing in his gut. "How long has she known?"

Something in his tone must have alerted Seth to feelings, because the younger man turned suddenly and looked at him. "I made her swear she wouldn't tell you."

"Why?"

Seth shook his head. "Funny how the obvious seems to escape everyone. You two may be my biological parents, but that didn't necessarily mean you'd be people I would want to know. So I made her swear she wouldn't tell you. She didn't like it, but I didn't give her much choice. Last night I just came by to say I was leaving tomorrow morning. I wanted to thank you for letting me ride with Micah, and I intended to just say goodbye to Mrs. Tate as her friend's kid. I never imagined the whole thing would blow up like it did."

Nate shook his head and walked a few more steps before replying. "No reason you should, I guess. No reason at all. No way you could know that she's been acting so strangely for the last four months that I half figured she was leaving me for another man." He shook his head and swore softly. "Damn! No wonder she's been acting like she's under a death sentence."

"Is she?"

Nate scowled at him. "She's been lying to me for twenty-seven years, son. You think about it."

They walked on a little farther before Nate said, "I guess you must have wondered about us."

"A lot. A whole lot. When I was growing up, I think I was angry more than anything about it, even though my parents always told me my mother wouldn't have given me up if she hadn't *had* to."

Nate snorted. "Right."

Suddenly Seth halted and faced him, forcing Nate to do the same. "Look, Sheriff, I know you're mad about this. You should have had some kind of preparation, some kind of warning. I can understand that you feel...betrayed. But in all honesty, I think you're forgetting she was seventeen, living in a small town where unwed pregnancies were about the worst disgrace that could happen, and she thought you were *dead*."

"What makes you an authority?"

"She told me. She explained to me, and I *listened*."

And I haven't, Nate thought. He turned abruptly and resumed walking. "I'll tell you, boy," he said finally, ignoring the fact that the SEAL beside him was far from being a boy, "what sticks in my craw is the *lie*. But that's between her and me. Let's just you and I get acquainted here, and you let *me* deal with my marriage."

"Aye, sir."

Nate glanced at him and smiled reluctantly. "You're making the navy a career, I take it?"

Seth nodded. "Not much use for my kind of talents anywhere else. I think I'd die of boredom doing almost anything else."

"I used to feel that way myself. Having kids changed my perspective quite a bit."

"It would probably change mine, too," Seth agreed. "But I haven't been lucky that way. Women get attracted to us crazy types, but not many want to live the life-style."

"Yeah." Suddenly Nate laughed, a genuine laugh. "We *are* crazy types, aren't we? Nobody who was sane would do the things Special Forces do."

It had once been a source of pride in him, he found himself thinking as he and Seth continued to walk. The gung-ho attitude remained even after all these years, the can-do mentality. Glancing over at his son, he felt an unexpected surge of pride.

"I imagine you saw action in the Gulf?"

Seth nodded. "Early on. We were well established behind enemy lines by the time Desert Storm was launched."

"I figured you all probably had plenty to do with guiding the air strikes."

"Something to do with it. And with preparing LZ's... landing zones." And other things. The words weren't spoken, but Nate heard them, anyway. Much that special warfare groups did could never be spoken about. Some SEALs had undoubtedly been in Kuwait and Iraq almost as soon as the decision to send troops had been made. Actually, they'd probably been going ashore a lot earlier than that, gathering intelligence. But these were not questions he could ask, because he was sure Seth wasn't allowed to answer.

And damn it, he had a *son*. It was the most incredible realization, and it suddenly seemed to become real. This tall, attractive stranger beside him was his *son*.

Abruptly he stopped walking and stood looking at Seth. The younger man halted, too, and waited patiently, bearing Nate's scrutiny calmly.

"Damn," Nate said finally. "Damn! You're my *son*."

Seth nodded. "It'll take a little getting used to, won't it? For all of us." He cocked his head a little and looked Nate straight in the eye. "And, of course, maybe we'll discover we have nothing in common and go our separate ways."

Nate shoved his hand into his jacket pocket and pulled out a roll of antacids. He popped a couple in his mouth. "Seth, we'll never have what we would've had if you'd grown up with us. It's just that simple. But I sure as hell don't see why we can't be friends. I'm kinda like Will Rogers. I never met a man I didn't like, and in your case, I already respect you."

"Because I'm a SEAL?"

"Partly. And partly because you were man enough to stand up for Marge when you sure as hell got as much reason as anyone to be mad at her."

Before Seth could respond, Nate heard the familiar growl of a Blazer engine coming up the snowy street behind them.

"Oh, hell," he said, turning, and recognized Micah Parish at the wheel. "Didn't anybody tell the troublemakers it's Christmas?"

Micah pulled to a halt and rolled the window down to lean out and speak to Nate. He barely spared Seth a glance and a nod.

"They found more barrels, this time at Winchester's ranch."

"Damn it! Same age?"

"Older. Leaking longer. Frankly, I didn't want to get too close. It doesn't look healthy at all. Some kind of chemical reaction must be going on, because the snow's all melted around it, and the ground is bare of growth. I called in the disposal team, but I don't think they'll get here before tomorrow."

Probably not, Nate thought. Everybody *else* was enjoying a holiday. Suddenly he laughed, a rusty, rueful sound. Work, he decided abruptly, was as good an excuse as any to put off his confrontation with Marge.

"Micah," he said, "meet my son."

Micah's expression didn't even flicker as he nodded to the young man.

"Now," Nate said, as if he hadn't just dropped a major bomb, "why don't we all go out and take a look at these barrels?"

They had been dumped in an old sandstone quarry in an isolated part of Carson Winchester's ranch. Standing at the edge of the quarry, Nate, Micah and Seth all looked down on the tumbled barrels. Whoever had dumped them hadn't even bothered to drive down into the quarry to unload them, but had dumped them right over the edge. All the barrels were badly banged up, and most were ruptured.

"Hell!" Nate growled the word and then looked over at the concerned ranchers, Winchester and his downstream neighbor Ransom Laird. Spring runoff ran through this quarry from the mountains and fed eastward into quite a few ranches. "Carson, you don't have any idea at all how long these barrels have been here?"

Winchester shook his head. "Haven't been out here in more than a year. Fence line runs a mile west and a half-mile south. If one of my hands wandered over this way and saw anything, he never said nothin' to me."

"Ask 'em, will you? If any of them saw these barrels before, I want to talk to them."

Winchester nodded.

"Damn," Nate swore again, and looked down at the barrels. Puddles surrounding them glistened with oil-slick rainbows of color, even on this gray day. And Micah was right. Something down there was generating enough heat to melt the snow for six or eight feet around. Antifreeze effect of chemicals, maybe. Or something far worse. Radioactive material generated heat, didn't it?

"Carson, I don't want anybody over here until the disposal team gets here. Until we know what that crud is, it's best to keep clear."

"No problem by me. Isaac only came out this way 'cause we're missing that calf and he mighta wandered this way."

"You find the calf?"

"Oh, yeah." Carson nodded and jerked his thumb in an easterly direction. "Up thataways. Damn critter must not have a brain, wandering so far from his mama that way."

"He seem okay? Not sick or anything?"

Carson tilted his head, then shook it. "Not so far as I could see...'ceptin maybe a little hungry. I'll watch him now, though. You can bet on it."

Nate turned to Ransom, whose golden beard and hair looked like burnished bronze even in the gray light. "You haven't noticed anything?"

"Not yet. But I think I'm going to start looking around. This is the second dump you've found, isn't it?"

Nate nodded. "Yep."

"Then I guess we *all* better start looking around in gullies and ditches."

Micah, who owned a ranch himself, agreed. "And my place would be a great dump, because I don't run a herd and there are places I haven't been to since I bought it."

They had plowed their way up the old quarry road with the plow attached to the front of Micah's Blazer, and now they turned around and headed back out. The police radio squawked from time to time, minor messages between patrolling officers, but nothing of great importance. It was Christmas Day, and most folks were home with their families, tucked in safe and tight and looking forward to Christmas dinner.

A glance at the digital clock on the console told Nate he and Seth would probably get back to the house just in time to sit down with Marge and the girls. On that thought, he leaned back in the seat and closed his eyes.

God, he thought, there was no choice but to get through it. It was a feeling he well knew from other times, but this was the first time he had ever felt this way about his home life. His private life. His wife.

Just get through it somehow. Anyhow.

"Been just about everywhere," he heard Micah say to Seth. "Everywhere that matters, anyway. Pleiku in the central highlands of Vietnam was where your dad and I met. He was my team leader."

Where your dad and I met. Micah's casual words, his casual acceptance of this unbelievable situation, pierced Nate sharply. *Your dad and I.*

Damn it, he wasn't this young man's father. Not in any way that actually counted. He had been denied that. Deprived of it. And there was no way he could ever recover what had been lost. No way. Seth would forever be someone else's son in the important ways. They might become friends, they might even manage to grow close, but it would never be father-son. Not really.

And Marge was responsible for that.

Initial anger had given way to a sick feeling in his gut, and thinking like this was only making it worse. Just get through Seth's visit, he told himself now. Just concentrate on the young man who was his own flesh and blood, and make whatever ties he could with him before the opportunity was lost.

When Micah pulled the Blazer into the Tate driveway to let him and Seth out, Nate didn't move. After a moment, Seth climbed out with a farewell to Micah and walked up to the house.

"I take it," Micah said after a moment, "that you didn't know about this."

"Found out last night when he showed up." He kept staring straight ahead, not even looking at the man he considered to be one of his two best friends in the world.

"Ouch."

"Yeah."

"While you . . . were in Nam?"

"Yeah. During my first tour. I keep wondering why she didn't call the Red Cross. I know her father destroyed all my letters to her, and destroyed all hers to me, but he couldn't have kept her from calling the Red Cross. She says everyone thought I was dead, and that was true, but only for a little while. Just for a little while. And you know, Micah, the worst is that she never told me the truth. Not for twenty-seven years."

"Probably scared half to death," Micah said quietly.

"I guess." After a moment, he turned and looked straight at Micah. "I'll handle it. Just need to . . . adjust."

Micah gave him the faintest of smiles. The big Indian seldom said much and smiled even less. "Adjusting gets harder as we get older, doesn't it?"

At that, Nate almost smiled himself. "Yeah. Damn near had a heart attack last night over this. Okay, scout, keep me posted. I'll be in the office in the morning."

He climbed out then, but paused to watch Micah drive away. *Get through it,* he reminded himself. *Just get through it.*

Chapter 4

Inside, dinner was ready to be served. A huge ham already stood steaming on the table in front of his place, where he would carve it. Marge faced him from the opposite end of the table as she had at countless mealtimes over so many years. Her eyes were red rimmed; her hands were knotted together at her waist.

"I told the girls," she said quietly.

She had told the girls. Part of him fiercely resented her taking this step without discussing it with him, and part of him was vastly relieved not to have to personally tell his daughters that he hadn't practiced the rules he had preached to them over the years.

One by one he looked at them, from eldest Wendy to youngest Krissie, and what he saw warmed him. No condemnation was in any of those eyes. There was simply breathtaking love.

Then he looked down at the waiting ham. Seth ought to carve it, he found himself thinking. If the young man had grown up with them, he would have wanted Seth to carve the Christmas ham this year, because he would be home for a holiday visit just like this, his eldest child and only son. If things had been normal....

"Seth, you carve the ham."

A sudden silence filled the large dining room. Marge seemed to stop breathing. All six of his daughters and Yuma stopped in midmotion and looked at him. Everyone sensed the importance of this...including Seth, who suddenly looked embarrassed and ill at ease.

"Come on, son," Nate said. "You can handle the SEALs, you can handle our Christmas ham. I want you to do it. I'd ask you to do it if you'd been with us since birth."

As easy as that, Nate thought. He made it real as easy as that. He even felt a faint smile on his face.

Then he looked straight at Marge and knew nothing in his life was ever again going to be easy.

It was late that night when he knew it wasn't going to be a simple matter of "getting through it." Yuma had left with Wendy, the girls and Seth had retired, and Marge had gone to bed.

He knew she was waiting for him. He knew he had hurt her by sleeping on a cot in the den last night. The reflection of the hurt had been in her eyes all day.

But what about *his* hurt? he found himself wondering savagely. What about his betrayal?

He could not—absolutely *could not*—get into that bed with Marge. Nor could he, he realized suddenly, stay in this house. With the girls around all day during the holiday break, he would feel as if he were trying to hold in an explosion. There would be almost no opportunity to even talk with Marge...not that he was ready to do that yet.

Finally he walked into the bedroom and closed the door behind him. Marge was sitting up in bed, leaning against pillows, a closed book in her lap. She simply looked at him, appeal, fear and sorrow filling her green eyes. Slowly, a tear trickled down her cheek.

"I'm leaving," Nate said. "Now."

She closed her eyes, squeezing them tightly shut, and stopped breathing. Finally the breath trickled out of her, a ragged sound of failing control. "We—" Her voice broke. "We can't work it out?"

"I don't know. All I know is if I stay here I'm going to explode. And if I explode I'll say things I'll never be able to take back. So..." He looked away, seeking the last crumbling remnants of his own control. "It's better if I clear out. When...I feel calmer...we'll talk. I'll stay at the office tonight. Tomorrow I'll find a room. Probably over Mahoney's bar, where Gage used to live."

She nodded slowly and drew a long, tattered breath. And slowly, very slowly, she opened tear-filled eyes. "I love you, Nate." Her voice was thick with anguish.

He couldn't even look at her. "I'm finding that a little hard to believe right now," he said finally. "And I'm finding it impossible to say. So I'm going. I'll come back tomorrow for whatever I need."

Five minutes later, with an overnight bag beside him, he was backing out of his driveway and trying not to remember how she had looked, how she had sounded. And how it had hurt him to hear those words from her when she had been guilty of the biggest lie possible.

Virgil Beauregard was on duty, sitting at the desk with his feet up, hands clasped behind his head. When he saw Nate, he arched a brow. "Something up?"

Nate shook his head. "I'm crashing on the cot in my office."

Beau's feet hit the floor with a thud. "What's wrong?"

"Damn it, Beau, I don't want to discuss it!"

"The whole damn town is going to discuss it if Velma finds you here in the morning. Maybe you'd better give me the official distribution so I can handle her."

Nate, halfway down the hall, whirled around. "It's nobody's damn business!" But even as he growled at Beau, he knew that wasn't so. In a community this size, everything was everyone's business. And the sheriff's personal business was apt to be the juiciest morsel of all.

Beau regarded him steadily, undisturbed by Nate's angry words. The two men had been working together nearly twenty years and weren't easily bothered by such things.

But Nate didn't want to speak the words. To speak them would be almost like making an official announcement of the rupture between him and Marge. Would make it real. Set it in concrete. Yet the rupture *was* real. He wasn't going back to that house in the morning. He wasn't going back to that house for a long time. Maybe... maybe he was never going back. Because he was married to a complete stranger.

A hollowness seemed to fill him, a cold emptiness that contained nothing but a wasteland scoured by an icy wind.

It was real.

"Marge and I," he said to Beau, "are separating."

Then he turned and walked with leaden feet down the hallway to his office.

Separating. Marge heard the word first from the lips of her youngest daughter Krissie two days later. Krissie had been asked by a girlfriend, who had heard her mother talking about it with her father. *Everyone* was talking, Krissie said tearfully.

Everyone.

And Marge heard the news last of all, from the lips of her daughter. Shock poured through her, stunning waves of heat and cold as her knees weakened and she collapsed onto a kitchen chair. *Separating.*

Oh, it couldn't be. Couldn't be! It was just gossip....

But wasn't that, in fact, what had happened? Nate was now living in that barren room above Mahoney's. Had come yesterday to take most of his clothes. The old stereo system. The small TV. The...

Grief welled in her, a sudden uprush that choked everything inside her, that doubled her over and ripped gasping sobs from her throat.

Separating. It was a death knell.

"Mom?" Krissie asked tearfully. "Mom? It isn't true, is it? Tell me Daddy's not leaving!"

But Marge couldn't answer her. Not to reassure her. Not to tell her the worst was coming to pass. The grief that consumed her didn't leave room for speech.

"Mom? Mom, why did Daddy leave?"

Still sobbing, Marge straightened and held out her arms to her daughter. Krissie flew into them, and together they cried and cried and cried.

Nate wasn't coming home. Maybe forever.

Reverend Fromberg had been pastoring most of the people in Conard County for over two decades, having come to the area as assistant to old Reverend Castille back when Marge and Nathan Tate had been young marrieds with two young daughters. Watching their breakup was almost as painful as having his own heart torn out.

And it was affecting an awful lot of good people. Marge and Nathan Tate, strongly married for nearly thirty years, pillars of both community and church, had become a constant in the lives of many. There was an almost universal sense of shock at their separation, and an almost universal uneasiness. If the Tates couldn't stay together, who could?

Well, this just couldn't be tolerated, Fromberg told himself as he stared out at a wintry morning several weeks later. Couldn't be tolerated at all. Two people who had come through so much over so many years had no business shattering their relationship. Whatever they thought was worth this pain simply wasn't. There wasn't a question in his mind. Whatever had happened wasn't sufficient to justify a rupture of this magnitude.

He knew both Marge and Nate well, and would have said there was no way on earth they would ever break up. It wasn't often two people who'd been together so long still felt the degree of love that those two felt. Or that Fromberg would have sworn they felt up until Christmas.

The difficulty was that, without knowing exactly what had caused Nate to move into that abominable apartment above Mahoney's, Fromberg didn't know exactly how to approach the problem. But he *was* going to approach it. It was his duty as pastor, for one thing. For another, they were his friends and it was killing him to think of how they must be hurting.

The easiest way to get information, of course, would be to talk to Marge Tate. Nate was as closemouthed as a clam about anything and everything. Marge would be more likely to confide in him as pastor. In order to help, he had to know the parameters of the problem.

And three weeks was long enough, he thought. Three weeks indicated that neither of them were likely to come to their senses easily. But the longer this separation dragged on, the deeper the wounds would grow. Someone had to intervene and try to patch things, and there was no one else but Fromberg in a position of sufficient authority to butt in.

Shaking his head over the mess, he reached for the phone and dialed Marge Tate. Five minutes later he was on his way to the Tate house.

Marge ushered him into the kitchen and served him the green tea he liked. He had long since ceased to be a formal guest in the Tate home, and Marge and Nate always welcomed him like one of the family.

She didn't look good at all, he thought, as he watched her pour the tea and set out a plate of cookies. Dark circles rimmed her eyes, her cheeks were too pale, and she'd lost even more weight.

"Marge, are you ill?"

Her head jerked a little, almost as if the sound of his voice startled her. She couldn't even manage a smile. "No, Dan, really. I'm fine."

"Horse pshaw."

"What?" Astonished, she simply stared at him.

"Horse pshaw. Neither you nor Nate are fine, and there's no use pretending otherwise, Marge. What the dickens is going on between you two? Nothing could be this bad...."

"Oh, it is," she whispered, her eyes filling with tears. "Oh, Dan, it's every bit that bad. And it's all my fault."

He felt his own throat tighten in the face of her patent grief. "But Marge...Marge, I've known you over twenty years. I can't believe you could have done anything that bad."

"But I did. Oh, I did!" The words came out on a tremulous breath, barely audible as she visibly battled tears. "Oh, Dan, I did something so awful—" Breaking off, she leapt up from her chair and ran from the kitchen, leaving Fromberg to stare into his cup of tea and try to conceive of Marge Tate having done anything awful enough to warrant all this.

No, he thought. It didn't add up. Marge Tate was a good woman, inside and out. Whatever she had done would be a minor transgression in most people's eyes. Surely. Marge returned a few minutes later, eyes red rimmed, nose shiny. "I'm sorry, Dan. That was rude."

"But forgivable, under the circumstances. Do you want to tell me what happened, Marge?"

She turned her head, looking out the window at the gray, snowy day. The cottonwood that she and Nate had planted when they built this house reached bony, leafless fingers to the sky. "Lies come home to roost, Dan. Sooner or later, they catch up."

Suddenly Fromberg was no longer nearly so certain this was a minor problem. "What lie are we talking about here?"

Marge continued to look out the window as if she couldn't bear to look directly at him. "Do you remember the naval officer who came with us to the candlelight service?"

"Why, yes. Seth . . . Hardin, wasn't it?" Marge couldn't possibly be about to tell him she was going to run off with a much younger man. No. Not that it was beyond the realm of possibility, but it didn't seem at all like Marge—

"Seth Hardin is my son."

There were times when even a man who had heard everything could be stunned. Not so much because of the news, but because of who it came from. For long moments, he simply stared at Marge while shock ricocheted through his mind. Realizing finally that his silence had grown far too long, he spoke. "Your son?"

"My son," she said raggedly. "Nate's son. Nate didn't know about him. Seth was—Seth was born while Nate was . . . before we . . ."

Patiently he waited as she struggled to tell the entire story, and as he listened a painful stillness grew in him. A silence compounded of deep grief and deep shock. Two people whom he loved dearly had been wounded almost beyond comprehension. And as a result, one of them was now wounding the other in a terrible way. In a way that might be irrevocable.

And he wasn't quite sure what to do about it. As understanding grew in him, he realized that the problem was even worse than he had imagined. In fact, he admitted now, he had come over here anticipating something relatively simple, like midlife crisis or another woman. Not something of this magnitude. Not a lie this big.

Reaching across the table, he patted Marge's shoulder and wondered how this could ever be mended. On the one hand, he acknowledged that Marge had really had very little choice, especially believing that Nate didn't want her, and later, that he was dead. Given the apparent circumstances at the time, she had done what she could. The only thing she could. She had done what was best for the child.

But he could sympathize just as strongly with Nate. For heaven's sake, Marge should have told him about the child as soon as he returned from Vietnam. Certainly as soon as he asked her to marry him. Yes, Fromberg could well sympathize with Nate's sense of betrayal. The lie was enormous, and far worse for having been kept so long.

Understanding the magnitude of the problem didn't help at all, either. This was no simple case of exhorting a man to exercise a little control over his hormones. Of reminding a woman what she was tossing away when she turned her back.

Rising from the table, he walked to the back door and stared out the window at the dismal day. Right now, Nate would be feeling that his entire marriage was a lie. He would be wondering how he could ever believe Marge again about anything. He would be wondering how many other lies he had been told over the years.

And there wasn't a whole lot his pastor could say. Because trust, once shattered, was hard to mend. The hardest thing of all.

But neither could Fromberg ignore what was happening here. Neither could he let it continue without making an effort to help resolve matters. There was little that couldn't be forgiven by a willing heart.

Turning, he looked at Marge. She sat staring at her hands in her lap, looking so defeated and alone that his heart went out to her.

"I'll speak to Nate, Marge," he said. "I'll speak to him."

Marge drew a long, shaky breath, but didn't look up. "It won't do any good, Dan. It won't do any good at all."

"Well, it sure won't hurt to try."

"It'll just make him madder. Dan, please!"

"No, Marge, I can't keep silent. You were wrong not to tell him about the child a long time ago. But what you did was perfectly understandable. And keeping the secret *is* forgivable, regardless of what Nate thinks at the moment. Maybe if he hears it from someone else, it'll hurry him back to his senses."

Marge lifted red-rimmed eyes. "He hasn't lost his sense, Dan. He's been wounded. By me. By his wife. He's always t-trusted m-me...." Biting her lip, she looked away. "I betrayed him. He's not going to forget that. Ever." Blinking rapidly, she drew a couple of ragged breaths to steady herself. "I thought—I thought I was protecting him. But I wasn't really. I guess ... I guess I was protecting myself."

"Don't be so hard on yourself, Marge! You were hardly more than a child! And I'm sure you meant to spare him the pain. I believe that. In all the years I've known you, I've never once known you to put yourself before Nate or the girls in anything. Not once. Not in the smallest way. No, I don't believe that and I won't believe that. And I'll tell Nate so to his face!"

Her reply was little more than a tremulous whisper. "He won't thank you for it, Dan."

"I don't expect him to."

No, Fromberg thought as he drove in the direction of the sheriff's office a short while later. No, he certainly didn't expect Nathan Tate to thank him for interfering. Nate was self-reliant, independent and absolutely determined to handle his life himself. He'd never asked for advice from anyone. And until now, he'd done well enough without it.

But now, Fromberg thought, Nathan Tate was in the process of making the biggest mistake of his entire life. The most catastrophic mistake he could make. No true friend, no pastor, could stand back in silence and just let him do it.

The rooms above Mahoney's were utterly depressing. So depressing that Nate was working record hours to avoid going back to them. Sixteen- and eighteen-hour days were becoming his norm. Anything to avoid staring at those dingy walls while thinking about what Marge had cheated him out of. Anything to avoid facing the fact that the bedrock of his world had turned into quicksand.

For the first time in more years than he wanted to remember, his desk was clear of all paperwork. Now time hung heavy on his hands even here, and he had to restrain himself from getting involved in his deputies' cases. At this rate, he thought with pained ruefulness, he was going to become everybody's least favorite person.

With effort, he resisted an urge to drum his fingers on the scarred desk top. Time, he found himself thinking, to drop in on friends. Like Ransom and Mandy Laird. Yeah. And he could use the toxic waste thing as an excuse....

A sigh escaped him before he could stop it. He felt like a leaf drifting aimlessly on the wind. Without Marge, his life was rudderless, purposeless, pointless. Without his family, he was a man without identity or meaning. His whole world had revolved around Marge, the girls, his job. But above all, Marge. His touchstone. His reason for getting out of bed every damn morning.

And he was getting awfully tired of feeling sorry for himself. Time to kick his butt into gear. Do something useful. Anything. Go out to the Laird place and ask if the sheep were showing any signs of poisoning. That'd take a couple of hours at least. Maybe longer, since Mandy would undoubtedly ask him to stay for coffee.

"Got a minute, Nate?"

As soon as he heard Reverend Fromberg's voice, Nate wished he'd escaped out the front door five minutes ago. He had hoped Dan would have the sense not to butt in, but he should have guessed that pastoring was no easier to stop doing than sheriffing. Suppressing a sigh, he rose and shook Fromberg's hand, before motioning him to a seat.

"Save your breath, Dan."

The pastor smiled. "Why? It's free."

Ordinarily Nate would have chuckled, but these were not ordinary times, and he was not feeling like his ordinary self. Instead, he scowled faintly. "Look, I appreciate your concern but—"

"No, you don't appreciate my concern," Fromberg interrupted. "But so what. You won't listen to me, at least not right now. But whatever I say will rattle around in your head until eventually you hear it. I know you, Nate. It may take weeks, but you'll remember this conversation. And when you do, you'll hear what I'm about to say. So I'm going to have my say."

Nate's frown deepened. "Look, I don't want to hear it."

"I know. Listen, anyway."

"I don't think you understand the problem!"

"The only way to determine that is for you to hear what I think the problem is."

Nate swore softly, uncharacteristically, and looked away. "There's no way on earth you can possibly understand, Dan. No way. It's not something a person can imagine."

"No, I don't expect it is. But some things are obvious to anyone. Like the fact that this happened twenty-seven years ago, when Marge was still very much a child. When she was all alone and didn't know if you were alive or dead. I imagine she felt even more alone than you did. At least on patrol you had your buddies who were trained to look out for you. She had no one at all."

"I understand that! Damn it, I understand that!"

"Do you really?" Fromberg leaned forward and slapped his palm emphatically on the desk. "I somehow suspect that you haven't yet tried to put yourself in Marge's shoes. Not seriously. I know you always wanted a son—"

"No!" Nate interrupted him ruthlessly, harshly. "This whole damn county's been pitying me for nearly thirty years because I never had a son. Let me tell you something. If I'd had one, it would have been great. Yes, I'd have liked to do all those father-son things. But it was never a grief for me that I didn't have a boy. Never a problem that I had only daughters! I will *not* have you or anyone else saying that I moved out because I can't forgive Marge for depriving me of a son. You can't love a child you never had, and you can't grieve for the loss of someone you never knew!"

"Nate—"

"No, I don't want to hear it. The lack of a boy was never a problem for me. Or between Marge and me. And it's not the root of the problem now! Damn it, Dan, I'd have moved out if a *daughter* had turned up on my doorstep!"

Fromberg didn't reply immediately, and in the silence the ring of telephones in the outer offices could be heard, as could Velma's raucous laughter at something one of the deputies said. Finally he spoke, his voice quiet. "I know that, Nate. I know that."

"Do you? Then why did you say I'd always wanted a son?"

"Because, whether it was a big wish or a small wish, or a wish so minor you dismissed it, the fact remains you wanted a son. And whether you want to admit it or not, you can't help but be a tiny bit angry that you had a son all along and never knew it. But that's not the issue here. I was just starting with the small things, because they're easier to dismiss. No, the real problem here is that you feel Marge betrayed you. Lied to you."

"I don't just *feel* it, Dan, I *know* it. There's no other word for it. And she kept the lie for our entire marriage. How many other lies have there been?"

"Nate, I'm sure—"

"Well, I'm not!" Nate interrupted savagely. "I'm not, and may never be. How can I be sure? She lied once about something so big, so important, that I still can't fully grasp the magnitude of it. If she can do that, she could lie about anything. Everything!"

"But why would she?" Fromberg asked reasonably. "She had a reason to conceal the boy's birth. Quite a bit of reason, actually, considering she probably thought you'd behave exactly this way if you found out."

"Look—"

"No, *you* look! Why don't you consider that she was protecting you at least as much as she was protecting herself!"

"And that's an excuse for lies?" Nate nearly growled the words. "You just don't get it, do you? I don't think she does, either! I don't think anybody does! You can't found a relationship on trust without truth! Everything I believed for the last thirty years may be nothing but lies! I can't trust a liar!"

"One lie doesn't make a liar."

"Oh, come off it! We're not talking about a little lie! We're not talking about her telling me I'm handsome when I'm not! We're talking about a *big* lie. About lying for twenty-seven years, every single day! We're talking about a lie that got repeated in every single passing minute that she didn't tell the truth!"

He shoved back from his desk and leaned over on his hands, glaring down at Fromberg. "You listen to me, Reverend. This is the bottom line. The only proof I have that Seth Hardin is my son is her word. Her confession that she's been lying for twenty-seven years. Makes it kinda hard to know the truth, doesn't it?" Turning, he grabbed his jacket and Stetson off the coat tree. "I've got work to do, Reverend. See you in church."

Fromberg remained seated and said nothing as Nate stalked out of his office and down the corridor to the front. Velma glanced up and nodded when he said he was heading out to the Laird ranch. The deputy at the duty desk didn't say anything at all. Nobody was saying much to him these days, he thought sourly as he stomped out to his Blazer. And that suited him just fine.

Sunlight poked through the clouds, reflecting off the snowy countryside with blinding intensity. Nate felt around on top of his visor for his sunshades and slipped them on. Damn county was going to hell in a hand basket, he thought irritably. Just one thing after another these days, and most of it related to outsiders. The creeping crud of the big cities was seeping even into these pristine spaces.

As he crested a low hill, he saw a dozen head of cattle in the road ahead of him. Pulling up close, he climbed out and used his hat to shoo the cows off the road. It wasn't too hard, given that the creatures were dumb and inclined to stick together. Once he got them moving in the right direction, it only took a few minutes to get them all behind the damaged fence line.

Using some wire from the back of his truck, he strung it between two fence posts, across the collapsed portion of the existing fence. It would hold the cattle for a while, anyway. Then he radioed Velma to call Tom Preston and let him know his fence was down and where.

And then he just sat there on the edge of the seat, door open, booted foot on the running board, and he looked at that fence and thought that maybe it was a little odd how it had fallen. For a fence to sag to the ground that way you usually needed more than a couple of posts to tip, unless the wire was snapped.

Wire broke; sure it did. All the time. But usually just one strand of it, not enough to bring the whole fence down. And Preston was a careful rancher—he'd have his hands checking the fence often enough that something like this wasn't too likely at all. Not that it couldn't happen. Anything could happen.

Bothered, Nate climbed down again and waded into the snow to examine the fence more closely.

The cattle had trampled the area pretty thoroughly, destroying any hope of finding footprints or anything else to identify the cause of the fence's fall. But after a few moments of examination, he pretty much knew all he needed to know, anyway. When he at last found the ends of the snapped wire where they lay buried in deep snow, there was no mistaking the fact that they had been cut. The disfiguring marks left by wire cutters were as apparent as a neon sign to a man who'd strung plenty of fence wire in his day.

Somebody had put down Preston's fence. And people pretty much only did that for a reason.

Hell! Rustlers? Or another waste dump site? Looking past the milling cattle, he scanned the snow for signs of vehicle tracks, but could see none. Which didn't mean diddly-squat, of course.

For a moment, just a moment, frustration as scalding as liquid fire poured through him. It was beginning to feel like trying to hold back a flood with a broom—the toxic waste crap, Marge, now this. He was only one man, and he could wield only one broom and . . .

He swore one short word and turned to stalk back to his Blazer. Climbing in, he turned over the engine and turned the heater on full-bore. His pant legs were thoroughly soaked now, and he was beginning to feel chilled.

"Velma," he snapped into the microphone, "get Gage out here on County Road 103, ten-mile mark. And tell him to bring whatever and whoever he wants. This fence didn't come down by accident."

"Funny you should say that, Nate. Those are the exact words Tom Preston said when I called him."

"Well, he sure as hell is right. If you can round up Micah, get him out here, too, will you?"

"Sure thing, boss."

And now he had to sit here and wait it out. No way could he just trot off and leave the scene of a crime. It might be something as minor as snowmobilers who wanted to run where they shouldn't. Or it could be as major as rustlers. Either way, he couldn't drive off and leave the area to the mercies of fate.

Which meant he had to sit here alone with his thoughts, something he had been steadfastly avoiding for the past few weeks.

From time to time, despite the best will in the world, he would suddenly see Marge in his mind's eye. Suddenly she was there, and the pain that ripped through him was invariably fierce. Several weeks had done nothing to ease the sense of betrayal he felt, nothing to ease the anguish of having lost nearly everything that mattered. The anguish of having lost Marge.

For he had lost the woman he loved. In plain terms, the woman he loved had never truly existed. She had been a chimera created by his imagination. The woman he loved could never have been capable of a betrayal of this magnitude.

But Marge was only the beginning and ending of the pain. His daughters were the rest of it. When Marge didn't pop into his thoughts, one of his girls did. And lately, their faces in his memory weren't smiling. No. Lately he couldn't stop remembering the way Krissie had looked at him when he had told her he wasn't coming home soon. Could only remember the way Janet's face had paled, the way Wendy would look at him from time to time and just shake her head.

The whole world, he found himself thinking suddenly, seemed to be on Marge's side. Everyone seemed to think he was wrong to have moved out. Nobody seemed to understand his point of view.

Not that it really mattered. He'd never been so concerned with what others thought that he let it influence his decisions. Never. He'd never have survived as sheriff if he were that susceptible to the opinions of others. Not in any way that would preserve his self-respect, that is.

It was interesting, though, that he was being perceived as the wrongdoer rather than the wronged party. Well, he guessed on the surface of it that it looked bad when a man walked out on his wife of twenty-six years, and their daughters. Not that he was walking out on his daughters.

And not that any of them were exactly speaking to him just now. Everybody, the girls included, seemed to think he ought to be able to forgive and forget. It had been more than a quarter century, after all. What nobody seemed to understand was that the wound was a fresh one, making a mock-

ery out of all those years. Out of all that trust. It was easy
for others to say that it had happened well in the past, and
the years since should outweigh what came before.

But it hadn't come before. This thing had erupted into his
marriage just before Christmas. This *thing* had been a lie
that had continued during all those years, not something
that had been started and finished so long ago. Nobody
seemed to understand that the wound was *now*.

Except for Marge. Oh, yes, Marge understood the im-
mediacy of it all. He gave her that much. She had never once
said that it was so far in the past he ought to be able to
overlook it. Had never once even said it was in the past. No,
she understood just how very much in the present it was.

It was, quite simply, a fresh, raw, gaping wound, and it
was nowhere near through bleeding yet. It might never stop
bleeding. And Marge had pulled the trigger.

Finally the sound of tires on snow and the familiar growl
of a large engine alerted him to the arrival of Gage Dalton
in his black Suburban. Gage pulled up right behind him and
climbed out, slipping on a pair of sunglasses as he did so.

"Turned into a fine day," Gage remarked as he limped
up. "What's this about the fence?"

"Wire was cut, two sections of fence are down. Those
cattle were in the road when I got here, and they pretty well
trampled up the area, but I'm sure the fence was put down
deliberately."

While Gage was examining the cut wire, Micah pulled up.
And with him came Seth Hardin, clad in jeans, cowboy hat
and a dark blue parka.

"What the hell are you doing here?" Nate growled. "I
thought you were shipping out!"

Seth half smiled. "I did. Now I'm back. Taking some
overdue leave."

"Figured you wouldn't mind," Micah said as he strode
past.

Nate turned, about ready to take a chunk out of Micah's
hide, when it suddenly struck him that he was behaving un-
reasonably. Had Seth been anyone else, he wouldn't have

minded at all. He'd given the young man permission to ride with Micah, and if Micah didn't mind . . .

Nate shook his head. "Okay. Okay."

There were more important things at hand, anyway. Like the busted fence.

"You got any floor space for me to crash on at your place over Mahoney's?" Seth asked as he and Nate watched Micah and Gage explore the area.

Nate looked at his son. "Who filled you in?"

"Nobody. Micah just said you had rooms above Mahoney's now. I haven't even been by to see Mrs. Tate."

"How long you planning on staying?"

Seth's dark eyes were steady. "As long as it takes."

"Takes to what?"

"Just that," Seth said levelly. "Just however long it takes."

Nate returned his attention to Micah and Gage, refusing to get into it any more deeply with this stranger who was his son. The young man evidently had some purpose in mind, and Nate figured it would out eventually. Things always did. And it was seldom useful to demand answers from a man like Seth Hardin. Seldom useful.

"Yeah," Nate said presently. "I got room." Plenty of room. There was nothing but room in his entire life now that he'd walked away from everything that mattered.

Yeah. He had room. One great big vast wasteland of it.

Chapter 5

There was absolutely no evidence of any kind that might explain why the Preston fence had been cut. Micah and Gage agreed with Preston that the wire had to have been cut recently, but that was the only clue they could find. No tire tracks led out across the range, or any hoofprints, except those of cattle and antelope. No sign someone had ridden through here since the last snowfall several days before. And Preston swore he'd driven up this road just two days ago, and the fence had been intact.

He would have noticed if it hadn't been, Nate was sure. So someone had come recently and clipped that wire and pushed down that post. Why?

Had someone been scared off before they could accomplish their purpose? Or had they done what they set out to? Preston said he'd get his men to count cattle in this section of his range and see if any were missing. It'd take days, though. Maybe a week. That was a lot of land out there, and a lot of cattle.

In the meantime, all they had was petty vandalism.

It was getting dark by the time they were convinced they weren't going to find anything useful. Nate figured it was too late to drop in on the Lairds and decided just to head back into town and get some supper at Maude's.

"Seth, you wanna ride back with me?"

The young man paused on his way to Micah's vehicle. "Sure, Sheriff."

"Call me Nate, for cripes' sake," Nate grumbled. "If we're gonna be roommates, we can't keep on being so formal."

With the disappearance of the sun, the partially thawed road surface froze to a hard glaze that crunched and crackled under the tires of Nate's Blazer. Wintry sounds, familiar from long custom, suddenly seemed noticeable. Even the air smelled different with snow all over the ground, he found himself thinking. Things looked different, smelled different, sounded different.

And everything was so barren.

The evening star, brilliant in the cold air, hovered over the eastern horizon like a beacon to guide him. So much, he found himself thinking, that he had taken for granted over the years. So much. And in a twinkling, it was gone.

He glanced over at Seth. The younger man's profile was sharply etched against the darkening sky. "How long are you planning to hang around for?"

"I'm cleared for thirty days' leave. If I need more, I ca get it."

"A month." Nate returned his attention to the road. The brilliant light of his halogen headlamps occasionally bounced back almost blindingly from the snow. "And I'm supposed to believe you don't have anything better to do than hang around in the backwoods of Wyoming in the dead of winter."

"That about sums it up."

"I'm afraid I'm more suspicious than that, son. So why don't you tell me what really brought you back."

They drove nearly two more miles before Seth spoke. "I came back because of Krissie."

"*Krissie?* My daughter Krissie?"

"She wrote to me, upset about the split between you and Marge."

Nate counted to ten. Then he counted to ten again. At last he was able to speak in a measured voice. "All of us are upset about it. But it's nobody's damn business but Marge's and mine!"

"Krissie's my business," Seth said flatly. "She's my sister. I kind of like having a sister, you know. I'm surprised how attached I got to all the girls in such a short time, but I feel especially attached to Krissie. So if you don't mind, I'm going to hang around for the next month and get to know my sisters. Some of us got cheated a little more than others by what happened."

Nate glared fiercely into the night and tried to adjust to this new upset in his life. Not bad enough his marriage had gone to hell, but now he had to adjust to this stranger who was his son, adjust to all the changes that would necessarily come about as Seth moved into the life of all the Tates. And Seth definitely intended to move in. Nate didn't like to think about anyone having the kind of influence over Krissie that a newfound, fully adult brother would probably have. Didn't like to think of Seth replacing him as Krissie's primary male confidant.

Stupid. Really stupid. But that's how he felt. Threatened. With some justification, considering that Krissie had turned to Seth in her distress. Oh, yes, his uneasiness was amply justified.

Yes, it was a selfish feeling. Utterly and completely selfish, but so what? He had been the center of the universe for his daughters for many years, and relinquishing that position to boyfriends and husbands was difficult enough. Krissie was a long way from having either. She should have been his for a few more years, but now...

The resentment and selfishness of his own thoughts appalled him, and he forced the jealousy down. He should welcome Seth for the girls' sakes, too. They had missed having a brother as surely as he had missed having a son.

Marge had cheated them all, he thought bitterly. She had cheated them all.

They found another dump site the next morning, twenty miles east of Conard City, back in a gully six miles off

County Road 14. This site, too, was found by accident, when some high school students, out cross-country skiing on the bright Saturday afternoon, came across some jumbled steel drums. Alerted by the recent publicity about the other dump sites, they called the sheriff's office as soon as they returned home.

They never would have reported the drums at all except for the publicity over the past weeks. Nate thought about that and didn't like it at all. But it was true. On so many ranches there were dumps where everything from old cars to bathtubs had been left by generations of ranch families. No one would have thought anything of a pile of drums in some remote locations if it hadn't been for the earlier spills.

And that meant there could be many, many other such dumps, found and overlooked for who knew how long. This could have been going on for years. *Years!*

"Seth says he's staying with you."

The sound of Marge's voice jerked Nate right up out of his chair. She stood on the threshold of his office, wearing the soft green jersey dress she knew damn well was his favorite on her. Over her arm hung her best wool coat. Dressy for coming down to talk to him. Dressy for broad daylight in Conard County.

Her hair—her fiery hair—waved gently about her face and her green eyes regarded him softly. He wanted . . . he wanted to reach out and pull her close, feel her pressed once again to him. To feel the singing arousal he always felt when she leaned into him. To feel that wonderful sense of strength that came to him only when she flung her arms around his neck.

And that was no longer possible, because that woman was a mirage. The woman he loved had never existed.

"What the hell do you want?" he asked roughly. As soon as the words passed his lips, he wanted to snatch them back. He had never once spoken that way to Marge, and not even his present anguish justified it. But the words hung in the air, unrecallable. Marge blanched a little, but didn't waver.

"To tell you that I'm going into Laramie for a few days."

Laramie? She never went anywhere without him. "Why?"

"I'm telling you because someone should keep an eye on the girls. Just check on them from time to time. Wendy will look in, of course—"

"I'll look in, too," he interrupted gruffly. "Of course I will."

"Seth said he would, too." She gave him a small smile and turned. "Thanks, Nate."

"Wait a minute!" Going off to Laramie without telling him why? Marge, who hated to travel any long distance alone?

She turned back to face him. "Yes?"

Damn it, he thought. She looked so calm. So . . . in control. As if this mess weren't tearing her apart. As if she didn't give a damn. Suddenly angry again, he came around the desk and closed his office door to foil potential eavesdroppers. "Why are you going to Laramie?"

At that, her chin lifted defiantly. "Why should it concern you?"

"Because you never travel anywhere alone! Is something wrong?"

She compressed her lips tightly and simply looked at him. After a long moment, it dawned on him that she was telling him it was no longer any of his business. For a moment, he was blinded by a white flash of rage so intense that its instantaneous passing left him shaking internally. It was the kind of rage he hadn't felt in many, many years, and it was a kind of rage he had never felt toward Marge.

But he felt it now, in an incredible burst that came and vanished in an eye blink. In its wake came a desolation so intense that it felt as if his soul were sundering. And through the pain of his own betrayal, came the anguished realization that he had betrayed Marge as surely as she had betrayed him.

The wounds were past healing. The marriage past rescue.

"You're right," he said, speaking numbly. "You're right. It's none of my damn business. Let me know when you get back."

Then he turned his back and picked up some papers. He heard her hesitate, heard her draw a soft, shaky breath. The door opened, her heels tapped . . . and she was gone.

Forever.

Marge halted on the sandy sidewalk in front of the sheriff's office and buttoned her coat to the throat, fiercely blinking back tears. She had hoped . . . she had hoped that her announcement of a trip to Laramie would shake Nate into jealousy. Into a rage that would generate an argument that might give her a chance to explain. Into any kind of a reaction that might open the door that he had so firmly shut between them.

For an instant, she'd almost thought she had succeeded. Just for an instant. And then that deathlike mask had come over his face and he had turned away.

She drew a ragged breath and blinked back more tears as the cold wind nipped painfully at her cheeks. Throughout the weeks since he had moved out, she had been telling herself that he hadn't stopped loving her, that he was just hurt and angry, that eventually he would calm down.

After what she had just seen, she no longer believed it. It was over. Done. Nate had stopped loving her. She wondered how she was ever going to survive the loss.

"Marge? Are you all right?"

Startled, she looked around and saw Peter Little, the railroad investigator. "Oh! Hi, Peter. No, I'm fine, thanks. Just thinking." She managed a smile, a slightly wobbly one, and shook his hand. "How's the investigation proceeding?"

"I was just stopping in to ask. It's really out of my hands now. Marge . . . are you sure you're okay?" His voice grew warm, gentle. "I heard about . . . If there's anything I can do . . ."

She shook her head quickly, trying to silence him. She couldn't stand it when people started treating her as if she were dying...even if it felt as if she were. "No. Thank you. I'm fine. Just getting ready to go to Laramie for a few days!" She managed a brittle laugh. "A change of scene is always great for the winter doldrums."

"It sure is." He smiled warmly. "Are you staying with friends?"

"No, I'm splurging on the Windbreak Hotel. I think I'll even be really bad and have room service for breakfast."

He laughed, and the corners of his eyes crinkled attractively. "That's the way to do it. Well, I'm headed back to Laramie myself tomorrow. Maybe I'll see you around."

"Maybe." Smiling more naturally, she turned away and started walking briskly to her red Fiero. She knew when a man found her attractive, and Peter Little definitely found her attractive. If they *did* run into each other in Laramie, maybe...maybe she'd spend some time with him. Maybe. After all, Nate had just turned his back on her.

It wasn't until she got all the way home and started packing her suitcases that she gave way to the tears. To the impossible, hopeless tears.

Peter Little's arrival provided a welcome distraction for Nate. The sound of Marge's heels tapping away down the corridor was surely the saddest, loneliest sound he had heard in his entire life. The end.

Well, of course, he told himself as he tried to concentrate on his job, of course it had already ended. Weeks ago. This was...this was just another step in their separation process.

So when Little stuck his head in the door and wanted to know if Nate had a moment, he was glad to see the railroad investigator.

"Sure, come on in. Grab a seat."

"I just wondered if you've had any success in the investigation. I know it's none of my business anymore, but..." He shrugged. "I'm curious about it."

"So far not much luck. I can't talk about it in any real detail. And I can't say anything at all about the federal investigation. Those guys would draw and quarter me if I spilled their beans. But from my perspective, it's not going so good. We're looking for anyone who might have a motive, financial or otherwise. Looking for this Westin Weatherill character."

"But no strong leads?"

"Not yet. Not on my end."

Little shook his head. "It's too bad there isn't a better description of Weatherill."

"Actually, it's a good description."

Little arched a brow. "A man in cowboy hat and jeans could be anybody."

"Not necessarily. What we know is that whoever picked up the shipments looked like he ought to be picking up that shipment. Like he belonged around here. So it wasn't some drugstore cowboy or Connecticut Yankee, if you follow me. Most likely somebody's hired hand. And if the guy works locally, we'll find him eventually."

Little smiled slowly. "I hadn't thought of it that way."

Nate managed an answering smile. "Well, it's not as good as a photo, but it's a start."

No, it wasn't as good as a photo, Nate thought when Little departed. Not as good as he'd made it sound, either. They were checking for anyone whose financial difficulties might have encouraged him to try to make some ready money this way. They were searching for any hired hand who might be Westin Weatherill, but in truth, they had a field of suspects so broad just within the county that it was nearly hopeless. And this Weatherill character could have come from outside the county, too. Hell, he could be from out of state, and might show up here only to receive the shipments.

About the only real information they had was a negative: it wasn't anyone who was familiar to the clerks at the railroad depot. No, if it were one of the ranchers who regularly picked up shipments, or one of the merchants or their employees, the folks at the depot would have known who they were. That knocked a hundred or so people out of the running, he figured. But it left an awful lot more.

And Fred still couldn't remember where he'd heard about that cowpoke named Westy. Questions put to the area ranchers had so far drawn a negative. None they had yet talked to remembered a hired hand by that name.

And Marge was going to Laramie. The thought sat uneasily in his mind and weighed on him like lead. And then he felt again that moment of furious recognition. No, she was not the woman he had always believed her to be. Not even in this small way.

"Nate?" Velma stuck her head in the door. "Nate, the school's on the phone. They want to talk to you."

"Thanks, Velma." He reached for the phone, but waited to lift the receiver until he heard Velma reach the end of the hallway. She wanted to know what was going on, of course, which was why she'd walked back here to tell him. Enough of his life was on display at the moment, however, and he was damned if he wanted any more of it laid out in public.

"Nathan Tate here."

"Nate, this is Jack Handel." Jack was the principal of Krissie's school. "I hate to bother you, but Marge isn't answering, and we've got a problem here with Krissie."

Nate felt every muscle in his body stiffen. "She's not hurt."

"Oh, no. No, she's not hurt. We've been having some discipline problems is all. I, um, don't know if Marge mentioned it?"

Nate closed his eyes and wondered with a sudden wave of despair just what else he didn't know. "No. Marge hasn't mentioned anything."

"Well, Krissie's...been causing some difficulties with her teachers. We understand that, uh, things are rough for her at home right now. We've been making allowances for circumstances, but...frankly, Nate, we have to consider the other students, as well. We're suspending Krissie for a week."

A week. "Good Lord, Jack! What can she possibly be doing bad enough to warrant that?"

"Disrupting classes. Starting fights. She gave one of the other girls a black eye this morning. Yesterday she tripped

Tim Creslin on the stairs. Oh, I've got the whole list here for you to look over. The point is, we can't allow this to continue any longer. She's out for the week. And if she causes any trouble when she returns, you'll have to arrange for private tutoring."

Stunned, Nate hung up and stared at the phone. Krissie. His sweet little baby. A delinquent.

Shock. That's what he felt when he saw her. She sat defiantly on a folding chair in the school office, her clothes mussed, her blouse torn and her cheek scratched. The glare she gave him could have melted steel.

Jack Handel came out immediately to shake his hand. "Why don't we go into my office, Nate? Krissie, you stay here with Mrs. Arno."

Inside Jack's office, Nate waved aside the offered chair and went to stand at the window, staring out over the parking lot. "It's that bad?"

"It's that bad. We thought she'd settle down when the first shock of your, uh, separation passed, but she's not settling, she's getting worse. While we understand her behavior, we can't tolerate it. Not any longer. She's just growing more and more disruptive, and the counselor thinks she'll continue to get more and more disruptive because she feels she's not being heard. We have to consider the other students, Nate."

"Yeah." The word came out roughly.

"I'm having a list of her infractions prepared for you, so you can discuss them with her, if she'll listen. And I believe the counselor is going to add a few suggestions, but... Nate, in all sincerity, I think you need to consider getting her professional help. Especially if you and Marge aren't going to be able to settle your differences."

Lips compressed, Nate managed a nod.

"Divorce is hard on children," Jack continued. "Very hard. It's hard even when parents are fighting like cats and dogs. In your case ... Well, it's even harder when the child can't see any reason for it. There's resentment, and hate, and anger, and hurt, and hostility, and . . . a feeling of complete insecurity. Whether you've considered it or not, Nate, you have to understand that you've created a situation where Krissie wonders if she'll be the next to be abandoned."

At that, Nate swung around. "She couldn't possibly think—"

"But she does," Jack said firmly. "Oh, she can't articulate the feeling, but basically, you abandoned her mother, so maybe you can abandon her just as easily. And there's no obvious justification in Krissie's mind. As I said, you and Marge haven't been fighting or anything like that. This kind of thing makes a child extremely insecure. So Krissie is pushing, and pushing hard, to find out if you'll abandon her. Unfortunately, the school is not a place we can let her work through her fear and anguish."

Twenty minutes later, driving Krissie home, Nate wondered if *any* of them were going to be able to work through their fear and anguish.

One look at his daughter's face after they got home told him she wasn't going to discuss anything. And for the moment that was fine. Coming back into the house for the first time in weeks was . . . affecting him.

"Go to your room, Krissie."

For an instant he thought she was going to argue with him, his daughter who had never been a discipline problem in her life. Oh, the other girls from time to time had defied authority, but never Krissie. She had been born with a sweet temperament and a loving nature.

Seeing the anger flash across her face shook him, really shook him. During that instant, he got a glimpse of just what all this was doing to the rest of the family. For that instant, he looked past his own pain into his daughter's pain. It was all he could do not to reach out and fold her into his arms, but he resisted. This was not the time, he felt. Not when she had just been suspended from school. Not when he wasn't quite ready himself to delve into all the reasons for his leaving.

Almost as soon as the flare of defiance appeared on her face, it faded and she turned, running for her bedroom as if she were fleeing him. And maybe she was, he thought grimly. Maybe she was.

He stood in the kitchen for a few minutes, letting the impact of being in this house again resound through him. It had been his home for nearly his entire marriage, which meant nearly his entire adult life. He and Marge had only been married two years when they used his VA entitlement to build this place. It had been their home since Marge had carried Wendy, their oldest daughter. Every room, every corner and piece of furniture, held memories.

Stifling a sigh, he passed his hand over his face and forced himself to confront it. All of it. The emptiness of the house with Marge away, the absence of his other daughters.... Echoing silence in which he could almost hear their voices, could almost hear Marge's quick, light step.

Gone.

All of it was gone. Each time another daughter left for college, there had been another gaping hole in the house, a silence nothing could fill. First Wendy. Then Janet. Then Cindy. Three left at home, and Carol would be leaving in another year. Then Patti in three years. Little by little it had all been going away.

But not like this. Not like this. Not all at one time in such anguish. And Marge... He had believed Marge would always be with him. Always. Couldn't have conceived that anything on earth would make him want it otherwise.

Until this.

The phone chirped, and he hesitated, wanting to ignore it. Work. It had to be work. Damn it, couldn't they get through a few hours without him? But duty tugged at him, so he reached for the receiver and lifted it to his ear.

"Tate."

"Nate, it's Velma. Gage wanted me to tell you he's going out to talk to Al Bryant at Lowlands Farm. Something about Bryant and defaulting loans. Do you want to go with him?"

Actually he did. He'd have liked to shuck his personal problems for business, even for a short while. But this time he couldn't do that. Walking out on Krissie right now would be a mistake. A big mistake.

"I've got my hands full, Velma. I won't be back in today. Tell Gage to go ahead without me. Have him call when he gets back."

And then he stood alone again in the echoing silence and tried to face the fact that he was wounding his daughters in a way that was every bit as bad as Marge was wounding him. But what the hell could he do about it? He couldn't act as if he hadn't been betrayed when he had. There was just no way he could live a sham.

But maybe, instead of keeping clear to avoid facing his own pain, it was time to face up to the fact that he had daughters who needed him. Time to realize that he needed to take care of them regardless of how it stirred up his own wounds. Time to take responsibility for what he was doing.

Sighing yet again, he stepped farther into the house, deeper into the depths of memory. He felt like a trespasser here now, he realized with a deep pang. A trespasser in his own house . . . in his own life.

Drawn almost against his will, he walked down the hallway and stood in the doorway of the master bedroom. The signs of Marge's departure were visible, looking as if once she had decided to go, she couldn't move fast enough. And maybe that had been the case. Maybe . . . maybe she was hurting, too.

Well, she deserved it. Lying all these years. She deserved it.

But the words sounded hollow even to him in the echoing emptiness of his house, in the emptiness of his life now . . . in the emptiness of a broken home. Hollow indeed.

He let Krissie stew until supper time. Carol and Patti arrived home at the usual time and swamped him in hugs and kisses of welcome that tightened his throat and brought him face-to-face with the price of his inability to forgive. But he pushed such thoughts away, squashing them sternly as he focused instead on the present.

The girls started dinner, and he helped, talking to them about their days. Neither Carol nor Patti was surprised to hear that Krissie had been expelled, and Nate was faced with the rather unpalatable realization that his wife had known this was happening but hadn't seen fit to tell him.

"Why didn't your mother call me?" he asked the girls. "If I'd known..."

"What would you have done?" Carol asked quietly. "Dad, would you have come home?"

Instinct was to say yes, of course. Honesty prevented it. Whatever his impulse was, the truth was inescapable. No, he wouldn't have come back. He couldn't have. He would have tried talking to Krissie, but he wouldn't have moved back in. Wouldn't have embarked upon a masquerade. He couldn't. It would have violated his soul.

Looking from Patti to Carol, he saw that they knew that. They didn't necessarily understand it, but they knew the family was ruptured for good. Patti turned away first, back to cleaning vegetables for salad. Carol hesitated, then shook her head and turned away, too.

And Nate Tate stood alone in the kitchen, within arm's reach of two of his daughters, and realized that he had lost more than a wife. He was losing his entire family.

Wendy showed up during meal preparations and joined in. She chatted cheerfully, as if sorrowful undercurrents didn't exist, and soon the atmosphere was almost normal.

Except for Krissie. Nate's youngest daughter sat sullenly at the table, picking at her food. After a couple of attempts to draw her into conversation, her sisters started ignoring her. Nate didn't even bother to talk to her. He had never indulged any of his girls when they were sullen, and long experience had taught him that even to acknowledge the mood was a no-win situation. So, from the moment he sat at the table, he didn't say a word to Krissie.

Conversation was a little stilted at first, but gradually, mostly through Wendy's patience, it began to grow easier. Soon Patti was talking about cheerleading practice and comparing her frustrations with Carol, who was on the basketball team. It seemed neither of them especially cared for their coach.

Wendy kept the conversation going by asking appropriate questions. Nate contented himself with sympathetic clucks. Krissie never uttered a sound.

But Krissie was going to utter a sound, Nate thought grimly after the girls cleared the table. Oh, yes. No child of his was going to get away with behaving like a juvenile delinquent.

But when he marched Krissie into the den, where such discussions were traditionally held, one look at her mutinous face warned him that his work was cut out for him.

He motioned her to the sofa and settled himself on the Boston rocker. When she steadfastly refused to look at him—even a sidelong, nervous glance—he wanted to sigh.

With each and every one of his girls, he and Marge had had to face a period of complete rebellion. It was never easy to get through.

"Young lady, suppose you tell me just what you're hoping to accomplish with this misconduct." He knew the stern tone had been a mistake the instant Krissie stiffened and glared at him, but it was too late to change his tack.

"What do you care? It's not *your* problem!"

"It's my problem because I'm your father."

"Yeah. Right." She hunched her shoulder and looked away.

Yeah. Right. That could mean any of a hundred things, and he considered some of the more obvious before he spoke again. The temptation to give her hell for her attitude was strong, but he battered it down, deciding this wouldn't be a good time to tell her not to speak this way.

"So you think that my being your father doesn't give me a right to be concerned?"

And suddenly he was staring into a face contorted with rage as his daughter leapt up from the couch and began to shout at him. "My father? My *father?* How can you call yourself that? You just walked away from all of us! Just like Mom did to Seth! My God, what's the matter with you?"

Then she turned and fled the room, sobbing wildly.

Stunned, Nate didn't move a muscle. He couldn't have moved to save his life. *Just like Mom did to Seth.*

He didn't stay for the night. The girls didn't need him to; it wouldn't be the first time they had stayed alone together. But even so, he couldn't stay. After Krissie's explosion, he didn't try to speak to her again. He'd talk to her tomorrow, when she'd settled a little. Right now he needed to settle with himself.

When Nate returned to the dingy apartment, Seth was in the bathroom showering. With a sigh, he tossed his gun belt on the rickety dresser and then emptied his pockets. Wallet, change, keys...

Just like Mom did to Seth.

A curse escaped him, a soft sound of anguish. He wasn't abandoning his girls. He wasn't. Not at all. Just because he couldn't live with them anymore...

Swearing again, he sat on the edge of the rickety bed and stared grimly at the messy vision his life had become. Living with Marge would do a violence to him he couldn't endure. He'd be faced every day with the realization that his trust had been utterly betrayed, completely misplaced.

"Something wrong?"

He looked up and saw Seth standing in the doorway, a towel slung around his neck. The proof of Marge's iniquity, that's what Seth was. And that wasn't fair to Seth, was it? Smothering another sigh, Nate shook his head and seized on the easy thing to talk about.

"Krissie's been suspended from school for a week for getting into fights."

Seth came into the room and sat down on the facing bed. "That's bad. What's she fighting about?"

"Anything and everything, evidently. She's angry about Marge and me splitting."

"That's understandable."

This time Nate didn't bother to stifle the sigh. "Yeah. It's understandable. But it can't continue. And I'm sure as hell not going to get anywhere with her. I'm heading up her blacklist at the moment."

"She won't talk to you?"

"Let's put it this way—the only talking she did was to shout in my face."

"Ouch."

"Yeah. Ouch." With another sigh he stretched out and clasped his hands behind his head. "It's my fault. Damn it. I've been . . . so wrapped up in myself that I haven't properly considered what all this means to the girls. And I guess I'd better think about it before I try to talk to Krissie again."

"I could talk to Krissie," Seth offered. "I know it isn't my place, but right now she isn't mad at me. And I *am* the one she wrote to when you, uh, moved out."

Nate turned his head slowly and regarded the man he was still trying to fully realize was his son. "You think she'd listen?"

"She might. She certainly seemed awfully eager to have me as a big brother."

After a moment, Nate shook his head. "In the first place, it wouldn't be fair to you. You're not her father, and there's no reason you should set yourself up for the flak if she *doesn't* want to take your advice. No, I'd better handle it. But if I can't get through . . . Well, we'll see then."

Seth nodded. "Okay by me."

Nate turned his head again so he could stare up at the ceiling. "Did Gage call, by any chance?"

"Oh, yeah. He said to tell you he didn't have anything relevant. It's this toxic-waste thing, isn't it? It's a bitch of a problem, trying to find out who received the stuff."

"And where it all is. We haven't got a single lead beyond a signature on some paper, and nobody's ever heard of a Westin Weatherill."

"Well, he probably doesn't exist. Not really."

"Except that Fred thinks he remembers some hired hand or other named Westy, but we can't even get a lead on that. *Somebody's* picking the stuff up, though."

"And no clues at the dump sites."

"Not a one, yet. If we could find a fresh dump, that'd help. We might find tire tracks, or boot prints, or something that might give us some idea...." He shook his head. "Right now we've got nothing at all."

"Something'll turn up."

"Well, I hope it turns up soon! I'd like to get my hands on the sumbitch just so I can find out where all this crap is stashed. What if some kids find it and get into something really toxic? What if an entire herd gets poisoned and some rancher is ruined because of it? What if the stuff gets into the groundwater and makes people sick? It's a nightmare!"

In fact, he thought a while later as he tried to relax enough to sleep, his whole life seemed to be turning into a nightmare. What was he going to do about Krissie?

No answers presented themselves, no revelations occurred. All he knew was that tomorrow he was going to see the divorce lawyer. Tomorrow he was going to put into motion the machinery that would end life as he knew it.

Chapter 6

"Good morning, Nate." Sandy Keller's greeting was pleasant as her secretary ushered Nate into the attorney's inner office.

"Morning, Sandy." He took the chair facing her across her cluttered desk and declined the secretary's offer of coffee. "You're looking well."

"Wish I could say the same for you." Sandy and Nate had grown up together, and both had left Conard County immediately upon graduation from high school—Nate for the army and Sandy for college. Sandy had stayed away a lot longer, working with a large law firm in Cheyenne before returning to Conard City to open a general law practice. Having been friends for their entire lives, they never needed to stand on formality... or pull any punches.

Nor did Nate expect Sandy to pull any punches this morning. She never did. Besides, they'd been friends too damn long to tiptoe around each other. So he wasn't especially surprised by her opening shot.

"I was hoping you'd cancel this appointment," she said bluntly. "And you look like hell."

He managed a rueful smile. "Sweet as always, I see. You know why I'm here?"

"Of course I know why you're here. The whole damn county is clucking about this!" Sandy shook her head, gray-streaked brown hair swinging. "Why don't you think about this a little longer?"

"Because my mind is made up."

"Is it?" She sighed and leaned back in her deep leather chair. "Twenty-six years of marriage is an awful lot to throw away. You better have a damn good reason, and you better be damn sure you're not going to regret this."

Nate shifted impatiently. The fact that she didn't pull punches meant that he didn't have to politely take it. "Look, Sandy—"

"No, *you* look," she interrupted sharply. "We've been friends a long, long time, and I'm not going to pussyfoot around you. Getting a divorce is a lot tougher emotionally and financially than working things out. A lot tougher. I know you're upset. Hell, the whole county is upset right along with you."

"Damn it, Sandy, I don't care what the whole county thinks! This is none of their damn business!"

"Of course it's their business. You've been the sheriff for the last twenty years. You've touched the lives of every single person in Conard County one way or the other. But that's neither here nor there. Bottom line is, striking back at Marge is only going to make everything a lot worse. Nate, it won't *fix* a damned thing."

"I'm not striking back at her!"

"Then what do you call it? A divorce isn't a bouquet of roses!"

Nate swore and surged up from his chair, scowling. He'd expected to hear some hard truths—Sandy always had a few to offer—but he hadn't expected her to react quite this way. Turning his back to her, he strode to the window and stared down at the snowy street. Nearly a full minute passed before he spoke. "It's not some kind of revenge, Sandy. It's just that... I can't trust her anymore. Every time I think of

her now I feel...as if I never knew her at all. I feel...
betrayed."

"What did she do? For God's sake, Nate, after all these
years nothing could be bad enough to justify this! Did she
have an affair?"

"No! No." He shook his head and settled his hands on his
hips, but kept his back to Sandy. "No. She didn't have an
affair."

"Nate, you're going to have to tell me. I'm your lawyer."

Nate turned to one side, as if trying to look away from the
whole issue. But then he shook his head and spoke. "She
gave my son up for adoption while I was in Vietnam. Before we got married."

"My God!" Sandy's exclamation was little more than a
hushed whisper. "My God! Oh, Nate..."

He shook his head again, sharply, silencing her. "I can
understand what happened. Really, Sandy. I can understand the pressures she faced. I can understand that she was
all alone and scared. I can understand that she thought I
didn't want her anymore. I understand all of that. What I
can't forgive is that she never told me. That not once in all
these years did she tell me the truth until my son showed up
in my living room. It kind of kills my trust. It makes me feel
I never knew her at all. Damn it, I was married to a
stranger."

Sandy neither spoke nor moved while seconds ticked by
in utter silence. It sounded, Nate found himself thinking,
stupid. Really stupid. Words couldn't convey what the loss
of trust meant emotionally. No way.

But Sandy seemed to understand. When she finally spoke,
it was to address the divorce issue.

"I see," she said. "What are you hoping to achieve?
Apart from legally severing your marital ties. What do you
want in terms of property and custody?"

He turned slowly from the window. "I want joint custody of the children. I don't care about property. Marge can
have it all. I'll even pay alimony."

There was another long silence while Sandy stared impassively at him. Eventually she spoke, her tone level. "You terrify me."

His head jerked as if she had slapped him. The simple statement struck him forcefully, jerking him out of his haze of melancholy. "What?"

She leaned forward abruptly and tapped her desk with her index finger, punctuating every word for emphasis. "It's my job as your attorney to act to protect your best interests. You don't even know what those are! If *you* don't know, how am I supposed to protect them?"

"Sandy..."

"Nate, just listen to me. Listen to *yourself* for the love of heaven! Do you hear what you're saying? You want to chuck Marge, keep the kids and throw away all your property and income. Now just think that through for a minute! Assuming any judge would think you were sane enough to keep the kids after hearing this, just how the hell do you propose to house and feed them?"

"Marge..."

"Marge is the woman you don't trust any longer, remember? You can't trust her so you're divorcing her, but you're still going to trust her enough to house and feed those kids with all the money you give her? Does that make sense? Did you ever consider that this woman you don't trust might get so angry, so vindictive, so *hurt* as a result of this divorce that she might want to get even?"

"Marge wouldn't—"

"If you're so sure what Marge will and won't do, then how come you think she's so much a stranger that you're divorcing her? How come you're telling me you can't trust her?"

"Because it's not the same thing!" He nearly shouted the words, and silence filled the room in their aftermath. It was Sandy who broke it.

"Okay. It's not the same thing. So let's move on to what a divorce entails. You're claiming irreconcilable differences because you can no longer trust your wife. The fact that she's given you no other cause to feel that way in twenty-six years is something we'll overlook for the moment. Say that Marge contests—she *can,* you know. It'll make things messy, but in the end, if you're determined enough, a judge will grant the decree because you'll clearly be an irreconcilable difference. But keep in mind that it could get really messy and expensive."

"Marge wouldn't..."

"Forget what you think Marge will do. I can guarantee you from experience that divorce brings out all the nasties in people. In fact, my dear old friend, there's really no such thing as a friendly divorce. By the time you get around to the property and the kids, things are pretty usually getting downright ugly. I wouldn't be too sure, if I were you, that Marge will take this with a sweet smile.

"But say she does. Just say she quietly lets her husband of twenty-six years walk out of her life. Maybe she won't want joint custody. Maybe she'll feel she doesn't want to *share* the children to that degree. Maybe she'll honestly feel it isn't in the girls' best interest to be shared that way. Maybe she'll just feel vindictive. So, what if she fights? She may have lied to you years ago, but just a couple of weeks ago *you* walked out and left your daughters behind."

Nate looked stunned; he hadn't thought of it this way. A sharp oath escaped him.

"Now you're beginning to see reality here," Sandy said. "The future of your children will not be in your hands or in Marge's, Nate. It'll be in the hands of the *court.* And the court might not see things the way you do. Moreover, from now until they reach majority, the fate of those girls will rest with the court. Either you or Marge can make life messy for one another over any little thing...like whether you should take your vacation for one or two weeks in either September or October. What if Marge has other plans of her own? What if she remarries and custody has to be handled in regard to her new husband's wishes? Things just get messy and stay messy."

Nate couldn't even speak. He just simply shook his head.

"Right," Sandy said. "Now, about the property. Custody, of course, gets taken into account. So let's say you *do* get joint custody. What if the judge decides in the property settlement that the house has to be sold and the gain evenly divided? Can you buy another house for your kids? What if Marge gets complete custody and all the property... and a new husband convinces her to dispose of the assets so he can take a cruise? You never know. What'll become of the girls? But you know, given that you walked out, it's always within the realm of possibility that Marge may get custody and all the property. How will you handle that?''

He hadn't considered any of this, and now he sat, trying to absorb what Sandy was suggesting. His instinct was to say it wouldn't happen, of course, that Marge would never... But he didn't know Marge. Not the way he had once thought.

"The point I'm making, Nate, is that this step is the first step on a long, messy, painful journey. Filing for divorce isn't the end of anything. It's the beginning of a lot of trouble, a lot of grief and a lot of anguish. I think you need to go back and think about whether it wouldn't be less painful to work out your problems. I know *I* need you to give some thought to what you want out of this. I'll file for you if you want me to, but you have to be clearer on why, how and what than you are right now.''

He nodded slowly, admitting the justice of what she was saying. And trying not to admit to himself that he was a tiny bit relieved not to have to go ahead with an irrevocable step today.

"I need you to think about why you're so willing to give away everything except custody,'' Sandy continued bluntly. "It's not simple nobility, Nate. Very little ever is. I suggest you go home and figure out what the hell you feel so guilty about.''

"I don't—''

Sandy stabbed her finger at him, interrupting without apology. "You do. You sure as hell do. Figure out what it is and then we'll talk some more.''

What the hell did he have to feel guilty about? he wondered as he drove to the office. Not a thing. Not a damn thing! He wasn't the one who'd been living a lie for the last twenty-seven years. Not him.

Krissie's face floated before his mind's eye, but he dismissed it. Other kids survived divorce without becoming delinquent. Krissie would, too.

Which reminded him he needed to call Wendy, who was watching Krissie today, to make sure that nothing had come up that required her to go in to work. And then maybe he'd go home over the noon hour and see if he couldn't talk some sense into his youngest daughter.

Somehow he didn't think that was likely to be very successful. Not yet, anyway.

An urge to growl almost overwhelmed him when he stepped into the office and everyone looked his way with expressions of sympathy. About the way they'd look at him if he had terminal cancer, he figured. And every one of them silently wondered if he'd set the divorce in motion.

Well, let 'em wonder, he thought sourly as he stomped back to his office. Let 'em wonder!

"Nate?" Beau stopped him halfway down the hall. "We picked up a DUI last night who turned out to have a couple of outstanding warrants in Laramie. I'm going to drive him up in the morning—"

"No, I'll do it." Before he even thought about it, he was speaking. And as soon as he said it, the surprised look on Beau's face told him he needed to explain. "I have some business to take care of and need to go, anyway."

After a barely perceptible hesitation, Beau nodded. "Great. Well, I'll have all the papers ready for you."

"Thanks." Yeah, personal business, he found himself thinking as he settled behind his desk. Like finding out why the hell Marge had gone to Laramie.

Coming to Laramie had not been one of her brighter ideas, Marge Tate thought as she threw her purse on the bed and paused in front of the mirror to survey her new hairstyle. A make-over sounded good in theory, but she got jarred every time she looked in the mirror.

But the primary reason she had decided to come was because at home, sitting around the house, she saw Nate in every nook and cranny, kept expecting him to round the corner—and couldn't forget that he was gone, apparently for good.

She had more spunk than that, she told herself. Her throat might be so tight with unshed tears that she felt as if she were being hanged, her heart might be breaking in two, but she wasn't going to take it lying down, like some kind of wimp. No, that wasn't her way. Somewhere over the years of raising six daughters and being married to a cop, she had developed some backbone.

A breath not unlike a sob escaped her, and she sat on the edge of the bed, fighting back the grief. If she'd had some backbone twenty-seven years ago, she wouldn't be in this fix right now. She should at least have had the gumption to tell him what had happened. To tell him about the baby.

But her father had insisted that it would only hurt Nate to know, and there was no reason to hurt him when he could do nothing. The reasoning had been seductive enough to sway her from her barely formed intention to confess all. But her father, she realized now, had had his own reasons for his actions, and they were not entirely altruistic. Her father had hated Nate. Had never become reconciled to their marriage. Had tried everything, including stealing her mail, to destroy her relationship with Nate. How could she have ever believed he had Nate's interests at heart?

Because he had been her father. Because she had always believed in his love for her, despite his harshness and his narrow-mindedness. Only in retrospect could she see that her father had been willing to do anything to keep her from Nathan Tate.

She drew a long, ragged breath and blinked back another tear. She couldn't cry. Peter Little was picking her up for dinner shortly, and she didn't want him to see her with puffy eyes and smeared makeup. She didn't want anybody to see her that way. She didn't want anybody to know how badly she hurt, or how much she missed Nate.

If pride was all that was left to her, then she would protect it fiercely.

But oh, it was hard! Her mind kept betraying her by wandering down corridors of memory. And there were so many beautiful, happy memories to remind her of all that she was losing.

Nate, as a youth, scraping against the edges of manhood, struggling still with the vestiges of boyhood. Tall, straight, a little gangly... and so very earnest about everything. Wanting to mend the world's ills. Learning to laugh with her on stolen summer afternoons.... She caught her breath and stifled another sob as she remembered how hard she had tried to make him laugh, because he almost never did. And how when she had succeeded she felt such incredible joy.

Nate, returned from Vietnam with a hard edge... a killing edge, he'd told her bluntly. With a disturbing way of staring into the distance, as if he could see through things. So tall and powerful in his army greens and green beret, no longer gangly or poorly coordinated. Taking down a couple of angry hotheads who were giving Marge a hard time over a fender bender on Main Street. Just... taking them down with deadly skill. Not hurting them, not killing them, just... putting them out of action. Nobody ever shouted at Marge again after that. Ever.

Nate after his second tour in Vietnam, the hard edge even more apparent... weeping at the birth of his first daughter. Actually choking up over Wendy's arrival and squeezing Marge until she squeaked. And the long, lovely afternoon a couple of months later in a secluded spot by the creek, Wendy sleeping in her travel bed while Nate made love to Marge until they were both too exhausted to lift a hand.

Nate the day he had first been elected sheriff, receiving at long last complete acceptance from the county that had scorned him in his youth. A sweet, sweet victory, a triumph over background and narrow-mindedness. A vindication for the man who had been the son of a woman of "dubious morals." He had celebrated by taking the girls on a camping trip.

Oh, it hadn't been perfect, not by any means, but for all these years, Marge had known she was luckier than most women. Far luckier.

And now this. No more Nate, turning over in the middle of the night and drawing her into a bear hug. No Nate to share the quiet early morning hours with. No Nate to keep her company in the waning years of her life.

No Nate.

She drew another ragged breath, almost a sob, and swallowed her tears once again. She had to be strong. For the girls. For herself. It only felt as if life were over, but it wasn't. No. It might have a gaping, painful hole in it, but she was still here, and she had to go on. For the girls. And for herself. There would be a future.

The phone on the bedside table rang, jarring her. She picked up the receiver and heard an anonymous voice announce that Mr. Little was awaiting her in the lobby.

Panic nearly seized her for a moment. In her entire life she had dined out alone with only one man. The thought of eating dinner with Peter Little was almost terrifying.

But life had to go on, she reminded herself. It had to go on.

Nate almost didn't recognize Marge when she stepped out of the hotel with Peter Little. He'd had no trouble locating her after he made the prisoner transfer; she had come to the same hotel where they'd always stayed when in Laramie.

Since pulling into the parking lot twenty minutes ago, he'd been playing an emotional tug-of-war with himself about whether he should go inside and talk to her. He wanted to know what she was doing here, but he didn't think she'd be any more forthcoming now than she had been in his office the other day. Most likely, she'd show him the door.

And he'd learn exactly nothing. Better to lie low and keep an eye on her. That might be devious, but she had forced him to it by not telling him what she was going to do here. And he had a right to know what the mother of his daughters was up to, especially since one of those daughters was in big-time trouble, and Marge hadn't seen fit to tell him anything was wrong.

Just more lies, he found himself thinking. More deception.

But when she emerged from the hotel into the bright lights of the porte cochere, he almost missed her because he didn't recognize her. And because he had never expected to see her with a man.

Recognition hit him like a blow to his chest. She'd done something to her fiery hair, something that made it softly curly and fluffy around her face. And her face...it was different in some subtle way. More beautiful than he remembered it. Far more beautiful.

And she was with a man. His shock was such that it took him a few minutes to recognize Peter Little, but when he did, a burning fury rose in him, scalding his guts and filling his throat with bile. His hands tightened around the steering wheel until they simply couldn't tighten any more, and he had to fight down an impulse to smash Little to a pulp.

He couldn't do that. No way. He had no right to do that. No right at all.

So he sat there, watching as Little helped Marge into his car, watching as the two of them drove off into the twilight.

He managed to keep from following them. Managed to retain enough sense to realize that if he *did* follow, he might well cause a scene that could cost him his career. Suddenly, he didn't trust his self-control.

And that was as disturbing as anything else that had happened.

He drove away after a while and looked up a favorite diner for a quick dinner. He tried to convince himself to head back to Conard County, but he couldn't quite make himself do it. Not quite. Instead he found himself back at the hotel, checking in.

And getting a room across the hall from Marge proved easy, thanks to his uniform and his badge. Easy enough that it made him uneasy. He didn't like feeling that just anybody could find out what room Marge was in. People were just too damn quick to assume a uniform was real. That the guy wearing it had a right to be doing whatever he was doing.

The disgruntled thought followed him upstairs and down the corridor to his room. He'd packed an overnight bag, and now he tossed it on the bed and looked around. Funny, he thought unexpectedly, to be staying at this hotel without Marge.

The thought caught him sideways, slipping past all the anger he'd been nursing since Christmas, reaching right to the core of the matter with all the force of a punch to the gut. *Without Marge.* Grief paralyzed him, locking him in place, blinding his eyes. *Without Marge.*

And down the corridor of the next forty years howled a desolate, icy wind.

Without Marge.

Peter Little was a charming companion, an easy talker with a knack for telling a good story. Nevertheless, Marge found him exhausting. Just before coffee, she slipped away to the ladies' room and considered her options for bringing the evening to an early close.

It wasn't that she didn't like Peter Little. He was a very likable and very attractive man. Engaging. But she wasn't interested in dating. She'd only agreed to have dinner because it seemed impossible to refuse the friendly invitation. And *he* was interested in dating. He was trying a little too hard, and kept talking about seeing her again and...

Oh, heck, she thought and moistened a paper towel. Pressing it to her forehead, she decided to fall back on the old headache excuse. In her entire life she had never dated anyone but Nate, and she had long since forgotten what a strain it could be initially. Or maybe it hadn't been a strain at sixteen. That was entirely possible. It wouldn't be the only thing that wore her out quicker now than thirty years ago.

God! Standing before the mirror, damp towel pressed to her forehead, she fought back another round of tears. Twenty-six years of marriage down the tubes. Just like that. Gone. And she didn't know if she'd ever have the heart, the courage or the energy to make that kind of commitment again. All those years of striving, trying, listening, caring, all the *work* that went into making a good relationship— well, she didn't know if she could ever do it again.

As it had so many times during the past few weeks, fugitive hope reared its head, but she dismissed it. Nate was *not* coming back. Any hope of that had died when he made that appointment with Sandy Keller for yesterday. Local gossip had carried the news to Marge's ears almost the instant Nate had made the call. And there could be only one reason Nate was seeing an attorney.

He was filing for divorce.

"Are you all right?"

Marge swung around to find a woman of about her own age regarding her with concern.

"Uh . . . yes, I'm fine. Thank you."

The woman hesitated just a moment, then smiled and went into one of the stalls. Marge turned back and regarded herself in the mirror. She looked like hell. Behind all that artfully applied makeup she had had professionally done, behind her new haircut and perm, there was a pale-faced woman who was barely holding herself together.

She threw the paper towel in the wastebasket and headed purposefully back to the dining room. Peter Little was just going to have to understand that she wasn't ready for a social life. She might *never* be ready for a social life again.

He stood as soon as he saw her approaching, and she thought yet again that he was a truly fine-looking man. Truly fine. A lot of women would probably have palpitations over him. Not Marge Tate, though. In her entire life, only one man had ever made her heart skip a beat, and that man was about to divorce her. Just the thought flitting across her mind was enough to tighten her throat until she could barely speak.

When she reached the table, she didn't sit. "Peter, I'm really sorry, but I'm feeling awful. Would you mind taking me back?"

He minded. She saw annoyance pass briefly across his face, but it was gone, smothered quickly. Of course he was annoyed, she thought. Having your date call it an early evening wasn't very flattering.

"Of course I'll take you back, Marge. Just let me get the check." He smiled warmly. "Maybe we can do this another time?"

"Of course," she hastened to say, not wanting to make him feel bad. "Of course." But she didn't think it very likely.

They parted in the hotel lobby, but Marge didn't go straight up to her room. Suddenly she couldn't bear the thought of sitting in isolation in a room that should have been shared with Nate. Just couldn't bear it.

So she went instead to the lounge, took a quiet back table and ordered a glass of wine. It felt odd to be in a lounge alone, listening to a couple of surprisingly talented musicians sing James Taylor songs.

But not as odd as staying alone in that room upstairs. And if an occasional tear slipped down her cheek here in this dark corner, no one would ever notice.

By midnight, Nate was almost out of his mind. Marge hadn't returned; he knew that for a fact because she didn't answer her phone. And he couldn't believe she would ignore the phone when she was out of town and the kids were home.

So what the hell were she and Pete Little up to? A dinner and a movie? Fine. But surely she should be back by now.

Unless . . . And it was that unless he didn't want to think about. Couldn't stand to think about. It made him want to tear steel with his teeth to consider the possibility that Marge might be with another man. And so soon after their breakup. As if he didn't matter at all. As if nearly thirty years accounted for nothing.

Damn it, he'd been the one lied to, and this breakup was tearing him apart! How could she calmly come to Laramie and go out to dinner with a man who had been a guest in their home? How could she do that so soon? How could she leave their daughters behind while she went to have a fling?

The picture in his mind was so ugly he couldn't stand it. But he also couldn't quite dismiss it. By eleven, he hadn't been able to sit still any longer, and time had begun to drag so slowly that seconds seemed like minutes. By midnight he was mad enough to kill, and scared to death something had happened to her.

Marge had never been one to want to stay up late, so she either had to be hurt or having a really wonderful time, and either possibility struck him as intolerable.

And the seconds just kept ticking slower and slower.

Marge left the lounge a little after midnight, sure she must look like hell but not caring. Sad songs sung by the duo with the electronic keyboard and guitar had kept her on the very edge of tears for hours. She had needed that. For weeks she had been refusing to give in to her grief and loss, to the sorrow that was never far away. Tonight she had indulged. Tonight she had wallowed. And maybe she had been needing to do that all along. Certainly she felt a sense of relief.

It wouldn't last, of course. She didn't think she would ever feel any lasting relief from the loss of Nate. Periodically, she looked down the corridor of the next forty years and just simply wondered how she was ever going to endure. Because enduring was all that was left to her.

Back in her room, she hung up her coat and tossed her purse down on the dresser. Pete Little and their dinner together now seemed like a distant dream. A slightly unpleasant distant dream.

Crossing to the closet, she kicked her shoes off and reached for the zipper at the back of her black dress. A dress that was one of Nate's favorites.

She was drawing a ragged breath, blinking back tears, when the phone rang. Her first thought was of the girls. It was late...something might be wrong....

In her stocking feet, she darted across the room and snatched up the receiver. "Hello."

She was answered by a click and a dial tone. Wrong number? Wrong number. The girls were okay. Of course they were! She'd spoken to them only a few hours ago, just before Pete had picked her up for dinner.

Just then, someone knocked on the door. At once her heart climbed into her throat and she hesitated, knowing no one could have a legitimate reason to be knocking on her door in a strange city at this hour of night.

Call hotel security.

But even as she had the thought, she realized she hadn't double-locked the door. First the lock, she thought. Then she would call the desk for assistance.

Hurrying on silent feet, she crossed to the door and turned the bolt. As she did so, she peered out the peephole.

And recognized Nate, in his uniform, without a hat or jacket. At once, her only thought that something dreadful had happened to one of their daughters, she threw back the bolt and opened the door.

Nate stepped in right past her and slammed the door. Its sound reverberated in the silence as Marge looked up at her husband of twenty-six years and realized he wasn't worried or concerned—he was angry. Searingly, seethingly, over-whelmingly angry.

He glared down at her, making her uneasy, and then strode across the room, turning away with an abruptness that made her feel he could barely stand to look at her.

"Nate? What's...going on?"

"Did you enjoy your evening?"

The question was loaded with sarcasm, but it clarified nothing for Marge. She remained by the door, her hands knotting into fists, as she warred against a need to fling herself into the powerful arms that had always protected her. She was no longer welcome in those arms. No longer to be protected by them. Grief welled in her, clogging her throat unbearably.

Nate turned when she didn't answer, and he scowled at her. "I can't believe you, Marge. But I guess that just goes to prove I never knew you at all. Never. How could you go gallivanting off—"

The tone, the choice of words, caused her to gasp. "Gallivanting?" Stunned by the unexpected attack, she simply stared at him.

"Gallivanting. The girls are home alone.... Do you have any idea how much trouble Krissie is in?"

"But I just talked— What happened?"

"Krissie's been suspended for a week for fighting and disruptive behavior!"

Now truly speechless, Marge simply shook her head, wanting to deny what she was hearing.

"But you already knew that," Nate continued harshly, hammering out each word. "I find out my daughter's getting into trouble at school and her mother can't be bothered to let me know! Didn't you think I should be involved, Marge? Didn't you think I deserved to know that something's wrong with Krissie? Why did I have to find out from Jack Handel when he was in the process of suspending her?"

Marge's chin lifted, a proud little gesture that had always had the power to tug painfully at his heart. She'd had a hard childhood with stern parents, and that lifted chin always signified to Nate that she was gathering her courage to endure. Always reminded him of how much courage she had needed as a child.

"You left," she said quietly. "You didn't come back. You didn't call. I presumed you didn't want to be bothered...."

She might as well have slapped his face. "Presumed I didn't want to be bothered! Damn it, Marge, how could you even suspect such a thing after all these years! You know better—"

Again that little lift of her chin as she interrupted him. "Until a few weeks ago I would have said you would never abandon your children. It seems I don't know you at all."

Chapter 7

The same way Mom left Seth.

At Marge's quietly spoken accusation of abandonment, Krissie's voice was suddenly loud in his mind. And in the wake of a mind-blasting sense of guilt came the white heat of blind rage.

"I didn't abandon anyone," he said succinctly, sounding all the more dangerous for the quiet of his tone. "I merely moved a few blocks away. I certainly didn't leave the girls to come to Laramie to whore around!"

Marge gasped and her cheeks turned as white as chalk. "Nate . . ." His name escaped her on an agonized whisper.

"I saw you leave with Little. You didn't come back in until after midnight. I sure hope he was worth it, Marge."

She raised a trembling hand, as if to reach for him, but he ignored it, brushing past her toward the door.

"I was going to ask for joint custody," he said, pausing with his hand on the knob, but refusing to look at her. "Not anymore. You're not fit to mother those girls. Not fit at all. I want full custody. And I'm going to get it."

*   *   *

Marge had no idea how long she stood there, so shocked she could neither think nor move. At some point, still almost numbed, she began to weigh options with the crazed mindlessness of a threatened animal.

Kidnap the girls, take them so far away he could never get them from her. Leave town with them before she lost them. Call Pete Little and ask him to explain to Nate. Call a lawyer. Call anyone at all who could talk some sense into Nate.

Call Dan Fromberg.

Shaking violently from head to foot, she sat on the edge of the bed and dialed Reverend Fromberg with fingers that didn't want to obey her.

"Dan...Dan, it's Marge Tate."

"Marge!" Fromberg's sleepy voice turned warm and concerned. "Marge, is something wrong? Where are you?"

"In—in L-Laramie. Nate j-just...Nate just... Oh, Dan, I'm so scared. H-he's going t-to t-take the girls!"

"Take the girls? You mean, take them away from you? Why would he want to do that?"

"Because he says I came to Laramie to f-fool around! Can you believe it?"

"No, I can't believe you'd do any such thing, and quite honestly, my dear, I don't think Nate does, either."

"Dan..."

"No, just calm down, Marge. Just calm down. In the first place, Nate will come to his senses. This isn't at all like him, and you know it."

"But he said—"

"Marge, listen. He's hurt. He's been hurting ever since he found out about Seth. Now, you cry when you get hurt, but men tend to get angry. So instead of dealing with what's happened, he's been walking around angry. Evidently, something tipped the balance and he blew up tonight. Now tell me, isn't that what happened?"

It took a few moments, but as she replayed the painful conversation in her head, she began to understand what had happened. Nate had probably been looking for her all evening while she was sitting in the lounge. He had evidently seen her leave with Pete—how else had he known she went out with him?—and had concluded that Marge had been with him all evening. So he had been angry already—about Pete, about Seth—and she had accused him of abandoning their daughters....

"Yes," she whispered into the phone. "Yes. I said something..."

"Okay. He'll probably feel like a fool before morning. You know Nate prides himself on his control, on his cool logic. He's not going to be very happy about how he behaved. And even if he really meant it, he wouldn't want to do this to the girls, anyway. You know that."

Marge drew a shaky breath. "I don't know what I know any longer, Dan. I don't know anymore!"

"It's hard. Marge, I know it's hard. And I can't honestly promise that Nate won't go through with any of this. But you know him better than anyone, my dear. Sit down and just think about it. Think about him. Ask yourself what the man you know would really do."

Ask herself what the man she knew would really do? The man she knew seemed to have ceased to exist the day he found out about Seth.

Minutes later, having hung up the phone, she stared at her reflection in the mirror over the dresser and wondered if she had ever really known Nate at all.

He couldn't sleep. That scene with Marge had been unforgivable. Completely unforgivable. No way could he excuse the things he had said to her. No way.

His temper had gotten the better of him for the first time in years. Truly gotten the better of him. Usually when he grew angry, he maintained *some* sense. Some control. This time he had retained none. This time he had spoken unforgivable words, made unforgivable assumptions.

Marge wasn't a whore. She may have kept a secret for twenty-seven years, may have committed a huge lie, but she wasn't a whore. She wouldn't give herself cheaply to anyone. He knew that as sure as he knew the rising of the sun.

Her date with Little had been perfectly innocent. If she had stayed out late with him, it had been for innocent reasons. So what if she had come to Laramie to meet him. Didn't she have the right to? After all, her husband was filing for divorce. That made her a free woman in all but the eyes of the law, didn't it?

How could he have accused her of whoring? How could he have threatened to take the girls away from her? God, what an awful thing to do! They were her daughters, too, and she loved them every bit as much as he did. Damn, he deserved to be whipped.

And the memory of how she had looked haunted him in the dark. So beautiful. A new haircut, that black dress that made her skin look like dairy cream. Huge green eyes. So beautiful. More beautiful than she had ever been.

But even more haunting was the way she had paled at his accusations, the anguish that had darkened her green eyes when he threatened to take the girls away. Her chin hadn't lifted then. No. For the first time in all the years he had known Marge, her chin had drooped.

And the memory of that cut at him like a knife.

He had to apologize, he realized. First thing in the morning, he'd tell her he hadn't really meant any of it, that he'd been upset. . . .

But in the morning, Marge was gone.

It had been so stupid to leave Laramie while it was snowing, Marge thought. Stupid. Stupid. Stupid! The wind had kicked up, blowing the fresh snow wildly until she couldn't see much beyond the front end of the car. The road had almost completely vanished, and she had to guide herself with the mile markers and reflector posts that picked up her headlight beams and flashed them back. It wasn't much, but she kept going now because there was no alternative.

She wasn't used to thinking about these things, and it made her furious to realize how much she had always depended on Nate. How she had utterly ignored weather conditions and all the rest of it, content to let her husband decide when they would travel, if they would travel. . . .

And that was only the beginning. She had let Nate handle everything for all these years, from the bills to repairs. And it had never once occurred to her she might need to know about these things.

And ignorance led to stupid decisions, like the one to start driving home while it was snowing. But she had passed the halfway point miles back and there was no choice but to forge ahead.

Nor did it help that she had to keep blinking back tears in order to see what little she could. She could hardly believe what a mess her life had become, could hardly believe that Nate had said those horrible things to her...that he had been that angry with her.

He was hurting. She believed that now. She couldn't forget his anger or his horrible accusations, but she could understand what led to them. He was hurting. But she was hurting, too, and so were the girls, and now Krissie was suspended.

Oh, dear God, were they ever going to get their lives sorted out again? Ever? Were they ever going to reach a place where it didn't hurt all the time?

And whatever was she going to do about Krissie? She had talked and talked and talked to her daughter about her misconduct, and received nothing in reply except sullen glares. What more could she do? Get a counselor, she supposed, although that would probably send Nate through the roof.

Or would it? They'd never needed such a thing before, but that didn't mean Nate would object.

And what did it matter what Nate thought? He'd walked out.

On that thought, the tears began to flow again. And through the tears, she saw one of the dash lights flare red. The engine had overheated.

Cursing, Nate stomped out of the hotel into the chilly, snowy predawn air and climbed into his Blazer. It started on the first try, and he was out of town before the heater even began to blow warmer air.

Snow had been falling since midnight, the clerk had said, and Mrs. Tate had checked out around two.

Two. He had sent her into flight and she had run in the middle of the night. The thought filled him with self-disgust.

And guilt.

And for the very first time, he began to wonder if maybe Sandy was right, after all. Maybe he did feel guilty about a few things. Maybe he had some stuff to feel guilty about. Like the girls. Especially Krissie. Carol and Pat were nearly grown, but Krissie was only twelve.

Damn it! He slammed his palm on the steering wheel. Maybe it was time to consider something other than his own sense of betrayal. Time to consider that other people were being affected by what he was doing.

Time to consider his girls.

Guilt and concern swirled around him as the sun rose behind heavy clouds and the snow swirled across the wintry landscape. His wife had driven off into a snowstorm in the dead of night because he was such a bastard. His youngest daughter was feeling so hurt because of his actions that she'd gotten herself thrown out of school. And there was really no telling how this was affecting his older daughters.

Really no telling how they felt about the abrupt appearance of Seth in their lives. Maybe they were just covering, just being the polite people he and Marge had raised them to be. Maybe inside they were hurting, too.

And maybe it was time to reorder his priorities to take those facts into account.

The instant he saw Marge's car, his heart climbed into his throat. It sat forlornly alongside the road, gently nosed into a ditch. Oh, Lord, she might have been sitting out here in the cold for hours, hurt and bleeding from an accident! Considering when she had checked out . . .

But he didn't want to consider it. Because of the snowstorm, there had been no traffic along this road since he left the outskirts of Laramie, and as he eased his Blazer onto the shoulder behind the red Fiero, his gut tightened in anticipation of the very worst.

This couldn't be, he found himself thinking. This was not possible. Marge had to be okay. She had to be!

But even as he was flinging open the door of the Blazer, the door of the Fiero was swinging open. Marge levered herself out, then staggered a little, as if hypothermia were affecting her coordination.

Nate, in a burst of relief and concern, hit the ground running and caught her up into his arms.

"Sugar, oh God, sugar...."

Her teeth were chattering so hard, he wasn't sure if she spoke his name or merely moaned. It didn't really matter. Sweeping her up, he carried her to the warmth of his vehicle, tucking her in the passenger seat, wrapping her with blankets.

"M-m-m-my p-p-purse..."

"I'll get it, sugar. I'll get it."

He slammed the door behind him, to lock in the warmth of the Blazer's heater, and rescued her purse and suitcase from the car. He'd come back with help later and tow it in. For now he needed to get Marge warmed up. Maybe to the hospital. She might have frostbite....

When he climbed into the cab a few minutes later, she was still shivering with an audible rattle of her teeth. Reaching over, he pulled off her gloves and examined her fingers while holding them in the blast of warmth from the heater. Her fingers were icy to the touch, a little bluish, but he didn't see any of the whiteness of frostbite.

Bending down, he worked to loosen the laces of her boots and get her toes free of any constriction that might impede circulation. What he found here was a little more worrisome. That might well be frostbite on a couple of her toes. Just little patches, but they were white.

He turned up the heater even more and tugged Marge around until her feet were in his lap. Then he began to chafe them, encouraging the return of blood.

"Hurts..." she said between chattering teeth.

"I know, sugar, I know. But I have to get you warm."

And it was all his fault she was in trouble. All his fault. Damn it, she could have died out here, and for no better reason than that he'd blown his cork and made terrible threats to her. For no better reason than that he had stooped to using his own children as a weapon.

Hell, it made him sick to his stomach to even think about what he'd done in the heat of rage last night. What he'd said, what he'd threatened.

But now was not the time to apologize. First he had to get her warm, had to get that terrible marble paleness out of her poor feet.

Feet...such small, delicate feet. How many times over the years had he held them in his lap and rubbed them just like this, easing the day's stresses for both of them, building in the gentlest of ways toward lazy lovemaking. Marge had always loved to have her feet rubbed. Always.

A thumb pressing gently into her arch, rubbing in slow, deep circles. Under the toes, gently stretching and stroking, bending each toe upward in a way that relaxed muscles higher up. Warming. Relaxing. How he loved to do this for her. And soon she would start making that soft sound, so like a purr....

He looked up, recognizing that sound, and found Marge's green eyes regarding him steadily. Sadly. She still shivered a little, but not violently. The danger was past.

Bending, he opened his mouth and breathed warm air on her toes. The flesh was pink, all the dangerous whiteness gone. She was okay.

Slowly, slowly, he straightened and looked at her again. And met the same sad stare.

"We'll talk later," he said. "We have to talk, Marge. But after I get you home."

She nodded and looked away. He didn't miss the way she swallowed, though. He knew when she was trying to suppress tears.

Turning, he put the Blazer in gear and eased them back onto the road, heading for Conard City.

Tears. Marge's tears. He had a sudden, very uncomfortable view of himself from the outside. And he found himself wondering if anything Marge had done could possibly justify what he was doing now.

Two wrongs didn't make a right. The simple old axiom resounded in his head like an accusation. What the hell was he doing?

He didn't like any of the answers that occurred to him.

By the time they pulled up in the driveway at the house, Marge felt completely thawed. Even the painful burning in her fingers and toes as circulation was restored had entirely vanished. Nate wanted to take her to the hospital, but she flatly refused.

"I asked Mrs. Malcolm to watch Krissie," Nate said. "I'll need to drive her home."

"Sure."

He turned his head and looked at Marge. "I'll be back."

Her heart squeezed, but she could no longer tell if it was joy or dread that caused her reaction. No longer did she feel capable of predicting anything Nate chose to do. No longer did she feel she could trust him implicitly. Nor did the irony of that escape her.

According to Mrs. Malcolm, who had been baby-sitting for the Tates since the birth of their first daughter, Krissie had been a perfect angel, but that's what she always said, and Marge put only moderate stock in it. The girls tended to be good for Mrs. Malcolm, but they weren't always angels. And a glimpse at Krissie's face warned her that, regardless of how she had behaved for her sitter, she wasn't going to be an angel now.

When Nate had walked out the door with Mrs. Malcolm, Krissie spoke.

"How come you came home with him? Where's your car?"

"My car broke down." Marge turned and looked at her daughter, feeling a sudden sense of surprise at how close to adulthood her baby was. It seemed like only yesterday...

"What's *he* coming back for?"

"*He* is your father, and I won't have you referring to him that way!"

"Why not? He's not my father anymore! He walked out!"

"That doesn't mean—"

"Tell me what it means then! He hasn't talked to any of us since he left! He couldn't care less—"

"Krissie! That's not true! He's been hurt—"

"And the rest of us haven't been? What about you? What about Seth? What about *me?* He doesn't care about anybody except *him!*"

Suddenly Krissie looked past Marge and pointed a finger. "You're selfish! *Selfish!*"

Marge whirled around and saw a tight-jawed Nate standing in the doorway. And from the look of him, he had heard most of what Krissie had said.

"Go to your room, young lady. Now." There was a steely note to his voice that even Krissie couldn't ignore. With a sob, the girl whirled and ran from the kitchen. Nate closed his eyes a moment and then looked at Marge. "Mrs. Malcolm left her knitting basket in the living room."

"I'll get it." She needed to do something. Anything. She couldn't just stand there. Turning, she fled almost as quickly as Krissie.

A half minute later she was back with the basket, but hesitated when she saw Nate standing rigidly in the same spot, staring into space as if he saw something terrible.

"Nate?"

He turned his head slowly and regarded her from hollow eyes. "I'll be back. We have to talk, Marge. We really have to talk."

She nodded slowly. And then ached as she watched him walk down the driveway. The years hadn't diminished him at all, she thought as a tear ran down her cheek. Not at all. He still had the power to stir her pulse and make her need. And he still owned her heart.

She made them a lunch, heating up leftover homemade soup and some refrigerator rolls. Krissie refused to come out of her room, so Marge left her there. She really didn't feel like arguing. In fact, when it came right down to it, she was feeling emotionally exhausted, and she didn't especially want to talk to Nate about anything at all.

But there was the custody question, and the accusations and threats he had made yesterday. It was...it was every bit as bad as she had feared during the many years of her silence. Her initial youthful fears, encouraged by her father's insistence that knowledge could only be hurtful, had with time given way to the fear of losing her daughters, as well as Nate. Intolerable losses. And with time, it had become easier to convince herself that Nate would only be hurt.

Well, he had been hurt. And so had the girls. And she felt horribly responsible for all of it. What would Nate have done all those years ago if she had told him the truth right then? He'd been really angry to learn that her father had been intercepting all their mail, but so had she. Would he have understood how she felt when he failed to reply to her letters about her pregnancy? Would he have forgiven her fears?

Whatever he might have done, it couldn't have been any worse than this. Back then, at least there hadn't been the children to consider. Back then, there had been only them, and the rupture would have been so much less painful in the long run. So much less wounding.

Why, she wondered dismally, were young people so incapable of seeing past the moment?

The kitchen door opened with a blast of cold air to admit Nate. As was his habit, he paused on the mat to let the last of the snow melt from his boots while he hung his jacket and hat on the pegs he had placed there so many years ago—high ones for himself, a row of lower ones for the little girls to reach.

Marge turned swiftly away and swallowed hard, trying to ease the sudden tightness in her throat. "I, um, made us some lunch. Just soup and rolls."

"Sounds good. I've been eating at Maude's. She's a great cook, but the menu is limited."

Which Marge already knew. Aware suddenly that he was as uncomfortable as she, she turned again to face him. Yes, he looked as awkward as she had ever seen him. "Maude's cooking will kill you."

"Maybe. Mine'll kill me quicker." One corner of his mouth lifted in a tentative smile.

Despite her anxiety over the children, Marge felt her own mouth respond helplessly, and a warmth seemed to trickle through her to her womb. He still worked his magic on her. Still. Even after all these years.

They ate at the kitchen table, and for those few moments she could almost forget that this was no longer a daily occurrence. It seemed so right to have Nate here like this, and so wrong to have him gone. She wondered if she was always going to feel this way...and wondered why she should have to.

"You've always made the best soups," he said after his second bowl. "Always."

"Thank you." Too formal. Too stiff. Too stiff to ease her trepidation.

Nate sighed and pushed back from the table so he could settle one ankle on his other knee. For a moment he studied Marge while he tapped his fingers on his thigh. "I was out of line last night, Marge. I had no call to say those things. No call at all."

Her breath locked in her throat, leaving her incapable of speech. When she didn't reply, he shook his head and continued.

"I don't know why you went to Laramie, and it's none of my business."

He paused as if giving her an opportunity to tell him why she had gone, but how could she admit that she had wanted a make-over in the hopes that a new hairdo and better makeup would get his attention? Nor did she know if it was safe to admit that she was going slowly insane in this house without him, that everywhere she turned was another reminder that he had left. She was looking for a job, but they didn't grow on trees in this small town. So she had gone to Laramie to escape. And she couldn't tell him any of this.

"None of my business," he repeated when she didn't speak. "And considering that we're...separated, you had every right to go out with Little, and it's none of my damn business what you did with him. The things I said... Marge,

I know you're a good mother. I wouldn't take the girls from you...." He cleared his throat noisily. "I wouldn't. They need you. More than me, probably."

"Oh, Nate, they need you!" The words burst out of her. "Of course they need you! You're their father!"

"I haven't been acting like it. Krissie's right. I've been behaving selfishly." He shook his head again. "That's what we need to discuss, Marge. How to deal with this mess in the best way possible for the girls. Even Sandy Keller hollered at me to try to work this out."

"You mean—you mean you haven't filed?" Hope left her light-headed.

"No. Not yet." He made an impatient gesture with his hand. "I'm not saying I'm ready to forgive and forget. Because I'm not, Marge. I can't seem to get past the fact you lied to me. It's ... a little too big for me to get past. But I've only been considering myself, not the girls. And that's not right. So at the very least we need to try to cooperate as parents. You can keep seeing Little, of course."

All of a sudden, Marge was seeing red. Red haze seemed to fill the entire universe and suck all the oxygen from her lungs. "How very generous of you," she said acidly. "Just where the hell do you get the idea I need your permission to see anyone I choose to see? *You* walked out, Nathan Tate!"

He was visibly startled. "I didn't mean—"

"Sure you did! Last night you thought you had the right to make terrible accusations because I went out to dinner. Now today you think you have the right to give me permission to do something! Let's get something clear here, Nate. Very clear. When you walked out on me, you gave up any rights you had where I'm concerned!"

Now he looked stunned. And Marge, even as she exploded, was unhappily aware with some corner of her mind that this was not the wise way to handle this, that challenging him would only make him mad and cause more trouble. But she also felt he was suffering from an incredible tunnel vision that was keeping him from seeing anything but his own feelings, and she wanted him to know—*needed* him to know—that she had feelings, too. That the girls had feelings.

"You have nothing to say about what I do any longer," she continued, her voice quavering just a little. "We'll discuss how best to handle the girls, but we'll do it as equals."

"Well, of course..."

"No, not of course. You've been a good husband for a long time, Nate. And a good father. But now the situation has changed, and you're just going to have to accept that we don't have a united front on everything. Not now. Not since you shattered it."

Hard words. Very hard words, and she could see how they struck him. Her first instinct was to soothe him, to take the edge off what she had said, but she stopped herself. This was not a time to spare him. He wasn't sparing her or the girls. And she couldn't escape the hope that if she could just make him really aware of what it was he was doing to all of them, he might come to his senses.

Instead of replying, he lowered his foot to the floor with a thud and rose. Halfway across the kitchen, he looked back. "You shattered my trust."

Behind him, Marge gasped at the savagery of the unexpected blow. Come to his senses? As anguish welled with renewed force, she faced that fact that maybe he never would. Maybe he'd never be able to.

And why should he? He was right.

She had shattered his trust.

He found Krissie lying on her back on her bed, holding a throw pillow to her stomach. In the split second when he first opened the door, he caught sight of the little girl she had been, saw the desolation and fright that filled her. Then a mask of sullen rage dropped over her face.

"What do you want?"

"To talk."

"I don't want to talk."

"Fine. You just listen. Despite what you think, I'm still your dad and I still love you as much as I ever did. But if you think these shenanigans of yours are going to do a damn thing to get your mom and me back together, you're wrong. In fact, if anything, you're making us fight more. Now you just think about that, missy.''

"I don't care!"

"Really? Then how come you're so damn mad? I promise you one thing. If you give your mom any more trouble, if you give the school any more trouble, you're going to find out just how much your dad I still am. Maybe you ought to give some thought to how many privileges you still have and how easy it would be to lose them. Permanently.''

He waited a moment, considering it a major victory when she only glared at him, but didn't argue or shout that she didn't care. Which meant she *did* care. Which meant he still had enough leverage to straighten her out.

"I love you, Krissie,'' he said, then left without pressing his luck any further. She would never know, of course, just how terrified he'd been that she really *was* out of control. But relief was almost overwhelming as he walked down the hall.

Marge was still sitting at the table where he'd left her, looking pale and wounded. He felt a twinge in his heart and conscience both, but her lie stuck in his craw and never let him forget. Never let him forget he had been betrayed.

"I'm going to the office,'' he said. "I'll check back later, and we can discuss things when we're both calmer. If Krissie gives you any trouble, let me know.''

She raised glistening green eyes to his face and managed a nod. "Nate...''

He shook his head. "Not now, Marge. Not now. We're both hurting. It's not a good time. We need to let things settle. Talk to you later.''

Marge would never know how hard it was for him to walk past her, grab his jacket and hat and leave without kissing her. Without touching her. Without gathering her close and holding her. She'd never know. But he did.

He wasn't over her. And it was beginning to look like he never would be.

So how the hell did you handle that?

* * *

"Gage is chomping at the bit waiting to talk to you" was the first thing Velma said to him when he stepped in the front door of the sheriff's office.

"Well, that might be the best news anyone's given me in weeks."

"Not surprising," Velma said tartly. "Talking to you lately is like poking sticks at an angry grizzly. When are you gonna come to your senses?"

He glared at her. "None of your business, Velma."

"Good luck" was Beau's lazy remark from the duty desk. "Everything's Velma's business, boss. You know that."

He scowled at Beau for good measure and stalked down the hall to Gage's office. A "Come on in!" greeted his knock, and he stepped into the investigator's small, neat office.

Gage was sitting with his feet propped up on the desk, and a phone cradled to his ear. He raised one finger and Nate nodded, closing the door before he sat in the cracked leather chair facing the desk. After a moment, it registered that Gage was speaking to one of the federal agents who was handling the California end of the case. He leaned forward, listening intently.

"I agree, Brenda. One hundred percent. The organized-crime stench is thick, especially with that stuff about the cars. Well, I'll keep you posted. Yeah. You, too." Gage hung up and turned his scarred face toward Nate.

"Organized crime?" Nate repeated.

"It seems that the flatcars don't belong to Cheyenne Western Railroad, despite what's painted on the cars. The feds checked, and all of Cheyenne Western's cars are accounted for elsewhere."

"Which means?"

"Big money is behind the operation, first of all. Those cars ain't cheap. Secondly, it means they could have been loaded at a siding by nonrailroad personnel posing as Cheyenne employees. In effect, getting around the ICC rules by avoiding any extensive involvement by real railroads. Which makes sense. Somebody had to look the other way for those unlabeled barrels to get so far. The feds theorize that the loaded cars were transferred at the switchyard to the carrier who brought them this way, and since they were already loaded, nobody looked any closer. And if anybody saw the cars being loaded, well, it would be assumed that Cheyenne Western employees were doing what they were supposed to. This doesn't mean there wasn't any inside help at the railroad, but it probably reduced the amount of involvement to near zilch. Making it safer and easier."

"Harder to track than backing up a truck and loading the cars at the terminus, you mean?"

"That's the idea. Plus, if anything goes wrong, how the hell do you trace nonexistent cars and a nonexistent forwarding company? Another layer of security."

"And now?"

"And now I've got a list of six potential suspects. All of 'em are ranchers who were having trouble making their note payments for a while but now are doing fine. And three of 'em know Westy Weatherill."

Nate was up out of his chair like a shot. "What are we waiting for? Time to ask some questions. Damn it, Gage, I want to know where all that stuff has been dumped. I wake up in the middle of the night with godawful visions of sick or dead kids." He shook his head sharply. "Where do we start?"

"Hold your horses, pardner!" Smiling faintly, Gage held up a hand. "Micah's already making the rounds on the pretext of looking for additional dumps. That's how we know three of them hired Westy Weatherill. He's working on the other three right now."

"Why Micah?"

"Because everybody knows I'm your investigator. Micah's poking around seems more natural than mine. He'll be able to narrow the list, if it can be narrowed, and then we'll bring out the big guns."

"You."

"Me."

Nate shook his head. Railroad manifests from the last year indicated there were still dozens of barrels of waste they hadn't located yet, and the horrible possibilities arising from that made his stomach knot. "I can't imagine one of our local ranchers doing something like this, Gage. These folks respect the land. Respect the water. I just can't imagine any of 'em getting hooked up in a scheme like this."

"To save their homes? Besides, Nate, chances are they were misled about the dangers and the toxicity. You don't really suppose anyone told the consignee he was going to be handling stuff that could kill him, do you? No, they probably made the stuff sound almost innocuous in some way, made it look like the feds were just big baddies with all this environmental crap. And you know damn well a lot of folks consider the concern exaggerated."

And your average rancher was one of the world's most independent cusses, Nate admitted. Blindly patriotic, but foursquare in favor of less government. Less interference. And in Wyoming's vast open spaces, pollution was, for most, a distant problem of the cities. A few gallons of waste dumped in the middle of nowhere might appear to be insignificant to some.

But Nate knew better, which was why he had nightmares about sick kids and dead cattle. And now that they actually had some suspects, he was champing at the bit. "When's Micah due in?"

"Soon. He figured he'd be back here by five."

"I can wait that long."

Gage chuckled. "Glad to hear it."

Just then, Velma knocked, poking her head in. "Nate? I didn't want to take a chance on anybody overhearing me. Jeff Cumberland just called, and if you think he was mad over the cattle mutilations, you ought to try how he's feeling right now. One of his hands found another dump site."

Chapter 8

It was a depressing rerun. A dozen or so steel drums tossed into a wash, barely visible through the snow. These, at least, hadn't spilled, as far as anyone could tell. Small blessings.

Jeff Cumberland, the county's biggest rancher, wasn't in a mood to count his blessings. "They found another one," he told Nate grimly when they met near the gate at the southwest corner of Jeff's spread.

"Another one? You mean this one."

Jeff shook his head, his jaw working tensely. "No, I mean another one. I've had my hands checking the gullies and draws ever since we realized there were multiple dump sites around the county. Well, Nate, the good news is that we found one out here today. The bad news is that another of my hands just radioed in that he's found one, too. And we're nowhere near through checking all the possible dump sites. Damn it, Nate, do you have any idea how many square miles we have to cover?"

"You're using your plane, aren't you?"

"Of course! But the snow cover makes it nigh impossible to find anything unless the snow's melted off it. When you see this dump, you'll understand what I mean. Until it spills, we can't see it through the snow. And I want to get it before it spills!''

A reasonable desire, Nate thought.

"We'll have to drive out there. It's nearly a mile from here. Which means somebody drove onto my land at some point to dump that crap! Deliberately!''

Velma was right, Nate thought as he looked at Jeff. The rancher's anger over the mutilations more than a year ago didn't begin to approach this. And it was understandable. A handful of slaughtered cattle would raise a rancher's ire, but not like the thought of losing a herd, which is exactly what Jeff stood to lose if poison got into his water.

Nate climbed back into his Blazer with Gage and followed Jeff's truck along a rutted, snowy track. Going was slow, but that was okay—it gave him time to control his own anger and shift into a more clear-thinking mode.

Time bombs. That's what these dumps were. Time bombs left all over his county. God, the water could be poisoned for years, the land ruined for decades.

Somehow they had to find this Weatherill character and get him to tell them where he'd left all this stuff. If he could remember. The alternative didn't bear thinking.

The site was exactly like the others. A dozen barrels tumbled haphazardly, as if they had been carelessly rolled off the back of a truck. Covered in snow, they were almost invisible; Jeff was certainly right about that. And once again they had been dumped in a place where they could do maximum damage if they leaked, right in a gully that carried spring runoff. Nate found himself wondering if that was the intent, rather than simple concealment. But that was another thought that didn't bear thinking.

"I'll have the team come out tomorrow and clean it up,'' he told Jeff. "What about the other one?''

"About the same, from what Larry radioed in. He said he couldn't see any evidence that anything had spilled.'' Jeff tilted his head up and looked at the sky. "We might just have time to get out there if we head out right now. Then again, maybe it would be better to wait until morning.''

"No rush," Nate agreed. "I'd rather have more time to look around, and I don't want to miss any evidence in the failing light. I'll get Micah out here to take a look at both sites in the morning, then."

"Fair enough. I'll take you out myself. Around eight?"

As Nate and Gage drove slowly back toward the road, Nate caught sight of Jeff in his rearview mirror. The rancher gave no sign of being ready to go. He simply stood beside the gully with his hands on his hips and stared down at this new disaster.

Nate swore under his breath. Damn county was going to hell in a hand basket.

Nor was his day over. He'd known it would come sooner or later, but after the uproar with Marge and Krissie, and the new dump site, he was not very pleased to find the mayor and one of the county commissioners waiting for him.

"We're not here to do any shouting," Mayor Stephanopoulos told him. "We just want to hear what the sheriff's department is doing about the toxic-waste problem. We need to explain to the council and the commissioners."

Nate looked from Steve Stephanopoulos to Henry Freitag and wondered just what he was supposed to say to that. "We're doing everything we can. We have a few leads I'm not at liberty to discuss just yet. The FBI is working on it from the other end." The worst part of small-town and small-county politics, Nate often thought, was the fact that volunteers filled the council and commission seats, with the inevitable result. Henry Freitag was a fine businessman, and his business sense managed the county coffers very well. But he didn't have the time or inclination to learn to do anything else, from road maintenance to law enforcement. The same could be said for Steve, who was a really excellent dentist. Period.

"Just what *is* everything?" Henry asked.

Nate had a sudden, strong, uncharacteristic urge to sigh, swear and turn these two over to Gage. Almost as soon as he felt it, he squashed it. He'd been dealing with politicos for all the years he had been sheriff, and he knew how to handle it. Handle them. Give them what they thought they needed in a way that would send them away satisfied and leave him unhampered in the performance of his job.

Today, he just plain didn't feel like it, but so what?

"Everything is *everything*," he said flatly. "Everything that's legal, that is. We're combing the county for suspects. We may have a few. I was about to check into what our investigator has turned up. We particularly want to find a Westy or Westin Weatherill. Would either of you gentlemen know him?"

Two heads shook.

"That's a big part of the problem. All this stuff was consigned to him, but nobody knows who he is. And with the snow cover, we can't really hunt up all the dump sites. Once the spring thaw begins, the barrels won't be so effectively hidden. In the meantime, our best hope of cleaning things up is to find somebody who can tell us where all the stuff is stashed. Our perpetrator is our best bet. And we're working on it. I promise you, we're sparing no effort."

Freitag and Stephanopoulos exchanged looks, and Nate realized he wasn't going to get out of the woods this easily. He smothered another sigh.

Freitag cleared his throat. "We hear another dump was discovered at the Bar C."

Well, hell, Nate thought with a sudden burst of irritation. Who had let the beans spill on that one? "Two, actually," he said through a tight jaw. He hated to admit it, but he couldn't let Freitag and Stephanopoulos go around thinking they had better information than the sheriff's department. No way. "We're taking the investigation team out first thing in the morning. Nothing has spilled, so there's been no pollution. And just as soon as we check the sites for evidence, we'll send in the cleanup team."

"We can't keep leaving the discovery of these dumps to chance, Nate," Freitag snapped.

"Chance is about what we're going to have to settle for until we catch the culprit!" Nate spoke with sharp-edged impatience. "Just how many men do you think it would take—and how many *weeks*—to cover every inch of this county, looking for steel drums? Especially when they're buried beneath snow! Be reasonable, Henry! Look how long it took Jeff to find the two dumps on his property! And he's been looking for them. It wasn't just chance. We've got nearly three thousand square miles in Conard County. You gonna pay for the search parties? We're looking for needles in the haystack, man!''

"Well, you're not looking fast enough!" Freitag snapped back. "The people of the county are getting worried and upset—"

"And you think I'm not? Damn it, Henry, I'm having nightmares about what could happen if we don't find that stuff. But there's no escaping that I need the ranchers to search their own land. Nobody knows it better than they do. Nobody can do the job better than they can. I don't have the manpower to do it from here. Besides, my deputies have other tasks, such as good old-fashioned law enforcement. I'm sure you wouldn't care for the outcry if we gave that up!"

"Is that a threat?"

Nate opened his mouth, then closed it, completely astonished by this turn in the conversation. "Damn it, Henry!" he said finally. "You know better than that!"

"Do I? We came in here with a simple request to find out what you're doing, and all you're telling us is what you *can't* do."

Nate counted silently to five before he replied. "Henry, I'm trying to explain the difficulties we face so that you can explain them to anyone who asks you. There's nothing I'd like better than to be in a position to conduct a massive search for the waste dumps, but I'm afraid that is simply impossible. That's all I'm trying to say."

But Freitag didn't look very mollified. Of course not. He'd probably had a couple of the ranchers breathing down his neck today, demanding to know what the county was going to do about the outrage.

"I think," Freitag said, "that you should be aware that people in this county are very dissatisfied with your performance, Nate."

Nate sucked air through his teeth and this time counted to ten. "The voters'll have an opportunity this fall to tell me that, Henry. And they know my phone number if they can't wait."

"That's a cavalier attitude!"

Nate came close to losing it right then. He had never suffered fools gladly, nor had he ever previously thought that Henry Freitag was a fool, but right now he was doing both...or trying to. "I'm not being cavalier, Henry. The folks in this county know how to find me, and they're not shy about doing it when they feel it necessary. So far, you're the only voice I'm hearing."

Steve jumped in. "That's because of your marital problems! Damn it, Nate, the whole county's tiptoeing around you because they figure you've got more than enough on your plate."

"Steve!" Henry rose to his feet. "That was uncalled for!"

"Unfortunately, it's true," Steve said, rising also. "It's true, damn it, and that's why we're here, Nate. Because people are getting upset, and they want something to be done, and they don't want to bother you right now. So we got the fun job of coming over here to ask how it's going. And all we get is a list of what you can't do! I'm sorry you and Marge are having problems, truly sorry, but the people of this county deserve to know what's being done, anyway. They have a *right* to know."

Nate sat rigid as stone for a long moment while he faced with stark clarity what was going on in people's minds. They were judging his work not by how he was doing it, but by the fact that he was having personal problems. And they were leaping to the erroneous conclusion that he wasn't doing all he could.

And that cut him hard. "Gentlemen," he said after a moment, his gravelly voice rougher than usual, "I'll ask Gage Dalton to talk to you. Maybe he can convince you *he's* doing everything possible. Maybe you'll listen to *him.*"

Two minutes later he was all alone in his office, staring out the window at the alley, at the snow, and the unutterably sad day, and he wondered why all of a sudden he couldn't seem to get anything right.

A familiar rap on his door told him Micah Parish was just outside. "Come on in, Micah."

The big man stepped inside and closed the door firmly. "What's with the political delegation?"

"Apparently people think I'm not doing my job because my personal life is a mess."

Micah snorted. "Hogswill. Got a minute?"

"Yeah, sure. Gage said you were checking out some suspects and that you'd run across some stuff about the Weatherill character?"

"That's what I'm here for. I wrapped up with Gage just before you took Freitag and Stephanopoulos over there. Since he's not going to be able to tell you right away, I thought I would."

"Thanks. So what have you got?"

"Not a whole hell of a lot. None of the ranchers look like their lot has improved any from a couple of years ago. Three of them are making their note payments by the skin of their teeth, and only because of their wives. One woman went back to teaching, another started selling pottery to some place back East, and the third guy married a public health service doctor. So they've got additional income that can be explained. The other three... Well, I got stories about better management, better profits on the herds... nothing you can really pin down. They need to be looked at closer."

Nate nodded. "And the Weatherill character?"

"Now, that's where life gets interesting." Micah leaned back in his chair. "A couple of these folks say a Westy Weatherill worked for them, but only briefly, a long time back. Pay records show it. Like most cowpokes, he was paid in cash, so he probably didn't leave much of a paper trail around the county. No bank account, no merchants who would have known his name. So all we really know is that he existed. Nobody knows if he still exists. But he signed the pay logs, and I've got one of the logs with me so we can compare signatures with the railroad records."

"Good. That's good."

"But it doesn't amount to a whole hell of a lot," Micah observed. "It's possible one of the ranchers is paying him to pick the stuff up, but any of those guys I talked to today has enough smarts not to put him on the payroll while they're involved in something illegal. We can subpoena the records, I suppose, but right now I just don't see any point in it."

Nate shook his head. "None yet. Besides, I don't like to make suspects too nervous too soon. They can throw too many monkey wrenches into the works. What did these guys have to say about Weatherill?"

"Not much. Nobody seems to remember him very clearly. Crittendon said Weatherill was quiet, claimed to have worked at the Bear Creek Ranch in Niobrara County just before he headed this way, but Crittendon never checked it out. Didn't pay, he said, to call that far when he could find out just by putting the man to work. Evidently Weatherill knew what he was doing—Crittendon kept him for nearly three months, then turned him off because the work load fell off. Hasn't seen him since."

"And the others?"

"Basically the same. Weatherill knew what he was doing, worked hard enough. Shreeve was the only one with a complaint—said Weatherill drank a little too much."

"Shreeve's a teetotaler, so I wouldn't put much stock in that. But...maybe it wouldn't hurt to check around some of the roadhouses and see if anyone remembers Weatherill."

"We'll get on it."

"Anything else?"

Micah shook his head. "Like I said, it's not much. We need a break."

"Yep." He shook his head. "Like the link between organized crime and a down-at-the-heels cowpoke in Wyoming. That's a long stretch, Micah. A long stretch."

"Maybe not so long. Somebody probably came looking for someone like him. And his type isn't hard to find around here."

But one particular man could be very hard to find. Very hard.

He and Micah kicked the ball around for a few more minutes without getting anywhere, and finally Micah said good-night. Alone again, night falling swiftly beyond his window, Nate tried to concentrate on the case.

Instead his mind kept wandering back to Marge. How scared he had been this morning when he had seen her car off the side of the road. How relieved when she had staggered out of it. How much it had hurt when she reminded him that he had relinquished all rights when he walked out.

It was true, and it hurt. Hurt to realize that he still wanted her as much as he ever had. Every bit as much.

But he couldn't trust her. Without trust, there was nothing. Nothing at all.

Except hurt.

He got back to his room above Mahoney's to find Seth had left a note saying he was going out to play pool with a couple of the deputies, and that Marge's car had been towed in and was at Bayard's Garage.

Out with some of the deputies. Nate crumpled the note and threw it in the wastebasket, thinking that Seth was fitting in awfully well at the department, and wondering if he'd been serious when he'd said he was thinking about leaving the navy. But, hell, he must be halfway to retirement by now, or close to it. Why would he want to give up all that to work in a backwater sheriff's department?

He yanked off his boots, stripped his uniform shirt, pulled the tails of his T-shirt out and just generally made himself comfortable. He didn't feel like eating at Maude's tonight so he warmed up some canned soup and ate it with a stack of soda crackers. Bachelor fare. Seemed like everything reminded him of what he'd left behind.

There was a hockey game on TV, and boring as he found spectator sports, he settled in to watch it, determined not to remember any more of what he'd left behind. Not tonight, at any rate. He'd had quite enough for one day. Now it was time to vegetate.

During the closing minutes of a game he wasn't really watching, there was a knock on the door. When he answered it, he was surprised to see Paula Sibert standing on the landing, holding a large casserole dish.

He wanted to close the door on her. The longing was intense. Paula had a bit of a reputation around the county, and being seen with her would start up all kinds of gossip. But on the other hand, she was a member of his church, and a constituent, and you didn't slam doors on such people, however much you wanted to.

Not that she gave him a chance to. The instant he opened the door, she slipped past him as easily as a puff of air.

"I just wanted to leave this with you, Nate," she said. "It's some of my seafood casserole that you liked so much at the last potluck."

Oh, Lord, he *had* complimented her on that, hadn't he? "Uh, thanks, Paula. Seth and I will enjoy it."

"Seth. That's the young man who's staying with you?"

"My son." And damned if he was going to say any more than that. Half the county probably thought that Seth was one of his indiscretions and never dreamed Marge was in any way involved. Well, that was fine. He'd rather shoulder the blame than have her take any of it. People had a terrible double standard when it came to things like that.

"He's a fine-looking young man."

"Yes." He kept the door open, despite the temperature, which hovered around zero, and politely waited for her to leave. Instead she reached for the top button of her coat.

"Can I make us some coffee?" she asked.

Suddenly he was a man fighting for survival, and the rules of the game changed. "No, I don't think so, Paula. Thanks for the casserole, but you have to leave now."

For an instant he thought she was going to argue, but she apparently thought better of it. Instead she managed a bright smile and walked past him to the door.

"I'll pick up the dish tomorrow," she said as she stepped out.

"Pick it up at the office," he said flatly. "I'll leave it with Velma."

Her smile never wavered. "See you tomorrow."

He watched her descend the salty steps, her boots crunching on each one, and then she disappeared around the corner.

And only then did he realize that someone else was in the alley. A movement caught his attention, and he turned to see his dark blue van, and standing beside it in the shadows was Marge. As soon as she realized he had seen her, she turned and fumbled at the door handle.

"Marge, wait!"

She kept pawing at the handle, as if she had forgotten it was locked. Nate didn't wait. She was going to flee, and he had to stop her.

In his stocking feet he tore down the stairs, risking his neck, and across the snowy alley, catching her just as she opened the van door.

"Marge, no!"

She tugged against his hold, trying to back out of his arms. "Nate...let me go. I'll just go home. Just want to go home...."

He heard the tears in her voice before he saw them. Then he saw them glistening on her cheeks, and he knew with sudden, vicious certainty just how much he had hurt this woman.

"No, sugar. No...." His voice was little more than a husky whisper as he swung her up in his arms. God, she didn't weigh anywhere near what she ought to, he thought as he carried her toward the stairs and up to his apartment. She must have lost another five or so pounds. "Hush, baby," he murmured. "We'll talk. God, Margie, let's talk. Let's talk."

"I was... I wanted to t-talk about K-Krissie...."

"We'll talk about Krissie. I promise."

He stepped into the apartment and kicked the door closed behind them. This wasn't a place for his Marge, he thought. Not a place for her at all. It was dingy, poorly furnished, almost squalid. The smell of stale beer and fry cooking rose from the bar below so that the room reeked.

But for now it was the best he had to offer. He settled on the couch with Marge on his lap and ignored the spring that poked him. With one hand, he struggled to loosen the snaps and zipper of her parka, while he held her close with his other arm and dropped helpless kisses on her eyes and cheeks.

Marge didn't cry easily, and the fact that she was crying now disturbed him almost beyond bearing. For the moment, in concern for her, he forgot his distrust, his own hurt, his anger.

"I—I'm sorry," she said in a small broken voice. "I didn't m-mean to invade your privacy."

"You weren't. You absolutely weren't, Marge. Paula—you know about Paula—she brought me a casserole and I essentially told her to get lost. That woman scares me."

Marge caught her breath and lifted her tear-streaked face. For an instant a smile almost seemed to dance around the corners of her mouth. "She scares you? *You?*"

"Terrifies me. She's always hunting, and I never see her without thinking of a hungry lioness."

"I didn't think anything scared you."

Nate looked away, suddenly uncomfortable. "Things scare me," he said after a moment. "All kinds of things. I'm only human."

"But you never admit it."

"That I'm scared? What's the point? It doesn't change anything." He looked at her again. "What's wrong with Krissie?"

Marge stared at him almost as if something she saw saddened her. Then she wiggled. "Let me off your lap, Nate."

Reluctantly he let her go, watching her slide away down the couch as if he were a stranger. Only then did he become aware that his socks were soaked and his feet frozen. They felt as frozen as his heart. Bending, he tugged the socks off. "What's with Krissie?"

"Nothing new. It's just that . . . There must be something we can do! I'm so worried about her!"

He was, too, but he didn't want to admit it. Marge would only get more upset if she knew how concerned he was. "I think we're doing everything we can at the moment. Let her think about it for a few days, Marge. If she doesn't wake up, we'll see about counseling. She isn't home alone, is she?''

"No, of course not. Carol and Patti are with her." Marge picked at an invisible speck of lint on her jacket, then slipped the jacket off and folded it over the arm of the sofa. "The counselor at school says she's just trying to get our attention."

"I gathered that."

"That she's angry, and hurt and really furious with us. That she thinks she can make us feel guilty enough to get back together."

"It'll take more than that."

Marge flinched, and Nate immediately wished his words unsaid, even though they were true. There was no way he was going to live out a lie because Krissie was having temper tantrums. No way.

Nor was he in any mood to be patient and understanding. Holding Marge in his lap had awakened urges he'd been forcibly burying since he walked out. What he wanted, all he wanted, was to find the comfort he had always found in Marge's arms, in Marge's body. The edgy yearning in his body was hard to ignore, almost as hard as his emotional longing for things to go back to the way they had been.

But they couldn't go back, he reminded himself, tearing his gaze from Marge. They couldn't go back. Trust had been sacrificed.

Marge spoke. "Nate, I don't think my feelings, or yours, are as important as our daughter. Krissie needs to get back to school, and she needs to pay attention to her studies."

The implied rebuke stung, and he rounded on her. "I didn't say she wasn't important! But what are you going to teach her if we give in to emotional extortion? That she can have a temper tantrum anytime she doesn't like the way things are, and that they'll get fixed? No way, Marge. No way am I going to teach any kid of mine that kind of lesson!"

"That isn't what I was saying!" Marge's temper could be even quicker than his to flare.

"Well, that's sure as hell what it sounded like!"

"You know, sometimes you can be too damn quick to jump to conclusions!" She hopped to her feet and grabbed her jacket before turning toward the door.

"Where the hell do you think you're going?"

She turned and glared at him, her chest heaving, her green eyes flashing. "Who the hell do you think you are, talking to me that way?"

"You can't just come in here and start an argument and then walk out! We haven't discussed Krissie!"

"I didn't start the argument, and we're not going to discuss anything when you're in a temper, Nathan Tate! We need to have a reasoned, adult conversation about a lot of things, but lately...lately... Oh, damn it!" With a frustrated lift of her chin, she turned away and headed for the door.

"Marge, damn it!"

But she just kept walking, and when her hand closed on the doorknob, he lost it. Completely and totally lost it.

He shot across the room and slammed his palm against the door over her head, holding it closed. She whirled around immediately and tilted her head back so she could glare up at him.

"Don't you try any Neanderthal tactics with me, Nate!"

"Then don't you turn your back on me and walk out! Ever!"

"Why not? I have nothing to say to you in this mood! And you turned your back on *me* and walked out! How does it feel, Nate? How does it feel when somebody won't listen and just walks away?"

"I listened to you!"

"No, you didn't listen. Not really! You didn't honestly hear a thing I said!"

"Are you trying to tell me that what you did was right? That it was okay to lie?"

"I'm trying to tell you that I did the best I could! That I did what I thought best! Right or wrong, I did the best I could! Now let me go!"

"No! We still haven't discussed Krissie!" He was being an ass. Some corner of his mind, unaffected by the anger that seethed in him, registered his stupidity. But as with riding a sled down an icy hill, there was no stopping.

"We'll discuss Krissie tomorrow! Damn it, Nate, you can't hold me prisoner!"

Marge seldom swore. Watching those words come out of that beautiful mouth of hers made him even madder, another stupid reaction among his many stupid reactions. Nothing, it seemed, was going to cool him down. Everything fueled the rage he was feeling. Everything.

And in the strange way of such things, his anger heightened his senses, made him aware of his need for this woman, of his almost insane need to crush her mouth under his.

To silence her, soften her, take the edge off her. To turn her into the Marge who had haunted his every dream from his fifteenth year.

She was close, so close that he could smell her wonderful scent, the scent of Marge the woman, Marge the wife, Marge who had lain so sweetly in his arms so many times over the years. A scent that meant home to him more than any other in the world.

He could feel her warmth over the few inches that separated them. Exquisite, human warmth. Marge's warmth. Soft, loving, giving warmth, his refuge from care for so many years.

His hands suddenly remembered every contour of her, remembered how he had loved to stroke her smooth, soft skin. His mouth suddenly remembered the taste of her. The textures of her. His ears suddenly remembered her softly splintering breaths, her quiet little moans.

And he was on fire. Completely, totally ablaze with need for her.

Breathing hard, he looked straight into her eyes and saw his need reflected there.

Slowly, slowly, he bent his head and kissed her. Found again the exquisite secrets of her mouth. But this time was different. This time he felt almost as nervous as he had the first time, and every bit as concerned about whether she would like his kisses, his touches.

Whether she would reject him.

With painstaking care he sucked gently at her mouth. Nibbling softly with his lips, then his teeth. Sensitizing her. Drawing at last from her the soft sigh that parted her lips and beckoned him within her.

Oh so carefully, he slid his tongue into her warm depths, tasting her sweetness. Playing gentle, erotic tag, tongue against tongue, until powerful rhythms built, rhythms that seemed to pulse in every cell in his body.

Slowly his hand slid down the door and then tangled in Marge's hair, holding her mouth to his, while his other arm closed around her waist and at last—at last!—pulled her snugly against him.

He felt a tremor run through her, then, miracle of miracles, her arms closed around him and hung on tightly.

"Marge...oh, sugar, it's been too long...too long...." His whisper was ragged, rough with hunger. He needed this woman with every fiber of his being.

She shivered as he spoke and seemed to sag against him, yielding and warm. Softly eager.

"I need you, honey. Need you so bad...."

"Nate..." His name escaped her on the softest of sighs. "Nate...we can't..."

But her body was saying something else, and he knew her well enough to read it. He didn't argue. He simply closed his mouth over hers and took her on a wild ride with him, a ride along splintered sighs, ragged moans, soft whimpers. A ride through raging fires.

She had always melted for him in the most beautiful of ways, and she was melting now, leaning into him, shaping herself to him, hanging on to him. Giving in to the hunger that burned between them.

And he was scared to death, suddenly, that she would change her mind. Come to her senses. Remember how he had hurt her and pull away. There were so many reasons for her to refuse him, and there were at least as many why he should pull back.

But he couldn't. He simply couldn't. He was trapped in a web of aching need so great that it far exceeded anything he'd ever felt before. He needed her warmth, her heat, her love, her nearness, her caring.

He needed everything he'd thrown away when he walked out.

"Nate . . ." Marge whispered his name brokenly, clinging to his shoulders with a desperation that told its own story. "You don't want . . ."

"Yes, I do. I do." And he did. They might both regret this afterward, but right now he couldn't think that far ahead, could only feel.

Feeling drove him to take her mouth again while his hand inched up under her sweater, seeking soft secrets so long denied him. Up his fingers climbed, over satiny, quivering flesh, to slip beneath her bra and capture one small breast.

The contact electrified him. Gasping for air, he threw his head back and savored the feel of her in his palm, the hard point of her nipple poking softly at him, speaking eloquently of her arousal. Yes, she wanted him.

With a groan, he lowered his head to rain kisses over her face, to find her ear and gently thrust his tongue into it, causing her to gasp. And with his hand he kneaded her soft, aching flesh. When her nails dug into his shoulders, he groaned again with delight.

"Yes," he muttered against her ear. "Oh, yes . . ." He tongued the delicate shell, tracing the whorls until she shivered helplessly against him, and then again he slipped his tongue into her ear, a gentle in-out movement that soon had her whimpering helplessly. Ah, she'd always loved that, and he'd always loved doing it for her.

There were so many things he loved doing for her. So many. When she moaned and leaned back against the door, he bent and took her nipple into his mouth. Her reaction was instantaneous; she arched into him, pressing her breast harder into his mouth while seeking him with her hips.

The purely unconscious surrender to the moment filled him with fierce joy, and fed his own hunger until his very blood seemed to throb. She was his. She had always been his. Always.

And he had always needed her in ways he had never needed any other woman. She satisfied his very soul.

But he didn't want to think about that right now. Didn't want to consider what that meant. Didn't want to ponder all the misery that had become his lot in the past few weeks.

What he wanted—*all*—he wanted, was Marge. Marge under him, around him, taking him, receiving him, loving him.

Just Marge. Right now.

Chapter 9

Nate lifted Marge into his arms and carried her toward the bedroom. *Now!*

"Nate..."

He glanced down, saw uncertainty in her eyes...and then, with heart-wrenching trust, she turned her head and buried her face in his neck.

He kicked the door closed behind them, then lowered her to his creaky bed. A moment of acute awareness almost stopped him, an instant in which he acknowledged that this might be a mistake, but it swiftly disappeared in more compelling, more primitive awareness.

He locked the bedroom door.

Then he returned to stretch out on the bed beside Marge, to kiss her sad green eyes closed, to press her to him. And for the most exquisite moment, he closed his own eyes and savored the absolutely beautiful pleasure of holding Marge. For a moment, just a moment, he allowed himself to forget that everything had gone wrong, that this woman had betrayed him. For a moment he was simply a man holding the woman he loved in his arms.

And during that moment, a fugitive thought flitted through his mind, the thought that perhaps he had been too harsh. Perhaps forgiveness wasn't beyond the realm of possibility. Perhaps...

Then the thought drifted away on the rising sea of need, tossed about on the foam among the flotsam before being swept swiftly away into forgotten lands.

A tremor ran through Marge, a soft head-to-foot trembling, and then her arms rose, wrapping snugly around his neck as she offered herself to him.

And the last rational thought spiraled away. He took her mouth again, this time with an almost savage intensity that she greeted with complete surrender. Her head tipped back, her mouth opened as widely as it could to receive him. She was his!

And he took full advantage of her surrender. Full advantage. His hands became restless, sweeping over her back and hips, finding familiar contours eagerly. An upward sweep tugged her sweater up and brought him to the clasp of her bra. He released it, and as it gave, they both groaned softly in mutual pleasure.

Moving swiftly, he straddled her and tugged her sweater over her head, tossed her bra across the room after it.

"Oh, sugar, you're still so pretty...."

And she was. Oh, she definitely was. He'd always loved her small breasts. Something about them was so much more feminine because of their delicacy. Their fragility. The fact that his hand could have nearly swallowed them both at one time. Just so perfect.

Reaching down, he cupped her and squeezed gently, causing her breath to catch and her eyelids to flutter. So sweet. So incredibly sweet. Spreading his fingers, he rubbed his palms round and round in gentle circles, stimulating her with a caress that was not quite enough, enjoying every moment of watching her sink deeper and deeper into their passion.

Until at last she reached up and covered his hands with hers, pressing them to her in a plea for more...more...

Which he wanted so badly to give. And receive. Rising on his knees, he bent down and took her into his mouth, sucking her deeply into him, listening to the muted whimpers and moans that escaped her with each movement of his mouth. Feeling his own body respond to each of those whimpers as if to an electric shock.

Too long . . . it had been far too long. . . .

"Oh, Nate. . ." Her fingers were in his hair, clutching him closer, holding him to her as if she never wanted to let go. Never. Her response loosened a knot deep inside him, a knot that had had him strung tight since he learned about Seth. And now, in these blessed moments, it let go.

She tasted so good, so sweet, a taste that he was sure was imprinted on his soul, the way everything about Marge was stamped there indelibly.

He moved to her other breast, cherishing her equally there while he fumbled at the snap and zipper of her slacks and started to tug them down. She helped, lifting her hips eagerly. Then her hands slipped to his shoulders, to tug urgently at his T-shirt.

With a groan, he reared up and pulled the shirt over his head. Even before it was gone, her hands were plucking at the button of his pants, trying to free him.

Swiftly he rolled from the bed and stood, shoving his pants and briefs down and stepping out of them. Then, bending, he tugged Marge's shoes and slacks away. She was wearing panty hose, and a reluctant chuckle escaped him.

"Damn things ought to be outlawed," he rumbled.

And Marge giggled. The sweetest sound on earth, he had often thought. The very sweetest. He felt himself smiling at her as he reached for the hose. They came away with a rip that caused her to giggle again, and this time his quiet laugh joined hers. The last weeks spun away as if they had never happened. It was just Marge and Nate, loving as they had always loved.

Nate's laugh reassured Marge as nothing else could have. Earlier, at the door, she had seen something almost grim and frightening in him, a glimpse of the man who had once been in Special Forces A-Teams. A man who could do whatever was necessary to accomplish his goals. A man with a certain amount of arrogance that put him above others because he feared nothing.

But now he was *her* Nate again, a man who smiled and laughed while making love, a man who made her feel precious and special. A man she didn't hesitate to reach out to.

She reached out. Lifting both arms, she held them out to him and silently asked him to join her. He paused a moment, sweeping her from head to toe with his gaze, then lowered himself to the bed so that he lay half over her, his leg across hers, his arm over her, his chest on her breast.

"Sugar..." His breath was softly ragged. "Sugar...I missed you."

Her heart took wing. He'd missed her. *Missed her.* Oh, God, he'd missed her. He was saying words she thought she would never hear again. Deep inside her, something opened, opened wide to him, to his love. She unfurled for him like the petals of a rose.

Tears spilled from the corners of her eyes and ran down into her hair. "Nate...oh, Nate..."

"Don't cry, Margie. Shh...don't cry...."

He rained kisses all over her face until finally, finally, she managed to connect her mouth to his, and this time it was she who kissed him, with every ounce of the yearning in her soul.

It was as if she couldn't get close enough, and she writhed, trying to bring him over her, into her, but he wouldn't give in. He seemed determined to tease her mercilessly, and his hand wandered from her breast to the juncture of her thighs, where it played with her curls but refused to give her the deeper touches she was craving.

She wiggled her hips, trying to press against his hand, his fingers, but he moved away with a throaty chuckle and came back to tease her some more with light brushes and gentle tugs. Until she groaned and rolled her hips helplessly. So helplessly. She was his and she reveled in it.

So long. Too long. Far too long since the last time they had made love. Since the last time she had felt this close to Nate. A feverish need was building in her, but the need was for far more than a moment's satisfaction. And maybe, maybe, if Nate was admitting he missed her...maybe he wanted to resolve this, too. Maybe he still cared for her. Maybe it could be all right.

Oh, please, let it be all right!

Exquisite moments, glistening like dew drops on the morning grass, followed one after another. It had been years since last she had savored her moments with Nate with this kind of intensity, this kind of awareness.

But now she fought to store up each beautiful moment, to capture every wonderful sensation...because she might never know them again.

Shimmering sparkles of sensation ran into rivers of fire and centered in her womb, creating a clenching need, a heaviness that grew and grew as Nate's fingers continued their teasing dance.

Feeling an almost desperate need to give him all that he was giving her, she slipped a hand around until she found one of his small nipples and gave it a gentle tug.

A throaty laugh escaped him, and he bent his head, drawing the aching peak of her breast into his mouth and sucking hard...so hard it would have hurt if it hadn't felt so good. Arching her hips sharply in helpless response, she found his hand at last...and at last he didn't deny her. Gentle fingers slipped into her wet, hot folds and stroked knowingly. Just the way that drove her crazy. Just the way that turned her into a helpless wanton.

She reached her first peak almost immediately. Nate released her breast and kissed her deeply as his fingers continued to stroke, taking the embers and turning them into a new and greater conflagration. In moments she was at the top again, straining toward him, pulling him closer.

And this time he let her. Settling between her raised knees, he slid slowly into her. Watching as they joined. Marge gasped and watched, too, savoring...savoring....

And then he was deep, deep inside her where he belonged, and she felt complete for the first time in forever. Whole.

One with Nate.

And free-fall had never been so easy.

The afterglow, usually the very best part of their love-making, a time when they talked in soft whispers and laughed quietly, didn't last a full minute.

Marge knew it was fading when Nate grew stiff and un-yielding. Moments later he was off her, off the bed and reaching for his clothes.

"Nate?" Something inside her felt as if it were going to shatter. All the tenderness, all the vulnerability, all the openness she had felt in the last hour left her utterly de-fenseless. "Nate?"

"You better get dressed."

Her world turned dark. So very, very dark. So incredibly bleak and black and unbearable. It hurt to breathe, sud-denly. Every hammer of her heart was sheer agony. There was no way, no way she could survive this.

"Here."

As if she stood at the end of a long, dark tunnel, she saw Nate hold out her clothes to her. With numb fingers, she accepted them. With limbs that felt as if they belonged to someone else, she slipped from the bed and dressed.

The anguish that gripped her was too great to feel, like a noise too loud to hear. A pressure that gripped her in a smothering vise, that held her without escape like an insect trapped in a web.

No escape.

One thing and one thing only kept her going—the need to hide her tears. Not to let this man know just how deeply he had wounded her. How carelessly he had crushed her. It was a blind protective instinct, and it kept her moving as she dressed, as she descended the stairs and climbed into the van, as she drove home alone. Her body did what her mind could not, and soon she was in bed.

Alone in her own bed, staring up at the ceiling, and wish-ing she could just shrink into nothing so that she never had to feel again.

* * *

God, after all the things he had said, how could he have taken advantage of Marge that way? The question was still roiling in his mind and knotting his stomach the next morning as he drove himself and Seth out to the Bar C to investigate the toxic-waste dumps on Jeff Cumberland's land. Behind them came Micah, in his Blazer, with Gage in the passenger seat.

He'd taken advantage of her response to him. It was just that simple. Had taken advantage of her to satisfy his own needs without regard to how he might be hurting her. And he *had* hurt her. There had been no mistaking the wounded look in her eyes as she dressed. No mistaking it.

And he had done that to her.

Damn, he wanted to kick himself. Had been wanting to kick himself since he had seen that look and had known himself responsible. He'd needed to get her dressed before Seth returned, but had been planning to offer her coffee, to ask her to stay and try to talk. But one look into her eyes, and he had let her go.

"This Weatherill character has probably left the county," Seth remarked.

"Probably left the damn state," Nate growled back. "There's been enough uproar since the derailment to warn him off ten times over . . . unless he's a total jerk."

"Probably close to it," Seth said. "Had to be a jerk to sign his own name to those receiving papers."

"Yeah. I'd almost bet he didn't know what exactly was in those barrels, but he had to know he was doing something questionable. You don't dump things in the middle of nowhere without realizing there's something fishy going on."

"Easy money keeps a lot of people from thinking."

"Willful ignorance. The world is full of it." Nate snorted. "I still think there's gotta be another connection somewhere. One of these ranchers that Micah talked to, maybe." He drummed his fingers on the steering wheel. "Damn, this case is driving me crazy. I've *got* to find somebody who can tell me where all this stuff is dumped. We've *got* to clean it up before the water gets poisoned, or somebody gets sick."

He knew he was beginning to sound like a broken record on this subject, but it was running in his head like a broken record. Toxic waste and Marge. Marge and toxic waste. An endless merry-go-round of terrible worry. Trying to shake free of it, he glanced at Seth. "How long are you staying with us?"

"Till you and Marge get things settled between you."

"Now, look—"

"It's my business, you know. I helped bring this about. If I'd minded my own business and stayed out of the way, you two would still be together."

"There's not a damn thing you can do! It's between Marge and me."

"It's not just between you and Marge, Nate. Other people are involved. Your daughters, to name six. Your friends. Even me. I'm involved because I feel responsible. There may not be a hell of a lot we can do, but we're involved. When are you two going to sit down and start talking things over?"

"It's not that easy."

"Nothing worthwhile ever is."

Nate scowled at him, but didn't bother to tell Seth to mind his own business. The young man was going to speak his piece regardless of what anyone else thought, and since Nate possessed a fair measure of the same trait, he knew he'd be wasting his breath to argue.

Jeff was ready for them, already warming the cab of his truck when they pulled up. Greetings were exchanged, and then the convoy set out for the first dump site. They followed county roads for a while, but eventually they had to drive along a nearly invisible track leading deep into Jeff's rangeland.

"It's beautiful out here," Seth remarked as they bounced and slid along the track. "Like a white sea with mountains in the distance."

"Think you could settle here?" Nate was surprised how much he wanted that. For the last few days he and Seth had been roommates, sharing a laid-back kind of relationship but nothing intense. He had figured they were becoming friends of sorts, but he hadn't foreseen the strength of his unexpected desire to have Seth stay in the area. He felt his son look at him.

"I'm seriously thinking about it," Seth said. "Seriously. I thought I'd die of boredom, but what I'm actually doing is relaxing. And when you come right down to it, it's been at least as interesting as nonstop training. Maybe more so."

"It's rough to train all the time and never get to use it."

"That's a fact. Gets to be a real strain maintaining an edge. Anyhow, it hasn't been boring around here. Not at all. I can see why you're happy here. I think I would be, too."

"Well, I got two deputies scheduled for retirement in the next year. You think about it."

"Thanks. I will."

Jeff Cumberland at last pulled over in the bed of a wide wash that was lined by leafless cottonwoods and brush. The barrels here numbered in the dozens, tumbled every which way so that it was impossible to be sure just how many there were, or whether any were leaking.

"This wash feeds from the mountains in the spring," Jeff told them. "Until mid-July or so, when the runoff completely dries up, I water a lot of cattle here. Those barrels couldn't have been here last spring or early summer because my men would have seen 'em and got curious."

Micah approached the tumbled hill of barrels cautiously and squatted down, studying them. "It's impossible to tell exactly how long they've been here, but they're not weathered too badly. Probably wouldn't be any tire tracks under the snow, either, since we had a dry autumn. Ground was probably hard as rock most of last fall."

"It was," Jeff agreed.

"And nobody'd roll these barrels around without wearing gloves, so there's probably no prints." He shook his head and rose to circumnavigate the dump and look for clues. Gage wasn't far behind him, and minutes stretched into more than an hour as they first did a quick overview, and then settled in for the serious stuff, taking photos, dusting away snow, looking for bits of evidence.

About the only unique thing they found was a Skoal can, and Nate figured that dozens of men in Conard County chewed that brand of tobacco. Unless the can, which didn't look very old, contained some fingerprints that would tell them something they didn't already know, it was virtually useless. Micah slipped it carefully into an evidence bag anyway.

And that was it. Frustratingly enough.

They set out for the dump they had looked at yesterday afternoon, to give Micah and Gage a chance to check it out. Jeff led them, taking a shortcut across his rangeland. The driving was rough, forcing Nate to concentrate, preventing him from thinking about things he didn't really want to think about.

Things like Marge. Like last night. Like her lie.

He glanced at Seth and wondered if the younger man could even begin to understand the heart of the problem, or if he thought Nate was being an ass about the whole thing.

And maybe, Nate found himself thinking, he *was* being an ass about it. But how could he ever trust anything she said after this? How?

There just didn't seem to be any answer to that one.

A flare of brake lights from ahead warned him Jeff was stopping. Moments later he halted his Blazer behind Cumberland's truck and climbed out. Jeff was already standing by his truck looking at something ahead.

"What's up?" he asked as he slogged over to the rancher.

"Somebody's been out here since last night. See those tire tracks?"

"One of your men?"

"Not likely. I told everyone to stay clear until Micah had a chance to check it out."

Micah joined them and studied the path the tracks took. "That leads right to the gully where you found the barrels?"

"Hard to see in this light with all the glare off snow, but the gully is only a quarter mile ahead."

Gage took pictures. Micah squatted and drew the tracks in his notebook, making margin notes on his impressions.

Seth and Nate walked ahead, following the tracks, looking for anything at all.

"Why would the culprit come back out here?" Seth asked. "Assuming that was who was here."

"Oh, lots of reasons. The likeliest is that he heard we found the site, and he got nervous, wondering what we saw, if he'd left any obvious clues. But it's just as likely somebody else came out here out of simple curiosity, just wanting to see what's going on."

Seth glanced at him and smiled. "We can always hope for a break."

Nate actually chuckled. "Yeah. We can hope."

They reached the edge of the gully without finding anything significant. The tire tracks continued past, toward some heavy brush and leafless trees.

But the vehicle had definitely stopped here, and there were footprints in the snow leading down into the gully.

"Well, well, well," Nate remarked. Taking care not to disturb the prints, he began to work his way into the gully, Seth right behind him.

Maybe just a curiosity seeker, he told himself, but his hope rose anyway, hope that they were about to get some kind of a break. Some kind of a lead that would close this case and allow him to get the county cleaned up. Before the spring rain. Before the spring thaw, which would carry these chemicals everywhere if the containers were ruptured.

He slipped once on the way down and swore. Behind him, he heard Seth's chuckle. "Yeah, go ahead and laugh, son. You'll get yours."

Moments later, Seth did. They reached the bottom with snow in their boots and wet butts, and the cold, gray day did nothing to help. They looked at each other and broke out laughing. Nate clapped a hand to his son's shoulder and thought that it was pretty nice to have him around.

Somebody had been messing with the barrels, all right. The snow was a great record keeper, and showed them at a glance that some of the barrels had been moved and that somebody had trampled all around them.

"Curiosity seeker?" Seth said as Nate swore. "A reporter, maybe?"

"Nah. All the news interest died down after the first couple of discoveries. One pile of barrels looks the same as another. And I can't for the life of me imagine why anybody who was just curious would want to move any of these barrels. No, it looks as if someone was looking for something."

All of a sudden, Seth shoved him to one side and he fell facedown in the snow. Almost simultaneously he heard a sharp crack and felt a searing pain in the back of his head.

And for one soul-searing instant before rage filled him, he thought of Marge. Thought of never seeing her again.

In the distance, he heard the growl of a truck engine, and suddenly Seth was beside him, kneeling in the snow. "Nate?"

He opened his eyes and lifted his face out of the snow. "Yeah. I'm okay."

"Don't move. The back of your head is bleeding pretty badly. Looks like a rock fragment grazed you."

"The gunman . . ." Nate waited while Seth felt gently at the back of his head.

"He's gone. I saw him take off, and I'd bet that was his truck engine. Just a surface wound, I think. Hold still, I'm going to put on a pressure bandage."

Lying facedown in the snow, feeling the icy water soak into him, he let Seth perform first aid, a strip of cloth torn from Seth's shirt wrapping around his head. "I'm gonna get frostbite on some of my more important parts, son."

Seth chuckled. "Nah. Half a second, then I'll help you up."

"It doesn't make any sense, Seth! Why the hell would he take one shot and run? Why didn't he stay and finish it?"

"You're gonna have one hell of a headache. Okay, let's get you up."

Getting up sounded great until he was actually upright. Woozy just about described it, and he staggered a little before Seth steadied him. "Maybe you ought to stay down until the others get here."

"I'll be okay." And he would. Already things were settling. Taking care not to move too quickly, he looked up at the rim of the gully. "What did he hope to accomplish?"

"To kill you?" Seth suggested. "You've got enough blood all over the back of your head to look like a serious casualty. Maybe he thinks he killed you."

Hell. "What would that accomplish? This county isn't going to forget this stuff just because I'm dead!"

"Maybe somebody doesn't know that."

Just then, the roar of powerful engines told Nate that Micah and Gage were pulling up, probably with Jeff. Moments later, Micah appeared at the top of the gully.

"You okay?"

"Yeah," Nate answered and pointed with a finger. "He went thataway."

"Gage is going after him, but I wouldn't hold my breath. He took off like a bat outta hell. You need some help getting up here?"

"What I need is for you to get down here and figure out what he was looking for."

"Kinda hard to do if he found what he wanted. What's wrong with your head?"

"Scalp cut," Seth answered. "He needs attention."

"Damn it," Nate growled, turning on Seth. "I don't need you or anybody else telling me—"

"Okay," Micah interrupted. "Bring him up here, Seth, and take him in my Blazer. I'll hang around here and check things out until Gage comes back."

"Where's Jeff?"

"Right here." Jeff Cumberland appeared at the lip of the ravine with a rifle in his hand. "You need some help getting up?"

In the end he *did* need a little help. His head was throbbing fit to bust, and his legs felt just a little shaky. Mild concussion, he thought. Once up, he had more hands than he needed, or wanted, helping to strap him into the Blazer, until finally he exploded and told everybody just to stand the hell back.

Which immediately brought a chorus of chuckles, but he ignored them. Just before Micah closed the door, Nate reached out and stopped him. "He might have shot at us because we were too close to something he didn't want us to see."

Micah nodded. "I'll keep that in mind. Explains why he'd run, too. Somebody would chase."

"And maybe forget what they were looking at—or were about to."

Micah gave him another nod. "I'll look."

And with that, Nate had to be content.

They reached the hospital nearly an hour later. By then Nate was convinced his injury was minor, just uncomfortable. Still, the county wasn't used to its lawmen getting shot at, so Nate's arrival caused a considerable stir.

In no time at all he was facedown on a gurney while the back of his head was being shaved and Doc Randall was clucking over him. The worst of it, of course, was the novocaine injections, but once that was done, he didn't even mind the scrubbing.

"Oh, Nate!"

Marge was suddenly there, standing beside the gurney, touching his cheek with tender fingertips. Marge. After last night, Marge was here.

"Don't move, Nate," Doc Randall said. "Not a bit."

"Nate, Velma said you'd been shot!"

In that instant, he would have liked to throttle Velma Jansen. The woman was an inveterate gossip, but even she should have known better than to carry such a tale to Marge.

"Not shot," Doc Randall said. "Nope. A close encounter of the uncomfortable kind with a rock. Nate, I told you not to move."

"Mmmph." It was all he could do to hold still. He wanted to throttle Velma and hug Marge, and he couldn't do either. "I'm okay, Marge. Honestly."

"Why did Velma say someone shot at you?"

"Because someone did," Doc said.

Nate decided he wanted to throttle the doctor, too. "Damn it, Doc—"

"Hold still!"

"Shh," Marge said softly. She bent over so she could look into his eyes. "Oh, Nate, I was scared to death."

He felt her hand cover his, capture his fingers and squeeze gently, and suddenly he found himself thinking that he was the world's biggest ass. Absolutely the biggest ass on the planet.

"Velma never should have called you. Never."

"Velma called me because she's a woman and understands. Nate, how could you think I wouldn't want to know? Oh, darling..." Her voice quavered and broke.

A warm, salty tear dropped on his cheek, and was followed by the brush of soft lips. He wanted to tell her how sorry he was for last night, how wrong he had been to take advantage of her, but there were too many ears around.

"Why would anybody want to shoot at you?" she asked, her voice little more than a husky whisper. "Why?"

"I think he was just trying to scare me away, sugar. Just scare me. If he wanted to kill me, he had plenty of opportunity."

He heard her swiftly drawn breath and knew how much he had upset her with that comment. He guessed he deserved throttling as much as Velma and Doc. "Honey, I'm *okay*."

"He sure is," Doc said. "Listen to him. Head's as hard as it ever was. He'll need some watching for a few hours, though. Until tomorrow, to make sure the concussion isn't worse than it seems right now. You take him home with you, Marge, and keep an eye on him."

There was a silence so full of unspoken words right then that the clatter of something in the hallway sounded distant. He should have immediately refused, but he didn't. Instead he held his damn breath and waited to see what Marge would say.

"I— Of course I will, Doc. You know me." There was only the slightest tremor in her voice, but Nate noted it, noted that it wasn't easy for her to say. And why should it be? After all he'd said and done.

"Good," the doctor said. "You're the only person in this whole damn county who can make this hardheaded fool behave. I'd have to keep him overnight otherwise. In restraints, probably!"

A small giggle escaped Marge, and Nate felt his own mouth curving into a smile, but before it was fully born, Doc started taping a bandage in place, and he winced.

Marge saw it and squatted so she was at eye level. "Okay?" she asked softly.

"Fine," he answered gruffly. "Doc's as ham-handed as always." What he really wanted to do was ask a perplexing, almost childish question: Why was she being so good to him after last night?

Again there was the fluttery touch of her lips on his cheek, and the warmth of her hand covering his, and then she straightened, listening as Doc gave her instructions.

"You don't have to watch him every minute," Doc said. "If you want to go out to a movie or something, fine. One of the girls can keep an eye on him. Basically I just want to know if he acts funny, woozy, forgetful or in any other way that doesn't seem normal. Beyond that, I just want him to take it easy until tomorrow. You hear that, Nate?"

"I hear."

"I'm not kidding. You can watch TV, read a book, whatever, as long as you're taking it easy. No power tools or knives, in case you *do* get woozy. And those are orders."

"You got it."

"That's it, then. Keep the bandage dry. Here's a scrip for pain pills—you're gonna have a helluva headache when that novocaine wears off, Nate. These pills shouldn't make you woozy, though. Good stuff."

Nate felt Randall clap a hand to his shoulder. "Thanks, Doc."

"All in a day's work. Just behave!"

The nurse helped Nate sit up, and then he and Marge were all alone in the cubicle, eyeing one another uncertainly.

Finally Nate felt he had to do the honorable thing and give her a way out. "You don't really have to take me in, you know. I can stay at my place."

Marge shook her head swiftly. "Oh, no! You heard Doc. Somebody has to keep an eye on you."

He could think of a whole bunch of reasons he would have liked better than that one. Which was ridiculous, he tried to tell himself as the nurse returned with his uniform jacket and his hat, which he didn't think he'd be wearing for a while. Seth had rescued it from the snow, but it would sit right on his stitches. Damn, he felt naked without it.

Outside it was still bright afternoon. The sun glared, and he missed the protective brim of his hat. He missed his sunglasses, too, but they were in the Blazer. In fact, when it came right down to it, he just felt plain grumpy.

It seemed strange to be entering the house again, and that jarred him something fierce. This had been his home for the better part of a quarter century. How could it seem strange? But it did. As if he were a trespasser. And maybe he was.

"Why don't you go get comfortable on the couch in the den," Marge suggested. "I'll bring you some coffee. Did you have any lunch?"

She'd always cared for him this way, and he'd always appreciated it, but it had never been more apparent how little he deserved such attention. He thanked her, as he always did, but this time with more than ordinary emphasis. She seemed not to notice, which left him feeling guilty again. He wasn't quite sure for what, but he felt guilty.

Krissie appeared in the hallway and paused to look in on him. For a minute he thought she was going to refuse to answer his greeting, but after a perceptible hesitation, she entered the room and flopped onto the chair facing him, her legs dangling over the arm.

"You didn't get shot?" she asked.

"No. Just grazed by a piece of rock."

"Oh." Like all of Nate's daughters, Krissie had learned how to handle guns and knew what he was talking about. "You were lucky."

"Seth pushed me out of the way. Light reflected off something the guy was wearing or carrying, and Seth's no slowpoke."

Krissie almost smiled. "He's pretty neat, isn't he?"

"Yes, he is. Pretty neat."

"He's upset about all the trouble he caused."

Nate sat up a little straighter. "I know. He told me. But he didn't cause the trouble, Krissie."

She was playing with the end of her braid and didn't look at him. "He feels like he did. He said if he hadn't spoken to Mom, none of this would have happened."

Marge's voice interrupted from the doorway. "He's wrong, Krissie." She stepped into the room carrying a tray which she placed on the end table at Nate's elbow. "If I hadn't lied, none of this would have happened."

Nate felt her words like a shaft to the gut. It was what he'd been saying all along, but coming from Marge's mouth, it sounded different. Entirely different. "Marge . . ."

"Oh, no," Krissie said suddenly. Standing, she looked at both of them. "None of this would have happened if you'd practiced what you're always preaching. None of this would have happened if you'd kept your pants on."

"Krissie!" Marge gasped her daughter's name, but the girl turned and ran from the room.

Nate didn't move. Not a muscle. Didn't say a word when he felt Marge look at him, awaiting his disapproval.

Couldn't say anything at all. Because Krissie was absolutely right.

Chapter 10

"Are you going to let her go?"

Nate was stretched out on the couch, his head throbbing fit to bust, when he heard Krissie's belligerent question from the doorway. "Let who go where?" he asked without opening his eyes.

"She has a date with that railroad guy, Pete Little. Are you going to let her go?"

That opened his eyes. His initial reaction was no, by God, he was *not* going to let her go. But even as rage and jealousy rose in a consuming wave, reason rescued him. He'd left her. He'd told her he was filing for divorce. He'd told her she could date Little or anyone else she wanted, because the simple fact was that he no longer had anything to say about it.

But that didn't mean he had to like it.

"Dad?" Krissie stood beside him, calling him *Dad* for the first time since he'd walked out. "Are you okay?"

"Just a bad headache, honey."

She dropped to the floor and sat cross-legged beside him so that they were eyeball to eyeball. "How are you going to sleep when you can't lie on your back?"

"If my head keeps hurting like this, I'm not going to sleep in any position."

"Don't you have some medicine? Want me to get it?"

"Thanks. I'd appreciate it." And it'd give him a few minutes to figure out what to say to his daughter if she brought up the question of Marge's date with Little again.

Gingerly, he pushed himself up and sat. The throbbing in his head didn't seem to change any, so he might as well face the world upright. And maybe face what was going on in his life. What he was doing to himself, to his daughters, to his wife.

"Krissie said you have a headache." Marge came into the room carrying a glass of water and the prescription bottle.

And she was dressed up. Sort of. The way people around here got "dressed up" to go to the Elks, or the movies, or the town's only real restaurant, Aiello's. More dressed up than you got to go to Maude's Diner, but not church dressy, either.

He eyed her trimly cut slack suit, the jewelry glinting at her ears and wrists, and decided that yes, he wanted to kill Peter Little, but that really wouldn't be wise. "Krissie said you're going out."

"Yes, with Pete." She didn't elaborate, just tipped a pill into his hand and offered him the water.

"Thanks." He glanced up at her, thinking he'd never before seen her look quite so... steely. That chin of hers was lifted and stubbornly set, making it plain she didn't think she owed him any explanations.

And she didn't. Intellectually he realized that. Emotionally he didn't realize it at all. "I didn't know he was in town again."

"Got in this afternoon, I guess, on some kind of railroad business."

"I'd like to talk to him."

Marge looked straight at him then. "No, I don't think so, Nate. Not here. Not tonight."

Before he could figure out how to reply to that, she had left him alone with Krissie, who looked at him and asked, "You aren't gonna stop her?"

"I can't, baby. I can't."

"Why not? You're still married!"

Reluctantly, Nate looked at his daughter. "It doesn't work that way, honey, and you know it. I've never told your mother what she could or couldn't do, and she's never told me."

"But she never wanted to do anything like this before! This is different!"

Yeah, it was different, he thought, staring past Krissie at the doorway Marge had disappeared through. Very different. And it was all his own damn fault.

"Krissie?"

"Yeah?"

"I could sure use a hug." And much to his pleased surprise, she settled on the couch beside him and gave him a great big bear hug.

"Dad?"

"Yeah?" His heart nearly broke when he heard the forlorn crack in her voice. She was crying.

"I wish— I wish y-you could fix this."

"I wish I could, too, honey." He patted her shoulder and wished it could be just that easy. Just that easy.

Carol and Patti were home from their after-school activities when Pete Little came to pick up Marge. Their hostility was a palpable thing, and they made no effort to conceal their disapproval. Nate could hear the frost in their voices all the way down the hall, and he heard Marge's tone grow a little sharp in warning.

And then his wife went out with another man. Carol and Patti came back to the family room and dropped unhappily on chairs, from which they regarded their father glumly. They didn't have to say anything; their silence spoke as clearly as any words. They held him responsible.

Well, he was. He admitted it. And if he could just find a way to get Marge's lie unstuck from his craw, maybe he could work at putting things back together. If it wasn't already too late. And it was beginning to look as if it just might be. Two dates with one man in less than a week. Two. His stomach twisted into a painful knot.

Damn!

"Guess we should make dinner," Carol said finally. "You hungry, Dad?"

"Not a whole hell of a lot. Why don't you order up some pizza?" That was always a popular suggestion, and gloomy as the girls were this evening, everyone seemed to think it was a good idea.

The medicine was helping his headache, so he settled back a little on the couch and tried to figure out what the hell he was going to do about this mess.

He'd been a fool. He shouldn't have been so quick to walk out. He'd been too damn wrapped up in his own hurt feelings to think about all the things he should have been thinking about, first among them his daughters. They should have been uppermost on his mind, his primary consideration in all that he had done.

But they hadn't been. He'd been appallingly selfish. He'd acted irresponsibly, had reacted to a situation without thinking it through fully. He knew better than that.

"Dad? Phone for you. It's Deputy Parish." Krissie handed him the cordless phone.

"How's the head?" Micah wanted to know.

"Sore but intact. Ten stitches and a headache. You find anything?"

"Boot prints that might help if we catch the so-and-so. Another Skoal can, so I'd guess our perp has a heavy habit. A bunch of beer cans all close together, so I'd guess that whenever he dumped the stuff he hung around for a while. Might be some prints on the cans. And—really interesting—the shipping papers."

"But we have that from the railroad."

"Nope. I'm not talking about the bill of lading. I'm talking about the originator's shipping documents. The company that transshipped the stuff to the freight forwarder. The company who will know who originated all this waste."

Nate sat straight up. "Hell! No wonder he came back and wanted us out of there."

"Yeah. Stupid move. Anyhow, the papers got wet, they're all stuck together, and the feds want them shipped to the national crime lab."

"That's good. Any of the information will be more useful on their end of the investigation, anyway. Anything else? Did Gage get a make on the gunman's vehicle?"

"Not really. Late-model pickup, white, no distinctive features. He never got close enough to get any identifying information. Gage spun out on Chancellor Road and went into a snowbank. By the time he got out, the guy had disappeared. We had other units looking, but nobody picked up the suspect."

"So he must have gone to ground somewhere."

"Or off the road somewhere. You know how rugged the terrain is out that way. Lots of good cover, and no way to track anybody since the high school kids like to ski and sled out there. The place is always full of tracks. Gage tried to figure out where he might have gone off but . . ." Micah let the sentence dangle incomplete, his shrug almost audible.

"It wouldn't hurt to search the area, though," Nate said. "He may have just ducked there because he's smart, or he may actually hang out around there. There's at least one abandoned line shack out that way."

"We'll do it first thing in the morning. Will you be in?"

"I think so. Once this headache quits, I'll be just dandy, and the only reason I'm taking it easy is because I'd feel so damn stupid if I didn't listen to Doc and something happened."

Micah chuckled. "Yeah. And, damn it, it would. It always does. Marge called and said Doc thought you had a very mild concussion. How is Marge, by the way?"

"Out to dinner with Pete Little, that railroad investigator."

Micah paused almost imperceptibly before speaking. "Yeah, he was in today, asking how the case was progressing. He's taking an awful lot of interest in it."

He's taking an awful lot of interest in my wife, Nate thought sourly. Probably using the waste problem as an excuse to come to Conard City and hang around Marge. "If he's bothering you, tell him to get lost. The railroad's out of it, as far as the police investigation goes."

"I don't know that I'd say he's bothering anybody, precisely."

He's bothering *me,* Nate thought. Considerably. And it was infuriating to have to admit that he'd set himself up for this by walking out. By reacting from the gut. "Well, he doesn't have any need to know anything that isn't generally known."

Nate disconnected and set the phone beside him on the table. Damn Little, he thought. The man was probably even charging the railroad for his travel expenses. Sleaze.

But as soon as he thought it, he castigated himself. He was just being jealous, and not being fair to Pete Little at all. The guy had seemed regular enough ... until he had started pursuing Marge, but that was his own problem, not Little's.

And maybe instead of being nasty about Little he ought to spend some effort considering the fact that he *was* jealous. That the thought of Marge being with someone else was eating at his insides like acid. That maybe he'd better find a way around the distrust before it was too late.

But God! Every time he thought about it, really thought about how she had kept that secret for so many years, he felt as if he'd never known her at all. It was like putting on a pair of glasses and discovering the soft, fuzzy world you had been seeing all your life was full of sharp angles and edges and pitfalls.

He'd thought he had known her. Now he felt as if he didn't know her at all. And that realization was what kept jerking him up short and hard. Did he really know Marge at all? Or had he imagined her all these years?

But did one person ever really know another that well?

The girls joined him in the den to watch a sitcom, and for a little while, it felt as if he had never left. Carol lay on the floor, chin propped on her hands, her ankles in the air and crossed. Patti sprawled across the recliner as if it were a hammock, and Krissie sat on the other end of the couch with her feet tucked up beneath her.

The girls chuckled frequently, but Nate hardly heard a word of the dialogue. Hardly saw the screen. Instead he thought about the fact that Marge still hadn't come home. And he tried not to think about what she might be doing.

But his mind wouldn't quit, anyway. Jealousy roiled in his gut, and images of Marge and Little kept creeping into his head, and he kept telling himself that Marge wouldn't do any such thing.

But he didn't know Marge at all.

Yes, he did. He really did. Of course he did. Enough to know she wouldn't go to the Lazy Rest Motel with a strange man. Enough to know that she wouldn't want any gossip to get back to the girls, so she would behave. Enough to know she couldn't give herself without love.

But what if she were falling in love with Pete Little? He was an attractive man. A very attractive man. Just what Nate figured a woman would find almost irresistible, unlike himself with his weather-burned face and graying hair.

And after the way he had treated Marge last night, he really didn't have a damn thing to say about any of it, did he?

The girls didn't go to bed at ten as they usually did. Instead they hung around watching the news and weather, which didn't surprise him. He suspected they wanted their mother home every bit as much as he did. And he suspected that they were keeping silent only with great difficulty, that Patti and Carol felt, as Krissie did, that this was all his fault.

And it was. It really was. After all these years he should have stayed to work things out. Some kind of compromise could have been reached.

Which was easy to say, but there was no compromise on trust. None. Either you trusted or you didn't, and the discovery of Seth's existence had dealt a fatal blow to his trust. Or had seemed to. If he lived to be a hundred, the moment where he realized that Marge had lied to him for twenty-seven years was going to be vivid in his mind and soul.

But maybe if he worked hard enough he could get around that somehow. Deal with it somehow. Live with it somehow.

"Dad?"

"Hmm?" He looked over at Krissie.

"When's Mom coming home?"

"She didn't say." He glanced at Patti and Carol, who both shook their heads. She hadn't told the girls, either.

"I can't believe she's doing this!" Carol suddenly burst out. "I can't believe either of you! Is this all you mean to each other?"

She leapt up and hurried out of the room, tears running down her cheeks. Patti followed, giving her father a hurt look as she did so. Krissie remained a few minutes longer, but finally, with a mumbled good-night, she went to her room.

Leaving Nate alone with the mocking silence of an empty family room.

Was that all they meant to each other? A damn good question, he realized with heavy reluctance. A damn good question.

And maybe the only one that really mattered.

Marge came in just before midnight. All she wanted to do was crawl into bed, but when she opened the front door and saw Nate standing in the hallway looking like an angry father, she knew her wish was not about to be granted. Turning, she managed a smile for Pete.

"Thanks for a fun evening, Pete."

"You're welcome." He looked past her at Nate and nodded. "We'll do it again sometime. Good night, Marge."

She closed the door and bolted it before turning to look at Nate. "Is something wrong?"

He started to shake his head, then paused. Finally he grated out one word. "Everything."

Her concern was instant and swift. "The girls?"

"No, the girls are fine." Fine, considering they were hurting as bad as he was, something he hadn't wanted to think about before. "We need to talk."

"We tried that last night and didn't get very far."

"Well, sugar, we're sure as hell going to try again. Now."

Marge stiffened, and her green eyes snapped. "Nate, I don't like it when you take that tone of voice with me, and you know it."

He tilted his head back, drew a deep breath and tried to collect his patience. "All right," he said after a moment. "All right. But we're going to talk."

Now it was Marge who sighed. "Nate, I have an awful headache. You know what smoke and noise do to me...."

"Where were you?" He managed, by dint of strenuous effort, to make the question sound casually interested when what he really wanted to do was demand an answer.

"At the Lariat."

"The Lariat? He took you to the Lariat?" The place was a dive. Right then he could have popped Pete Little in the jaw.

"It wasn't so bad. There was music and dancing, and you know there's no place else to do that on a weeknight."

"He could have waited for Friday and taken you to the Elks Club!" And he could hardly believe he was suggesting where his wife's date ought to take her.

"Shh!" Marge's admonition was sharp. "Come into the kitchen before you wake the girls. And it's none of your business where we went."

"Yes it is," he argued, following her. "You're the mother of my girls. That makes it my business. Besides—" He caught himself and bit off the word. No way was he going to admit how jealousy was chewing him up inside.

"Besides what?" Marge asked. When he didn't answer, she let it go. She went to the sink and took a couple of aspirin before she turned to face him. With her arms folded, she didn't look especially receptive.

But they had to talk, he thought. Sooner or later they really had to talk, and later wasn't going to be any easier. In fact, it might be too late for both of them.

"Sugar, tell me again. Tell me again why you never told me."

Her chin lifted. "I already told you why."

"I know. But this time I'm really listening. I need to understand. If—if I can understand, maybe we can get past this and..." He didn't finish. Couldn't finish.

Marge looked away for a moment, shaking her head slightly. "Do you understand why I gave him up? Or do I need to explain that again, too?"

"I understand that part." He did. It made him sick at heart, but he did. "You thought I didn't want to know. You thought when I didn't answer your letters about being pregnant that I never wanted to see you again. I understand that. Damn it, I *do* understand that. I was feeling the same way because you weren't answering me. I thought— Oh, hell, Marge, there were about six months there when I really didn't give a damn if I lived or died. That's when I won all those damn medals. I think I was trying to get myself killed."

Marge drew a sharp breath and looked at him. "Oh, Nate," she said sadly.

"Yeah. Your dad screwed us good, didn't he?"

"You never told me you wanted to die. You never even hinted..."

"I didn't want to upset you. What was the point?"

"That's why I didn't tell you, Nate. What was the point? What was the damn point! It couldn't be undone. I thought it would only hurt you to know. I really, honestly believed it would only hurt you."

He believed that. He honestly believed that. But that didn't help with the basic problem, which was the lie. "How many other times have you lied to protect me?"

Marge gasped as if he had struck her. But she wasn't going to take this lying down anymore. Not anymore. "I didn't think of it as lying, Nate. I still don't actually. I never *lied*. I simply didn't tell you something which only would have hurt you!"

"And because you were afraid."

"Yes! Yes, I was afraid. With plenty of reason! Look at how you're acting now! I thought I'd lose you...."

And she had. She didn't have to speak the words. He heard them in his heart. Breathing was suddenly painful, but he still couldn't find a way around the core problem, and that was driving him crazy. "I need ... I need to figure out how the hell I can trust you again."

She flinched visibly.

"And then—and then when Seth showed up, you kept it a secret still," he continued. "Because he asked you to, you committed another lie by omission."

"It wasn't my secret to tell, Nate. It was his. And he asked me not to tell anyone. I tried to talk him into letting me tell you but...he wasn't sure he wanted to know you. I think he explained that to you."

"Yeah. He explained that. I don't really understand it, though. Crap, Marge, he's a full-grown man. He doesn't have to know anybody he doesn't want to. If he decided I was some kind of crud, what was I going to do about it?"

"Oh, I can understand it, Nate. It's very easy to embarrass people and make a nuisance of yourself. People do it all the time, and he had no way to know what kind of people we are. I understand it perfectly."

"You could have told me, anyway."

"I could have broken a promise, yes." She turned a little so that she was no longer facing him. "I was in a delightful position, Nate. Delightful. How would you be feeling right now if I'd broken my word to Seth?"

"About like I'm feeling right now. But you didn't have to give him your word."

"No. I could have told you that you had a son and then tried to explain why he wouldn't see you, didn't want to know you and wasn't going to have anything to do with either of us because I refused to give him my word." She shook her head. "When he turned up, Nate, I knew this was a chance to give you back something I'd stolen from you. And I was willing to do anything—*anything*—to make that happen."

She turned her head and looked at him. "Willing, even, to give you up."

He didn't reply. He couldn't even speak. Because, despite everything, despite the ache in his soul for her, the lie remained between them.

So much was founded on trust. Everything he knew about her. Everything he believed about her. Everything that he believed she felt about him was founded on trust. On the belief that she spoke only the truth. That she lived honestly.

Twice now, she had deceived him with silence. Twice. And that meant he couldn't trust anymore. And without trust, he couldn't rely on her love, on her feelings, on his perception of the kind of person she was. One little lie could mean so very many lies.

Without trust, there was nothing.

Marge sighed and stirred. "I'm going to bed, Nate. I'm exhausted."

He watched her turn and walk from the kitchen. Her head was held high, just as she had used to hold it when her father had accused her of some awful thing. Just the way she held it when she told her parents that she was going to continue to see Nathan Tate because he was a good person regardless of what others thought. It was a proud, defiant tilt.

"Marge?"

She paused at the door and looked over her shoulder. "Yes?"

"Are you going to see him again? Little?"

She gave a small shrug. "What the hell does it matter, Nate?" Then, steadily, she walked away.

In the morning, the throb in his head had settled down to a sort of weary drumbeat that had more to do with the bruising and slashed scalp than any concussion. He was going to feel naked without his hat, but wearing it was absolutely out of the question.

The girls left for school, except Krissie, who this morning was determined to be a little angel. She insisted on doing the breakfast dishes and the other morning chores for

Marge, who sat clad in jeans and a lavender sweatshirt at the breakfast table, nursing a cup of coffee as if it were a lifeline.

She didn't look good at all. "Are you okay?" he asked her as he slid into a seat facing her.

"I think I'm getting a cold."

"You look worse than any cold, sugar."

"Well, it might be flu. I'll live."

She always said that. Marge just kept going through illness, hardly ever giving in even to the worst sickness. Nate had lost count of the times over the years that he and the girls had been knocked down by some flu while Marge took care of them, sniffling, sneezing, aching and insisting she'd live.

"Maybe you ought to see Doc this morning."

"Nothing he can do for a cold or flu."

Nate sighed. This was a familiar argument, one he always used himself. Doc always complained that neither of them ever got to him before they were at death's door. "What if it's something else?"

Marge shook her head. "Aspirin and liquids. You know the drill." Turning her head swiftly, she sneezed into a tissue.

Krissie brought the coffeepot over and refilled Marge's cup. "I'll take care of her, Daddy."

Daddy. She hadn't called him that in a couple of years. He wound his arm around her waist and hauled her up to his side in a quick, tight hug. "I love you, Krissie."

"Yeah. Me, too."

He watched her put the carafe on the warmer and then walk from the kitchen, a bouncy little redhead who was the spitting image of her mother at that age. His chest tightened with emotion, and he looked away...and straight into Marge's green eyes.

"Come home, Nate," she whispered.

His chest squeezed even more, until it seemed as if he would never be able to breathe again. "I can't," he said finally. "I can't."

Not yet. Not until he made peace with his demons. And that might never happen.

The day was crisp, cold, brilliant. The first thing he did when he got to the office was dig his sunglasses out of his Blazer and stick them in his jacket pocket so he wouldn't be without them again.

"Cute headgear," Velma remarked as he passed her desk. "White bandages are gonna be the rage."

"Doc'll be glad to hear that. Is Gage in?"

"Ready and rarin' to go," Velma replied as she blew a cloud of smoke into the air. "Gonna take a bunch of deputies out to Chancellor Road, I hear."

"And I better not hear that anywhere else, Velma."

She cocked a brow at him. "P.O.'d about me calling Marge, huh?"

"She thought I'd been shot."

"Well, heck, boss, we *all* did! And I don't mind telling you right now, if somebody near and dear to me had been shot, somebody had damn well better tell me so I could be there!" She glared at him, blowing smoke through her nostrils like a dragon.

Nate leaned over the counter toward her. "Velma, it's been damn near twenty years, and you still haven't figured out who the boss really is around here."

"Sure I have. It's me. You're the only one who hasn't figured that out. Now git to work!"

Dave Winters chuckled from the duty desk. "Velma's got you on that one, Nate."

Gage was waiting for him with a topographic map of the area off Chancellor Road. "I wouldn't be surprised if we found some more dumps out here, too."

"Me either," Nate agreed. "What I really want is to get my hands on this Weatherill character. To find out who's behind all this. To get him to tell me where all the stuff is at. Mostly to find out where all the stuff is."

"Yeah."

Nate suddenly realized he was repeating himself again. He must have said the same thing to Gage at least ten times since this mess broke over their heads. "Sorry. I keep saying that."

Gage gave him a lopsided smile. "That's okay. I feel the same way. We're running against a clock here, as far as a serious disaster goes, and nobody knows when the time is up. And Westin Weatherill is our only link."

By nine-thirty, they were out at Chancellor Road and ready to begin. The plan was to check out the area approaching the old line shack first and, if they found nothing useful there, to fan out over a wider area, checking the arroyos that might provide good hiding places for other dumps.

There were only six of them to do the looking, on horseback. Nate had considered asking for volunteers—it would have made a sweep so much more efficient—but had decided against it. First, he didn't want to scare the Weatherill guy off, and second, if there were too many searchers, they would probably just trample up any evidence that might be out here.

They didn't waste too much time near the road. Youths with their snowmobiles, skis and sleds had pretty much chewed up the snow cover past hope of identifying anything. As they moved back into the gullies among the outcroppings, the surface disturbances lessened. Twice they came to an end of all tracks and turned back. They would explore those areas later for waste dumps. Right now they wanted to learn where the man who had shot at Nate and Seth had gone.

Seth was with them, and Nate couldn't explain why that made him feel so good. Why he was pleased by the way his deputies seemed to accept Seth as one of them, with respect and camaraderie. Why it meant so much that no one questioned Seth's right to be there. Except that Seth was his *son*, with all the emotional connotations that entailed. Despite all the years they had lost, and despite the fact that he had not reared this young man.

He cleared his throat, trying to ease the tightness there, and looked around at the barren, beautiful, snow-covered countryside. Somebody had violated Conard County.

That's how it felt to him. As if somebody had raped this pristine land. And that infuriated him.

At one o'clock they were nearing the abandoned line shack. Nate knew its whereabouts as well as he knew the back of his hand, because in long-ago summers, after he got his first car, he had cleaned it up so he could bring Marge up there. Initially they had used it only on rainy afternoons when the alternative would have been not seeing each other or sitting cramped in his little VW. Later they had spent more time there, needing the privacy and solitude, as only two people who are in love can need it. To be together and share countless hours of talk or silence, to be able to just reach out and touch as often as necessary.

And finally, they had made love there, just before he shipped out.

Over the years they had come up here a few times to reminisce. A couple of years back, they had brought the girls up here and told them stories of their courtship, of their long summer afternoons wading in the creek or lying beneath the clouds.

A couple of times, Nate had even come up to fix the place up a little and keep it from becoming totally dilapidated. And until he died, that shack was going to stand, because it held some of the happiest memories of his life.

And because Seth had been conceived there.

He glanced over at the young man who rode beside him, straight and tall in the saddle, handling the horse with the easy competence that came from knowing he could handle anything. That's what SEAL training did for a man. And that man was his son.

All of a sudden, Micah drew rein and waved everyone to stay back. He dismounted and squatted down. "Old tire tracks," he remarked. "Under the snow." Gently, taking great care, he brushed at the snow. After a few moments, the pressure-frozen track of a tire could be seen in a deeper layer.

"Somebody's been driving up here off and on all winter," Micah said, pointing up ahead at the rising slope between two rock faces. "See the depressions in the snow?

More tread marks under there. About the right size for a full-size pickup.''

"But not recently," Charlie Huskins said.

"Not here, no. Not since last snowfall."

"Doesn't mean anything," Nate said. "There's another way to get up to the old shack. Over on the other side of this ridge there's an easier access. I'd sure as hell choose it most of the time."

Six men exchanged looks.

"He's up there," Beau said after a moment. "I'd bet you anything he's hiding out up there."

"Okay," Nate said. "Micah, you take Charlie and Beau up this way. I'll take Seth and Dave with me around the ridge and up the other way. When we get up there, spread out and surround the shack." This way, if the guy tried to get out, he'd have to go through one group of deputies or the other to do it.

They paused a few minutes on horseback to eat some jerky and trail mix, and sip from canteens. Fifteen minutes later, they were on the move again.

Nate remembered a way over the ridge that the horses could handle, so they didn't have to backtrack all the way out of the ravine and back around the ridge. It was still slow going, though, and the afternoon was nearly over by the time they reached the shack.

And there had been plenty of tire tracks on this side of the ridge, just as he'd guessed. Recent tracks, since the last snowfall. He just hoped whoever was using the line shack was the character they wanted.

He was sure of it as soon as he saw the white pickup sitting under the trees. Smoke curled upward from a rusty stovepipe in the shack roof, and the one window was covered with cardboard. Somebody was at home here.

And Nate resented that. Resented it fiercely. His reaction was irrational, but strong. That was his and Marge's place, that old line shack. It was a shrine to memories. A shrine to all the good things in his life.

Good things he'd been busily throwing away. The thought caught him without warning, like a punch to the gut, and for several moments he couldn't even make himself breathe. What the hell was he doing?

He looked at Seth, and the younger man looked back at him from his own face. It was the strangest, eeriest sense of…of… He couldn't even name it. It was like…*destiny*, for lack of a better word. As if all the currents of fate had brought him to this shack nearly thirty years ago to create this young man and then brought him back here all these years later to meet him again. As if it had all been fixed and immutable.

"Nate?" Seth's voice was low, in deference to the quiet of the woods and the person in the shack. "Are you okay?"

"Fine, son. I'm fine." He'd called a lot of men "son" over the years, meaning nothing by it. A habit he'd picked up as an army NCO. Now he meant it. He wondered if Seth could tell that. Probably not. "Dave, radio the others and tell them we're here and ready."

They dismounted quietly, tethering their horses to trees. They'd walk the last little distance. A distance that would, Nate hoped, put an end to the blight on his county. His head started to throb a little as they climbed, but it was nothing he couldn't ignore. Far more than he wanted to get the man who had shot at him and Seth, he wanted to get the man who had put the lives, livelihood and health of the people of Conard County at risk.

He could almost taste victory.

At last they were in position, the cabin surrounded. Dave Winters had brought a bullhorn, and he used it now.

"This is the Conard County Sheriff's Department. You in the shack, come out, hands high."

For what seemed forever, nothing happened, no one moved. Nate was uneasy about just walking up to the door; after all, this guy had shot at him and Seth only yesterday. He wasn't your average, law-abiding citizen. Anyone going to the door might wind up with a bullet in him.

"In the shack," Dave said over the bullhorn. "We have you surrounded. Come out unarmed, with your hands in the air, now."

Again it seemed as if nothing was going to happen. Maybe there was no one in there. Maybe...

Then the door creaked open, and a tall, beefy man with a wizened face stepped out, his hands in the air. "What the hell's going on?" he demanded.

Dave and Micah moved in from opposite sides, and in moments had him frisked and handcuffed. Micah fished the man's wallet out of his back pocket. He flipped through it quickly and then looked at Nate across the clearing.

"It's Westin Weatherill."

Chapter 11

Sometimes the Miranda rule was a pain in the butt, Nate thought. He was far more interested in locating all the toxic waste than he was in sending Westin Weatherill to prison for dumping it. He'd have gladly violated the entire rule book to get Weatherill to talk...short of committing violence against him.

But it wasn't his decision alone. Micah was reading the guy his rights before Nate had even reached them. And Weatherill proceeded to clam up. All he would say was that he wanted an attorney.

He'd obviously been arrested before.

Because in Nate's experience, people who weren't familiar with being arrested and questioned usually blurted a great deal, despite having heard their rights. They tended to be nervous, off-balance and desperately eager to say something that might get them off. Later, when their defense attorneys had a fit, they learned that it *never* helps to talk to anyone before talking to their attorney. Weatherill had learned that somewhere.

So he probably had priors, and since none had turned up when they first checked on the name, Westin Weatherill wasn't likely to be the guy's real name. Which opened other interesting possibilities, such as what he was doing with ID in a name that wasn't his. Most people didn't go to those extremes.

And his fingerprints were probably about to become very informative.

They found the gun that had probably been used to shoot at Nate and Seth, and with the bullet that had splintered the boulder and sent the fragment flying at Nate's head, it was likely they could put Weatherill at the scene. One way or another, he was likely to be sent up the river for a while.

The truck, it turned out, was registered to Cheyenne Western Railroad, same as those flatcars. And probably didn't belong to the railroad at all.

It was with the greatest of satisfaction that Nate put Weatherill in a cell. There was more than enough circumstantial evidence for a conviction, he felt, even if the man never opened his mouth or they never uncovered another thing. But that left the problem of all the waste and where it was stashed. Maybe he could talk the prosecutor into cutting a deal in exchange for the information. They certainly had to do *something*.

"I want an attorney," Weatherill insisted yet again as the cell door closed and locked.

"You can have one," Nate snapped. "I told you that. Give me a name."

"I want that lady lawyer. Keller."

"I'll have someone call her."

Weatherill gave him a nod, but didn't voice any thanks. Not that Nate expected it.

"Call Sandy Keller," Nate growled at Velma when he got back downstairs. "Weatherill wants her to represent him."

As good a friend as Sandy was, he felt uncomfortable at the idea of seeing her again, after their discussion about divorce. Not that Sandy would allude to it in any way. No, not Sandy. But *he'd* remember. And while he was thinking about it, what the hell *was* he going to do about Marge?

"Nate?" Velma called him back as he started to turn away.

"Yeah?"

"Bethany Sykes made an appointment to see you at four. I told her you might not be back but..." Velma shrugged.

"Bethany Sykes?" He glanced at his watch, saw it was only fifteen minutes away. "Okay. Bring her back when she gets here."

And what, he wondered as he strode down the hall to his office, would the president of the Bible Study Group want with him? Other than at church functions, they never saw one another. And he couldn't imagine either her husband or her two sons *ever* doing anything of which Bethany wouldn't approve. She ruled with an iron fist.

Velma had left a stack of phone messages on the spindle on his desk, and a quick glance through them told him he was on the firing line at last over the toxic-waste dumping. Thank God they'd caught Weatherill. Now if they could just get him to say where he dumped the stuff....

"Nate?"

He looked up to see Sandy, decked out as usual in the neat navy blue suit that was her work uniform. "Howdy. The culprit's upstairs, and he hasn't said a word, Sandy."

"Well, that's good to hear. What are the charges?"

"I haven't seen Sam Haversham yet," he said, referring to the D.A., "but I'd guess it'll be illegal dumping and aggravated battery for the shooting yesterday."

She nodded again. "I heard about that. I'll go up and see him, then."

"Listen."

She paused, looking back expectantly.

"Sandy...he's the only person who knows where all that waste is dumped. The only person. It'd be real nice if you and Sam could cut a deal in exchange for info."

Sandy cocked her head a little and leaned against the doorframe. "I can't make any promises, Nate. My job is to give this guy the best defense possible. I can't let myself think about the waste issue. Because that's not *my* issue here. My issue is to provide a defense."

Nate sighed and rubbed his eyes. "I know. I know. But, damn it, just keep the possibility open. I'd rather see this sucker walk free than not find all the dumps. It's just that simple, and I'm going to explain that to Sam when I get a minute. In terms of the public good, the waste is a hell of a lot bigger threat than Westin Weatherill, or whatever his name is. By the way, I *don't* think that's his real name. We sent the prints in, and I'd bet my next paycheck that he's got prior felonies under another name.''

Sandy nodded but didn't reply directly. "You look like hell, Nate. I heard about your head.''

"It's okay. Just a crease and a few stitches.''

"You ought to get home, anyway. To Marge. I mean it.'' Without another word she turned and left.

Nate listened to her heels tapping down the hallway and wondered why the hell everybody in the world thought they had the right to offer an opinion on what he should do about his marriage. *Everybody,* from Seth to Sandy, seemed to have two cents to add.

"Nate, Bethany's here.'' The intercom reminded him that life offered no breaks.

"Bring her back, Velma.'' And somehow he knew he wasn't going to like this interview, either.

"Nate.'' Bethany nodded and entered the room, followed closely by Elvira and Endora Spitz, two spinster sisters who always wore black and invariably reminded Nate somehow of buzzards. Of all the people in his church, these three numbered among his least favorite, although Bethany managed to be charming enough when she chose.

He offered them seats, which they accepted, and coffee, which they declined. Then he returned to his chair, rested his hands on his desk and smiled. "What can I do for you, ladies?''

Bethany sighed; Nate recognized it as a prelude to unpleasant subjects. That was the unfortunate side of knowing people your entire life long. They became predictable.

She smiled sadly. "We have an unpleasant duty to perform, Nate.''

Nate felt the smile on his face freeze. All of a sudden he knew exactly what these women were here for. "Maybe you ought to just let it alone, Bethany.''

"I'm afraid we can't. The youth of the county have to be considered."

The youth of the county? He hesitated, wondering if he was misreading her intentions after all. "What's wrong with the youth?"

"Nothing is wrong with the youth. The problem is that we, as adults, must set a good example for all the children. You have an especially public position, Nate, and whatever you do is known by everyone."

Now he was sure. He let his smile vanish. "Be careful, Bethany. Be *very* careful."

She shook her head. "This isn't a time for caution, Nate. Your conduct is scandalous. You've left your wife for no apparent reason, and now you're letting her run around with some strange man! It's appalling, and it's a terrible example—"

"Bethany." He said her name quietly, flatly. A warning.

She shook her head. "Everyone's talking, Nate. A great many people are appalled by what's happening. It was bad enough that you walked out, but when everyone discovered it was because Marge was having an affair—"

He erupted then, rising from his chair and slamming his hand down onto the desk. Bethany gasped and recoiled in her chair as he leaned across his desk toward her.

"Let's get something clear here, Bethany," he said in a slick, deadly voice, "if I hear one word out of anyone's mouth against Marge, I'm going to commit violence!"

Bethany gasped again. One of the Spitz sisters—he could never tell them apart—leapt to her feet.

"Don't you threaten Bethany, Nathan Tate," she screeched, wagging her finger at him. "Don't you dare!"

Nate straightened and regarded all three of them from eyes grown as cold as a winter night. "Not one word about Marge. Not one."

The Spitz woman drew another breath, but Bethany forestalled her, reaching out to grip her arm. "He's right, Endora. Not a word about Marge. That isn't what we came for, anyway." She turned toward Nate. "It's your conduct we're concerned about. You're the law in Conard County,

Nate. Everyone looks up to you, especially the children. You need to go home and control your wife!"

It was a long moment before he could speak. During that time he fought for a self-control that seemed to be escaping him with increasing regularity. It would do no one any good for him to lose his temper, he reminded himself. No one at all. It wouldn't quiet the gossip or fix any of the problems, from the self-righteousness of these women to his marriage. No, it would only make things worse.

But still it took him nearly a full minute to find some calm from which to speak. And when he did, his voice held a flatness that was a warning. "Bethany, I don't control my wife. I never have. And it's none of your damn business, anyway. What happens between Marge and me is my business and Marge's business and no one else's. Period. As for setting an example for the youth of this county, their parents ought to be doing that. Like everyone else, I have feet of clay."

"Nate—"

He interrupted ruthlessly. "That's enough, Bethany. That is *enough.*"

And mercifully, it was. The women left, throwing him dark looks as they departed. Not two minutes later, Velma stuck her head in his door and gave him a thumbs-up.

"Good going, boss. That's telling them."

Her support genuinely surprised him. Velma had a heart as big as Wyoming, but she wasn't ever shy about telling everyone else how to run their lives. It surprised him that in this instance she thought the women should have butted out.

"Thanks, Velma."

"Don't get carried away," she said tartly. "That's not to say I agree with the mess you're making out of your life."

Before he could reply, she had turned and vanished. *Damn it,* he thought irritably. His life had turned into a three-ring circus with audience participation. *Everybody* had something to say.

And it didn't get any better.

Sam Haversham showed up just a few minutes later. "I hear you caught the dumper," the D.A. said.

"Sure looks that way. At least, he's wearing the name that was signed on the receiving papers. And I think we've got enough circumstantial evidence to charge him with aggravated battery in the shooting incident yesterday."

"I hope so, because we can't do much with an illegal dumping charge. Oh, we can fine him, but that's practically worthless if he's indigent."

"I don't think he's indigent. He *hired* Sandy Keller to defend him."

Sam's eyebrows took a quick upward hike. "Very interesting. You're thinking of the organized-crime connection."

"You got it."

"Then we need to get this guy to talk."

Nate smiled. "My thought exactly. I suggested to Sandy that she might want to keep that in mind. First of all, I need to get that waste cleaned up. I don't care whether Weatherill rots in jail or walks free, I just want the damn county safe again."

Sam nodded agreement. "Then I'll press for a charge of attempted murder."

Nate was momentarily taken aback. "How can you do that? I can't imagine how you could prove intent when he only took one shot at us! Hell, Sam, even *I* don't believe he meant to kill anybody."

"But," Sam said, "the only reason he failed to fire again was that his gun jammed. Nobody in their right mind takes *one* shot at a law officer and then runs. That's crazy. It doesn't make any sense at all. Ipso facto, he was trying to kill you and the gun jammed. Or maybe the unexpected approach of Micah and Gage scared him off."

Nate shook his head, and a grin started to spread across his face. "Hard to buy."

"I'll work on it enough to scare Weatherill. When I've got him scared good, I'll start the bargaining. One way or another, we'll get him to tell where he dumped all that stuff. Who's writing the reports?"

"Micah and Gage should have just about everything you need. I'm going to fill in the rest of it on the shooting, and

Gage found the spent bullet, so we're going to do ballistics tests on the gun that Weatherill had with him.''

"Good enough. I'll get back with you tomorrow, then. Is the prisoner upstairs?''

"With Sandy, I think. Velma can tell you if she's left or not.''

Sam rose, then hesitated, finally blowing a long breath. "Nate, about you and Marge . . .''

Nate started to shake his head, but Sam just kept talking.

"Nate, go home. There isn't anything worth ending your marriage this way. Whatever it is, work it out.''

Then without another word, the attorney turned and walked out, leaving Nate to stare at his closed door and wonder, finally, if the whole world was right and he was wrong.

Because he was sure as hell beginning to feel as if everything was wrong. Everything.

"Nate?'' Marge's stuffy voice filled his ear the following morning. "I just wondered how your head is.''

"It's fine. Marge, you sound like hell. Have you seen Doc?''

"No, I'm fine. Really. Krissie went back to school this morning.''

"But didn't she have more of her suspension left?''

"Yes, but . . . Oh, Nate, I'm so proud of her. She called Jack all on her own and promised she'd behave if he'd give her another chance. So Jack told her to come on back.''

Nate felt his chest swell with one of those wonderful bursts of pride and love that came all too rarely in life. Damn, she was *his* daughter. "But that means you're home alone.''

"Nate, I'm just *fine.*'' Marge's voice took on a slight edge, the way it always did when she thought anyone was babying her. Independent, that was Marge. Just look at the way she was already dating. . . .

And that didn't seem at all like Marge, he found himself thinking. In all honesty, despite all his doubts because of her lie, he really didn't think Marge wanted to be dating. It wasn't vanity on his part, just the simple, inescapable conviction that she had always loved him, and that she wouldn't forget that love any sooner than he would.

Which was an unsettling realization for a man who had until just days ago been hell-bent on divorce.

After he hung up the phone, he simply wasn't able to work. Marge had sounded sicker than he'd ever heard her, and she was home alone... and not getting any younger.

That thought floated to the surface of his mind and then clung like ice. It wasn't that either of them were old, because they were far from that. But... they weren't all that young anymore, either. The years were slipping past with frightening swiftness. Now here they were in their late forties and... Damn it, Marge shouldn't be sick and alone. The years she had given him deserved a hell of a lot better than that. A lot better.

In an instant he made his decision. The county owed him plenty of vacation time, and he was taking some of it right now.

Of course, that was easier said than done.

"The bail hearing is this morning before Judge Williams," Velma said, handing him a phone message. "Sam says with the attempted murder charge and Weatherill having no permanent domicile in the county, he should be able to keep him locked up."

"Well, that's good news. I'd hate to think of the sucker skipping the state. Velma, I'm going home to look after Marge. She's sick. You can reach me there if anything important comes up."

"It already has. The federal investigator is coming in this morning."

Nate swore. "Too damn bad. Tell Gage to look after him. And *Gage* can call me if he thinks it's necessary."

Suddenly Velma was grinning in a way that said she knew more than he was saying. The expression irritated him, but he couldn't say so.

"Fine, Boss," she said, and cackled. "Fine. You go on home, and I won't tell *anybody* where you are."

He scowled. "Except Gage."

"Except Gage." She laughed again and shook her head. "Get out of here before somebody finds you. Rumor is, the mayor is planning to drop in again, so scat."

Nate scatted. He liked Steve Stephanopoulos well enough, but their last meeting hadn't yet settled in his craw. He wasn't keen on a repeat. Although, with Weatherill in jail, that ought to help.

If they could find out where all the waste dumps were.

Ten minutes later he was pulling into the driveway behind Marge's Fiero and the van. Overhead, storm clouds appeared to be piling up, and he remembered that they were supposed to get some snow later today. More problems for the sheriff's department.

Inside, he found Marge drooped at the kitchen table over a cup of cold coffee. She raised her head to look at him from bleary eyes over a reddened nose. "What's wrong?" she asked.

"Not a damn thing. Sugar, you ought to be in bed." Pulling off a glove, he pressed the back of his hand to her forehead. "You've got a fever."

"Just a little one. I took some aspirin. Nate, I'm fine."

"I can tell. I'm calling Doc. You get your butt into bed."

She jumped up and glared at him. "I don't need Doc and I don't need you giving me orders. You walked out on me, Nate Tate. You walked out and you don't have a damn thing to say—"

He silenced her by the simple expedient of scooping her up into his arms and heading down the hall with her. She gasped, an outraged little sound, but he knew her anger wouldn't last. Marge always melted when he picked her up this way and carried her. Always. She loved it and had once confided that it made her feel small, safe and very feminine. He guessed with this cold she wasn't feeling very feminine, but the small and safe part were what he wanted, anyway.

She hadn't made the bed. That told him more clearly than anything how badly she was feeling, because Marge always made the bed the instant she popped out of it. He'd teased her about that over the years, but she always scowled back and told him it only took a half minute and made the room look so much better. . . .

And she hadn't even attempted it this morning.

"Nate, don't bully me." But she didn't sound very convincing, and when he lowered her to the bed, she gave a tired little sigh and relaxed.

"That's it," he said softly, brushing her tousled red hair back from her forehead. "Want me to get your nightie?"

"No." She sighed and shook her head. "I'll just take a little nap. Just a little one."

"That's good. Just a short one. I'll throw together something for lunch while you sleep."

"Why aren't you at work?"

"Because you're sick."

In the instant before he turned away, he saw her green eyes widen and heard the little catch in her breath. He didn't allow it to stop him. He kept walking, because she needed her rest. But it discomforted him to realize that in all these years he'd never stayed home from work to help her when she was sick. Never. After the girls were born, he'd hired help for her, but he'd never stayed home to do it himself.

All of a sudden that seemed like a terrible, terrible oversight.

Doc Randall said it wasn't necessary to bring Marge in; she was suffering from some goop that was running through town and she'd start getting better in a day or two. Plenty of rest and liquids. Nate almost laughed as he hung up. Marge had been right.

He fed her soup for lunch, and then when her fever climbed in the early afternoon, he sat beside her and mopped her face gently with a damp cloth.

And he wondered why he had never before taken the time to do such a soothing, caring thing for her. He'd been busy a lot. Sure. Always busy. So they'd set aside the morning hours, before the day began for the rest of the world, and sat together at the breakfast table and talked.

He missed those mornings. He missed them desperately. They had been the anchor to his days, a precious quiet time of peace. Without them he felt rudderless, adrift in strange seas. And it was affecting everything, he admitted. He didn't seem to have a life any longer, just an existence.

Marge fell asleep finally, cooler now, and he tiptoed out of the room, wondering if he wasn't being the world's greatest ass.

But truth had always been so important to him. He had always insisted on it and had very little respect for people who lied. Could he compromise a personal standard he'd held fast to for his entire life? Could he get past the lies?

But even if he did, little would be the same, he thought. Very little. He had ruptured his marriage, walked away from his wife and daughters, and broken his vow to remain through better or worse.

In the end, he found himself thinking, his transgressions were far worse than Marge's. What if she couldn't forgive *him?*

"Are you moving back home?"

Krissie asked the question the minute she got in the door from school. Before Nate could marshal a reply, a gasp from the doorway alerted him to Marge's presence. He looked that way and saw she had dressed in fresh jeans and a sweatshirt and, while still pale, she looked better than this morning.

"You shouldn't be out of bed," he said.

"I have to cook dinner for the girls."

"Since when can't I cook?"

A reluctant smile tilted up the corners of her mouth. "Since forever. I've never understood how you can cook anything over a camp fire but a stove completely defeats you."

"That's because it's electric. Sit down, sugar. I'll deal with dinner for the girls."

"Yeah," said Krissie. "We'll order pizza."

Which is exactly what they did in the end, largely because it made Marge smile and Krissie was so insistent.

Krissie brought up her question again while they ate. "Are you coming home, Dad?"

He looked around the table at each of them, at three of his daughters and the wife he had loved for so many years. Only, Marge didn't regard him with blatant hope. She kept her eyes down on her plate, but stopped eating. Stopped moving. Maybe stopped breathing. He couldn't be sure. Just as he could no longer be sure that she wanted him.

"That's something your mother and I will need to discuss just between us, Krissie."

It wasn't much of an answer, but it left the door open, and three faces, at least, looked relieved. Marge didn't look at him at all.

Maybe, he found himself thinking, he had let it go too long. Maybe she couldn't forgive him for the way he had made love to her the other night. Maybe there were too many hurts now. Maybe she was in love with Peter Little.

All the possibilities filled his head, leaving him with a horrible sense of hopelessness.

Maybe it was too damn late.

The last person Marge felt like talking to was Peter Little. If Nate hadn't still been there when he called that evening, she would have told the girls to take a message. But because Nate was there, she took the phone. What she was doing gave her a queasy feeling, but jealousy was her only weapon, the only thing she could do to force Nate to reconsider his position. It was evident to her that none of her explanations were satisfying him, that he was still completely hung up on her deceit. It seemed to her that this was the only way she could push him past the barrier and into thinking about what he was doing. About the actual consequences that would come if he pursued his course.

But she hated every moment of it. It wasn't that there was anything wrong with Pete Little; she just didn't love him. She would never, ever, love anyone but Nate. And she was willing to do just about anything moral and legal to get him back.

But this was a strategy that could easily backfire, and she knew it. It was backfiring already, as the ladies of the Bible Study Group ostracized her in subtle ways. And she'd heard about Nate's defense of her yesterday, and needed to thank him for that. She just didn't want to do it in front of the girls. They'd heard enough bad stuff since their father walked out.

And if Nate hadn't been there and listening, she'd never have agreed to go to the movies with Pete on Friday night. But because Nate was sitting there, she forced a smile into her voice and said she'd love to go to the seven o'clock show.

"I heard," Pete said suddenly, "that they caught the guy who's doing the dumping."

"Yesterday, I understand," Marge agreed. "He's in jail now. Nate's right here. Do you want to talk to him?"

Nate's ears pricked up at that, and there was a perceptible pause before Pete replied. "Nah, I don't think so, Marge. I was just making casual conversation. Wondering if the feds were getting anywhere on their end. But I can call the sheriff's office tomorrow. No point disturbing Nate during his time off."

And that was sure funny all around, she thought as she hung up the phone. A strange phone call.

"You sure you're going to be well enough to go out tomorrow night?" Nate asked gruffly.

She looked at him and had to fight an overwhelming urge to fling herself into his arms. Oh, how she needed to feel him holding her tight again, making her feel safe and loved. She needed it so badly that she ached inside. Just ached.

"Sure," she forced herself to say. "If not, I can always cancel tomorrow afternoon."

"I didn't know he was back in town again."

"He's really interested in the investigation of the dumping. He always mentions it." She tucked her legs up beneath her and folded her hands so she wouldn't reach out and touch the man she loved more than life. "He's always asking if the feds are getting anywhere."

"Why would he ask *you* that?"

Marge shrugged. "Maybe he assumes you mention your cases to me. I don't know. Does it matter?"

After the slightest hesitation, Nate shook his head. "No, I guess not. Just seems funny he'd even ask you when he always checks in with Micah or Gage about it."

Marge shrugged. "He's just making conversation."

"Yeah." He leaned over and touched her cheek lightly with the backs of his fingers. "You feel a lot cooler."

"I feel a lot better." She was almost reluctant to admit it, for fear he would leave now that she no longer needed him to look after her. But he didn't stir, just sat where he was.

And she found herself feeling as she hadn't felt since they had been in high school, not since their first few dates, when she had wondered so edgily if he would kiss her good-night. And later, when she was sure of the kisses, wondering if he would trespass just a little farther with her. Give her those delightful thrills, the heavy ache that made her yearn.

It had been so long, so very long since she had felt that anticipation and eagerness, that unsureness and fear that nothing might happen. And she was feeling it right now. Right now the heaviness was settling low in her center, making her conscious of her body, of the way her jeans hugged her. Making her feel as if something deep inside her had opened like a flower reaching for rain.

Oh, it had been so long since last she had wanted like this. So long.

"Good night, Mom, Dad."

Krissie called down the hallway, and was echoed by Carol and Patti. Marge almost smiled at the transparency of it. The girls never went to bed this early. A little matchmaking was in progress. She glanced at Nate and saw the twinkle in his eye. He knew it, too.

And that was the first twinkle she'd seen in his eyes in a long, long time. Not since before he'd found out about Seth. Her heart squeezed painfully as she faced yet again the magnitude of her crime, and the horror of the results.

And that reminded her that she owed him her thanks. "I hear you defended me to Bethany yesterday."

One corner of his mouth lifted in a wry smile she hadn't seen in a long time. "Velma?"

A soft laugh escaped Marge. "Who else?"

Nate shrugged. "It wasn't anything, sugar. She had no call to be talking about you that way. No call to be sticking her nose in somebody else's business, either. Self-righteous old biddy."

Marge laughed again. "She can be *awful*."

"Terrible."

"Overwhelming."

"Underwhelming."

"Officious."

"Cantankerous."

Marge grinned and sank back into the sofa cushion. "Cantankerous?"

"Yep. You should see how she treats her husband. A rattlesnake has a nicer temperament."

She tilted her head, unaware that her whole face softened. Indeed, everything inside her was melting with a need to reach out and touch this incredibly handsome, incredibly sexy man. Oh, Nate always joked that he looked like the weather-beaten side of a barn, but Marge thought he was good-looking. She always had thought so, even in youth, when for a while it had looked as if his face wouldn't ever grow into his nose.

And sexy as sin. He had a way of walking, of moving, of looking at people.... Well, she wasn't the only woman in the county whose heart went pit-a-pat when Nate Tate looked at her.

And Nate Tate was looking at her right now. In a way she knew as intimately as she knew his body. A way that said he wanted her. Her breath seemed to lock in her throat and she wondered achingly why he didn't reach for her. Why he didn't just hold out a hand and invite her closer. Oh, how she needed him!

And then she realized he wasn't breathing, either, that he was suspended in the same hellish anticipation and longing, that he was just as unsure about what to do as she. It

might be because of the way he felt about her since Seth. Or
it might be because she had been sick.

Slowly, as if compelled by a force out of her control, she
raised her hand and reached toward him. It was the biggest
risk she had ever taken, she thought suddenly, as her heart
hammered wildly. If he rejected her now...

His gaze lowered to her hand, then lifted to hers again,
and she saw all the tension drain out of him in the instant
before he reached out and gathered her into his arms.

At last! The feeling resounded through her in a warm
wave as Nate's arms closed around her at last. He drew her
across his lap and held her close and tight, and before she
could do more than draw a quick breath of pleasure, his
mouth covered hers and his tongue plunged into her as if it
were starved for her taste. An instant later her hand plowed
into his hair, holding him to her.

Oh, it was so beautiful! So beautiful! The dance of their
tongues was a familiar one, but freshened by separation and
fear. In fact, everything felt blessedly acute. Wonderfully
intense. She had forgotten that the touch of tongues could
be so arousing and so warming all at once. How could she
have forgotten?

But it was as if it were the very first time, and suddenly
she had no trouble remembering the sixteen-year-old girl
who had received her very first kiss from Nathan Tate, a
scruffy, angry, misunderstood young man. No trouble remembering what had impelled her to sneak away to meet the
town bad boy on lazy summer afternoons. No trouble remembering how every cell in her had yearned, until finally,
one hot afternoon, he had at last kissed her.

And how kisses had led to further excitements. How, once
his tongue had taken possession of her, it had caused her to
mewl softly and shift against him; his hands had seemed to
need to claim her, as well.

First kiss had been followed by the first touch of a male
hand to her breast, a touch that had sent an exquisite thrill
racing through her, waking her to a whole stunning new
world of sensation.

And it was happening again, right here and now as their tongues dueled and Nate's hand found its way up her side to her breast. The sensation was electrifying, and she arched eagerly into his touch, begging silently for more.

"Marge...sugar..." He lifted his head just a fraction; his mouth was still so close she could feel the movements of his lips as he spoke. "Sugar, about the other night...I'm sorry. I acted like an animal...."

"No...oh, no, Nate..." Her eyes fluttered open and her hand slipped from his hair to his cheek. "Oh, no. You didn't.... I..." There wasn't enough air to fill her lungs. She didn't want to think, didn't want to speak. All she wanted to do was love this man with every cell in her body. All she could think of was him touching her, entering her. "Nate, please...oh, please..."

He gave her a quick, hard kiss, and then astonished her by slipping one arm beneath her knees and rising with her as easily as if she weighed nothing at all.

"Nate..."

"Sugar, if you don't stop losing weight, you're going to blow away in the next squall."

She wanted to say, *Then come home, Nate. Come home.* But she didn't dare. Turning her head, she buried her face in his shoulder and said a little prayer that he was changing his mind, that he was thinking about coming back to her.

Beside the bed he lowered her feet to the floor and took her gently into his arms, holding her snugly against his chest. So much gentleness in this man, Marge thought as she often had. So much unexpected gentleness in him.

Her throat tightened and she had to blink back a tear, even as his hands began to stroke her back gently, as they ran up her arms and down to her hands.

Incredible gentleness. Sighing, she tilted her head back and offered her mouth to him. Offered herself to him. Offered everything she was and ever would be to the man she loved.

And hoped desperately that he would accept her complete offering. That he would, at last, come home.

Because she was sure she would die if he didn't.

Chapter 12

Nate backed away a step and stared deeply into Marge's eyes. Beautiful green eyes. So beautiful. His chest was so tight with a wealth of emotions that he couldn't even speak. Instead he reached for the hem of her sweatshirt and lifted it over her head.

The years had nearly made him forget, but now he remembered with a swift surge of feeling just what a priceless gift of trust she gave him when she allowed him to undress her this way. His hands trembled as he suddenly recalled the first time she had let him remove her blouse. It had been long before the first time they made love, just before he graduated from high school. Their petting had been steadily growing in intensity, their desire for one another an aching throb in the blood that just wouldn't quit. Long, lazy stolen afternoons in the barn loft or in their little shack had only fueled the need for closeness.

His hands had wandered nearly everywhere by then. Despite the impediment of clothing, he had learned all her contours, the shape of her breasts, the slope of her hips, the softness of her bottom...even the warmth between her legs.

They were driving themselves slowly crazy, but unable to help it.

Getting closer to the precipice in slow, terrifying, breath-takingly beautiful steps.

But then one May afternoon, sitting in the sunny glade just outside the shack, their kisses and caresses had become almost frantic, and without even thinking it through, he had reached for the hem of her top. He had heard her breath catch, and it had drawn him out of his haze just enough to make him aware of what he was doing.

And he had looked down into her eyes just as he was do-ing now, looked down into her heart and knew she wanted this every bit as much as he. So he had slowly, carefully, lifted her shirt off. The moment had been pregnant with significance, laden with exquisite awareness and over-whelming emotion. And all those feelings came back to him now, made his hands shake as he removed her shirt.

The sun had been shining then, brilliant afternoon light that had illuminated her creamy skin. Her bra, simple white cotton, had been so bright in that light that it almost hurt his eyes to look at it. These days she wore lacier things; then her underwear had been purely utilitarian.

And it had tightened his throat then, made him awk-wardly aware of his youth and inexperience, scared him half to death that he might hurt her as she looked so trustingly up at him.

The clasp then had been in the back; now it was in the front. Back then he had fumbled at it awkwardly, but now he released it with a practiced flip of his wrist. Back then he had nearly collapsed with sheer pleasure when he felt the clasp give. Now he almost did again just by remembering.

And for a long, precious moment, he was eighteen-year-old Nate Tate, removing Marge's bra for the first time with trembling hands and trembling heart, and a yearning so great it filled the universe. Her small breasts had been ex-posed for the first time in her life to the sun and his eyes in the same instant.

Now they were exposed once again to his gaze as he re-membered, and the love that filled him was overwhelming.

Her expression was shy, a shyness he hadn't seen in so many years... a shyness that helped sweep him back to the past when he had been a young man madly in love with a young woman who was the center of his universe.

Gently he cupped her breasts in his hands and ran his thumbs over her nipples. She drew a soft, shaky breath, telling him without words how much she enjoyed his touch. And man, did he enjoy her enjoyment.

"Lie down for me, sugar," he whispered huskily.

She folded onto the bed immediately, with an eagerness that warmed him to his soul. Bending, he unsnapped her jeans and tugged them off, along with her panties. He pulled her slippers off, too, and tossed them across the room.

She giggled.

He smiled.

And suddenly it was very all right. Standing between her legs, he undressed swiftly. And for the first time in weeks, he was fiercely glad he'd whipped his body back into shape for her, so that he could offer her a facsimile of the young man he had once been. The young man she had once, with a perfectly straight face, called a hunk. He had never been sure she wasn't teasing him, but that didn't matter now. What mattered now was that his body was once again the best he could make it... for her.

When he stretched out beside her, she turned to him eagerly, slipping her arms around his neck and pressing herself to him.

And suddenly he was back in the clearing, this time on another spring day a year later. This time he was a young man, a young man who had finished his Special Forces training and was getting ready to ship out to a distant war. And the shadow of coming separations lay like a blight on the day....

Until Marge opened her arms to him and drew him close, until her whispers and sighs filled his soul with warm balm.

Marge lay beneath him on his spread-out shirt, her eyes closed, her breath coming in soft gasps between parted lips, and his hands traveled over her with a freedom she had never allowed him before. Without clothes to come between them. Just skin on skin, heart on heart.

For the first time.

Sunlight filtered through green leaves blessed them as they rose on a rising tide of exquisite pleasure and need. As his hands learned how to give, as her inexperienced body learned how to receive. He had never been so intently focused in his entire life. He listened to each breath that escaped her, so he could tell what pleased her. Hardly hearing his own ragged breaths as he followed her up the mountain.

A bird trilled nearby as a deep, deep moan escaped her and her legs parted in ancient invitation. Marge beneath him, around him, taking him deep into the sanctuary of her love.

Marge in the grass of the clearing so long ago; Marge on the bed welcoming him now. Memory fused with the present in his mind, filling him with all the sharp need of youth, awakening a freshness within him that he had thought lost with time.

He drove deep and she lifted her legs, wrapping them around him, holding him to her.

"Nate . . . Nate . . ."

Her sighs were music in his ears, untying the last knots inside him. Unleashing him. Harder. Deeper. Faster. Feeling her nails dig into his shoulders, listening as her gasps turned into soft little whimpers and moans that fueled his passion.

"Nate . . ."

They crested together, locked in a moment of blinding intensity that left him drained.

And a few moments later, with Marge tucked safely into his arms, he drifted into warm sleep. This was how it was meant to be.

"You're not still going to the movies with Pete Little!"

Marge turned from the stove where she was frying bacon and looked at Nate. "Of course I am. He asked me, I said yes, and there's no reason I should cancel it."

"Yes there is! Last night!"

Reaching out, she turned off the element and settled her hands on her hips. "Yes, let's talk about last night. What exactly did it mean? That you're moving back in to stay? That you've forgiven me? Is that what it means?"

He opened his mouth and then snapped it closed. He wanted to say that was what it meant, he realized. He really wanted to tell her that he was coming back and ready to start over...but he couldn't. Much as he wanted it, he wasn't ready to do it. It would have been a lie to say otherwise.

Marge's lips compressed, and she whirled swiftly back to the stove. With a sharp snap of her wrist she turned the element on again. "I see," she said shortly. "Last night didn't mean anything at all." Her lower lip quivered, and she hoped he didn't see it.

"Of course it meant something!"

She blew out an impatient breath. "Right. More than Molly Garrity." The waitress at Mahoney's.

"Marge!"

"Oh, come off it, Nate. Every woman in the county knows about Molly. You men act like she's such a big secret, but we know, anyway. Just like we know you sometimes think with your hormones rather than your brains. And that's what you did last night, wasn't it?"

"No!"

"No?" She glared at him over her shoulder. "It seems last night wasn't a lot of things. Never mind. It's time you heard this from my perspective, anyway. I'm tired of feeling guilty for trying to protect you."

"Protect me?" He was nearly shouting, like a jerk, but he couldn't seem to stop himself.

"Yes, protect you, damn it! I didn't tell you about Seth after I gave him up because there was no damn point in it! No point at all! Damn it, Nate, use your head! It would only have hurt you! And I was trying to protect both of you when I didn't tell you about Seth's visit last fall."

Making a frustrated sound, she removed the frying pan to a cold burner and turned off the stove again. Then she faced Nate and let her anger bubble out. "Use your head, Nathan Tate. You're so hung up on the idea that I lied that you can't see the truth! And I'm through apologizing for trying to protect people I love. I'm through! Like it or lump it—I don't give a damn! All I ever tried to do was keep you from being hurt!''

Less than five minute later, still steaming, he was pulling into his parking lot in front of the sheriff's office. Protect him! Protect him? Hah. Sure. That's why she was going out with Pete Little tonight! To protect him!

Velma looked up when he stomped into the office, but compressed her lips and said nothing, once she'd gauged his expression. Sara Ironheart looked up from the duty desk, shook her head and resumed a report she was working on.

To hell with them, Nate thought as he stalked down the hall. To hell with them all.

"'Morning," Gage said from the opened door of his office. "How's Marge doing?"

"Fine. She's just fine." He kept moving and turned into his office. Gage followed.

"Good. Agent Lamare was sorry he missed you yesterday."

"I wasn't." Nate yanked out his chair, sat and glared up at Gage. "Did he have anything useful to say?"

"Only that there's a missing link somewhere. He's working on it. In the meantime, he wants to know anything we learn from Weatherill."

"Has Sam gotten anywhere?"

"Against Sandy? You're kidding, right? She's insisting to Weatherill that there's no way the D.A. can prosecute him for attempted murder."

"Hell!" Nate slammed his palm down on the desk.

"Come on, Nate! You know she has to do her job. Ethically she can't collude with the D.A. against her client."

"I know. I know." He sighed and passed his hand over his face. "I was hoping Sam might scare Weatherill despite Sandy's reassurances."

"Well, relax. Sam's going to push a little harder. He's insisting that he can convince any jury that Weatherill only took one shot because the approach of both Micah and me scared him off before he could take another.''

"Sounds good.''

"Good enough that Sandy made some remark about asking for a change of venue if he goes for the murder charge.''

"What? Why? Why should she need a change of venue?''

"Because she evidently feels that any jury in Conard County would be apt to convict anyone who took a potshot at our beloved sheriff, whatever his motive.''

"Oh, hell. That's hogwash!''

Gage chuckled. "Bottom line is, Sam would like the conviction, but at this point he's going to settle for cleaning up the dumps. He says he thinks he can scare Weatherill enough to bargain despite Sandy. He said to tell you that one way or another he'll make an offer than can't be refused.''

Nate nodded. "One way or another we've *got* to get to the bottom of this, and right now I feel like my hands are tied. That guy in the cell upstairs knows everything we need to know, and I can't even question him.''

"Well, you can question him, but it wouldn't do any good.''

"Not as far as a court is concerned. But it might get me the information I really need.''

Gage shook his head. "Weatherill knows the ropes, Nate. He won't say word one to you.''

"Did we ever get a rap sheet on him?''

"Not yet. We ought to have something pretty quick, I would think.''

"Yeah.'' He paused a moment, hoping that they might get something they could use as leverage on Weatherill. Not likely, but a man could hope. "Little is going to be back in town today. Second time this week.''

"Little? Oh, you mean the railroad investigator. Again?''

"Seems he's taking my wife to a movie tonight.''

Gage closed the door of Nate's office and came to sit across from him. "You want to talk about it?''

Nate shook his head, but spoke anyway. "I just don't get it, Gage. I just don't get it. Why's she dating him? I mean . . . it hasn't been that long since we split."

"Ah." Gage nodded and leaned back in his chair. "Yeah, that would get to me, too. Like maybe she never really cared about me."

"Yeah." Nate shook his head again. "I never figured her for this type."

"I don't think she is, actually."

Nate scowled at him. "Come on. She's dating the man!"

"Yeah. But there could be a lot of reasons for that. Like maybe she's trying to get your attention. Maybe make you jealous. Wake you up."

Nate once again started to shake his head, but evidently thought better of it. After a moment, he even smiled faintly. "You think?"

"I think. Come on, man. Make up your mind. Either you want to get back with her or you don't. And if you do . . . well, maybe you oughtta do something about it."

But there was still the lie, Nate thought a few minutes later, after Gage left. There was still the lie. What the hell could he do about the lie?

At noon he called Marge, thinking he could at least apologize for acting like a fool this morning, for yelling when he should have been listening. She didn't answer, leaving him even more frustrated, because now he had to wait to get this off his chest.

Just as he was hanging up the phone, Seth popped in and set some greasy brown bags on Nate's desk. "Lunch from Maude's. You haven't been eating."

Nate looked up at the tall, powerful young man who was his son and wondered if he wasn't sacrificing the present to an anger that should have burned out long ago. And would have, if the secret hadn't been kept for so long. *Protecting him*. Yeah. Maybe.

"Son," he said, "I just finished losing a middle-aged spread, and I don't want to get it back."

"No danger of that unless you eat once in a while. Maude sent steak sandwiches, fries—they're still piping hot, so why don't you start before they cool off. I hate soggy fries." As he spoke he was lifting foam containers from the bags.

"Now I can't eat dinner."

Seth shrugged. "You weren't going to eat dinner, anyway."

"Why not?"

"Because Marge is going out with Pete tonight. I figure you'll spend the evening growling and pacing." He looked at Nate and smiled faintly. "I'm getting to know you."

In spite of himself, Nate smiled back. "So I see. How'd you know about Marge's date?"

"She called me this morning, apparently right after you stomped off. She's fed up."

"No kidding."

Seth pushed the bags to one side so he could see Nate when he sat. "Well, maybe she has a little to be fed up about."

"Maybe." The uncomfortable realization had been growing in him for some time, and it was beginning to turn into a sharp pang of awareness. Walking out on Marge... Well, he'd broken his word to her. Had broken his vows. Had failed his promises. And that was surely a hell of a lot worse than a lie. Unhappily, he stared at himself and didn't like what he saw.

Then he looked across the desk at his son and wondered why he couldn't just be content with what he had now. Let the past be past and just thank God that Seth had found them, that Marge had been willing to risk everything to make sure he knew his son.

And that's what she had done, he admitted. She had made many, many hard decisions, beginning with the one to give birth to Seth and give him up for adoption. As she had thought Nate dead or utterly disinterested, it had been the best choice for their child. And look at him now, a son any father could be proud of.

And maybe it was time to acknowledge that Marge had been trying to do her best about everything, including not telling him. Surely it must have hurt, time and time again over the years, to keep her silence when she wanted to share the pain and the guilt. Surely there had been times when she had wondered about their son and longed to share her anxiety over what had become of him.

But through it all she had kept her silence so he wouldn't have to suffer, too.

Nate still didn't know what he was going to do about the lie, but there was one thing for sure. He looked at Seth. "Marge is one hell of a woman."

Seth nodded. "She sure is. You know, when I showed up here last fall, I didn't have any idea what I was going to find, but inside of three minutes she impressed the hell out of me. And it was because of her, because of her insistence that I should know you, that I came back. I started out with some kind of vague curiosity, and now I've got a whole damn family. And it's because of her, Nate. Because of Marge."

"And Krissie."

Seth smiled. "Krissie brought me back on this trip. She and I have an agreement, by the way. I told her I'd come back this summer for a visit if she'd knuckle down in school."

"Thanks." Nate cleared his throat. "I haven't told you . . . I'm glad you turned up, son. Real glad."

"So am I, actually. But I'd be a whole hell of a lot happier if you and Marge would get things straightened out."

Nate scowled. "This is between me and her."

Seth shook is head. "Everybody who cares about you two is involved. From the sound of it, that's most of the county."

"From the sound of it. I've had more two-bit advice, more busybody interference, more dire warnings . . ." He trailed off and sighed impatiently. "Don't you start now, or I'll give you what-for. I've had it with everybody sticking their noses into my business."

The intercom buzzed before he could say more, and he answered it. "Yeah?"

"Sandy Keller and Sam Haversham are here, Nate," Velma told him. "Evidently Weatherill is going to plea-bargain, and Sam wants you there during the questioning."

"I wouldn't miss it for the world, Velma."

He rose, ignoring his cooling lunch. "This is good."

Seth nodded. "I was getting around to offering to bend the guy's arm a little. Glad it's going to work out."

Upstairs, apart from the six cells, there was a small room with a barred window where prisoners could talk to their lawyers. It didn't get much use ordinarily, but it was getting used now. Nate could hear Sandy and Weatherill talking as the jailer opened the door and let him into the cell area.

"You don't have to bargain," Sandy was telling Weatherill. "They can't get you on attempted murder. There's just no way any jury is going to believe you meant to kill the sheriff."

"The aggravated battery charge'll stick," Weatherill said. "If Haversham is willing to let me go on a misdemeanor, I'll give him what he wants. No way I'm going to jail. No way. I'd never come out alive."

"Why not?" Nate asked as he stepped into the conference room. "Why wouldn't you come out alive?"

"I know too much."

Nate wanted to pursue that, but he hesitated when he saw that Haversham wasn't there. "What happened to Sam? I thought he was here."

"He went back downstairs for a minute," Sandy said.

"Yeah." Weatherill gave a sour smile. "I think my rap sheet just arrived."

More and more interesting, Nate thought. Stepping into the room, he settled on a chair against the wall and folded his arms across his chest. "I'll tell you, Weatherill, I'm giving you the benefit of the doubt on shooting at me and Seth. What I want is to know where you dumped all that crap before some kid gets poisoned or some rancher gets put out of business."

Surprising Nate, Weatherill shifted and looked uneasy. "I didn't think about that," he said after a moment. "I was just dumping that crap out of the way, you know? It was easy money just to stash some barrels where no one ever goes. I didn't think about the stuff leaking or making anybody sick.''

Nate actually believed him.

"Okay," said Sam Haversham, entering the room briskly. "I've got your rap sheet here, Weatherill. You've got an interesting record."

"I know it by heart."

"I'll bet you do." Sam pulled out a chair and sat at the table next to Sandy and across from Weatherill. "Okay, your real name is Gary Weathers, and you have priors for all kinds of little stuff. I'm not really interested in that. What interests me is your organized-crime connection."

Nate unfolded his arms and leaned forward. He gave a low whistle, and Sam looked at him. "The Corelli family," Sam said. "Mr. Weathers here evidently used to make his living by being muscle."

"Just little stuff," Weathers said. "Nothing big."

"Well, we know organized crime is involved in this dumping scheme," Nate said. "At least, that's the conclusion the feds have reached. The Corellis, huh?"

"I didn't say anything about the Corellis being involved," Weathers said hastily. "I never said they had anything to do with this."

"No, I guess you didn't," Sam said soothingly. "Look, I'm not trying to get you in worse trouble, Weathers. We just want to get the mess cleaned up before some kid gets hurt. That's all we're interested in. If the feds can draw the connection to organized crime, that's fine. For my purposes, I just want to know where all the dump sites are. Then I'll charge you with misdemeanors on the dumping, and you can walk, okay?"

"That's okay by me," Weatherill said.

Sandy spoke. "Okay, Sam, but I'm drawing some limits here. You can't ask my client anything about other possible crimes or about past connections to crime families. The questioning has to be strictly limited to the locations of the dump sites. If you step out of that narrow area, the questioning will be stopped."

"That's all I'm asking for."

Nate rose. "Let me go downstairs and get a map of the county. It'll be easier to mark the locations."

Weathers nodded. "It'd be a lot easier than trying to describe, that's for sure."

Two hours later, map in hand, Nate and Gage set out to verify the information Weathers had given them. By dusk, they had inspected four of the sites and found more barrels, none of which had yet spilled.

"I hope the news is as good tomorrow when we check out the rest," Nate said. In all, Weathers had marked fourteen as-yet-undiscovered sites. An appalling amount of toxic materials had been scattered around.

"I just hope Weathers has remembered all the places he dumped the stuff."

Nate glanced over at Gage, who was little more than a dark shadow in the dim light from the dashboard. "Thanks for the thought. It'll keep me up tonight."

Just then the radio crackled and Velma's voice demanded his attention.

"What's up?" Nate asked her.

"Amanda Laird just called. Says her husband found another waste dump and wants to know if you can run out there."

Nate glanced at Gage. "Oh, hell. Yeah, Velma. Call Mandy back and tell her I'll be there in about thirty minutes. And call Haversham and tell him that Weathers evidently neglected to tell us about a site."

"Will do."

A glance at the digital clock on the console told him it was only four-thirty, still early despite the darkness. Clouds hid the moon, but the snow reflected enough light to create an eerie sort of visibility.

"We'll have to question Weathers some more," Gage remarked.

"Yeah. But the real question is, did he just forget, or is he deliberately withholding?"

"Why would he do that? What possible reason could there be to conceal some of the dump sites?"

"Maybe because of what's there."

Gage turned to look at him. "Come again?"

"So far we've found the usual chemicals. PCBs, PVCs, just the ordinary carcinogens. What if something far worse has been dumped out here?"

"Like what?"

"Radioactive materials. Hospital waste. Something that would *really* get people bent. Something that maybe could cause big trouble somewhere up the line for the people who were getting rid of it."

"RAM would be the likeliest stuff to cause that kind of a problem," Gage said slowly. "All radioactive stuff is supposed to be very seriously controlled. Very carefully controlled. I don't have any idea what the penalties are, though."

"Well, I can tell you, folks around here would get so seriously bent about being used as a nuclear waste dump that there'd probably be a congressional investigation."

"Which could make life really hot for some folks."

Nate glanced at Gage. "Let's go see what Ransom found. Maybe it was just something Weathers forgot about. I hope."

Ransom Laird greeted them at his kitchen door when they arrived, and invited them in for coffee. Mandy joined them a few moments later carrying their seven-month-old son Justin.

"You'll have to look at it in the morning," Ransom said after he'd poured coffee for everyone, "but these aren't steel drums like were found elsewhere. They're smaller cylinders, and they're warm. They've melted the snow around them, which is the only reason I even noticed them. Either some kind of chemical reaction is going on inside them, or they're radioactive. Either way, I don't want to fool with it."

"We'll bring a disposal team out in the morning," Nate promised. He spent a few minutes holding Justin, who was his godson, and soaking up the little boy's ready smiles.

He'd missed that with Seth, he found himself thinking. Missed all these little things.

But the wave of resentment wasn't as strong, and it gave way readily to warmer feelings, memories of his daughters in their infancy and delight in the child he held right now. Grandkids, he found himself thinking. That's what he needed. Grandkids.

Ten minutes later, he and Gage were back on the road, headed into town. "I think we need to talk to Weathers again," Nate remarked.

"Sure looks that way. I don't like the sound of those cylinders at all."

"Me neither." In fact, his gut was knotting tightly again, an unpleasant, heavy ache that made him reach for the antacids he always had in his pocket. "Hell, how much you wanna bet we have a congressman out here by Monday? And the governor."

Gage snorted. "It wouldn't surprise me."

And the mayor and the commissioners, Nate thought with a weary sigh. Yep, as soon as they heard about this, they were going to be all over him. All over him.

And what he wanted to do right now was shake Gary Weathers until the man's teeth rattled.

Back at the office, he called Sam Haversham first. "Weathers didn't tell us everything. Ransom Laird just found another dump site, this one as suspicious as hell. Don't tell a soul, Sam, but I suspect it's radioactive material."

"Hell!"

"We need to question Weathers again. Now."

"Yeah. I'll call Sandy. Give me forty-five minutes to get there."

Velma had gone home for the night, leaving only the duty deputy out front to act as dispatcher. Beau Beauregard was on tonight, and willing to engage Nate in casual conversation as he waited for Sam and Sandy to show up.

It helped a little—helped Nate keep from thinking about Marge going out to the movie with Pete Little tonight. Hell, he didn't even know if she was going to the early show or the late show. Maybe he ought to go over and stay with the girls when he got done here. He was sure it had to be bothering them as much as it bothered him that she was dating. Maybe more.

And it was all his damn fault. Somehow, someway, he had to get around this lie hang-up. When he really, really thought about it, it seemed kind of stupid, actually. Apart from protecting him from knowledge that could only hurt, she had been protecting herself from losing him . . . and he couldn't tell her she wouldn't have lost him, not when he'd walked out over Seth all these years later.

It pained him to look back and remember the young soldier he'd been, back from his first tour in Nam, full of memories of the Montagnard people he had been living with, convinced of the righteousness of his cause, full of idealism and confidence. Seeing so clearly that everything was black and white, with no gray middle ground. He'd learned about grays during his next tour, learned them in agonizing ways, but at the time he had come back and married Marge . . . No, he wouldn't have understood why she gave the child up, why she didn't just tough it out. Full of his Special Forces confidence and arrogance, he wouldn't have understood. He'd have believed her weak.

And now, in a very similar black-and-white way, he was hung up on a lie that had occurred a long, long time ago. Damn it, it wasn't as if he thought she lied to him all the time about lots of things. It wasn't her basic truthfulness he doubted at all. He was just angry and hurt and acting like a fool. He kept calling her a liar when he didn't really believe it at all.

He was striking out at her because he felt she had hurt him.

And maybe it was time he got around to admitting that. To her. To himself. He didn't think Marge was a liar at all. He had been shaken; who wouldn't be? His internal image of his marriage, of himself, his wife, his children . . . all of it had been changed in an instant. Nothing would ever look the same again. And in reaction to that discomfiting experience, he had seized on the one thing he could grasp, the one thing he could rail at. The one thing he could blame.

But was anyone really to blame? Himself, for not keeping his pants on, as Krissie had said? Marge, for giving herself to him just before he left for Vietnam? Her father, for interfering with the mail? Marge, for believing he was dead?

If anyone really held any blame, it was Marge's father. And even *he* had been trying to do what he believed best for his daughter.

The road to hell was paved with good intentions. Yep. And they'd sure paved one hell of a road this time. But it absolutely wasn't fair to blame anyone for this. There was no blame. There was only a lot of people doing the best they could with the situation they found themselves in.

And that wasn't worth turning his back on the only woman he'd ever loved. The woman he still loved with his whole heart.

And all of a sudden he was damned impatient with having to wait for Sam and Sandy, with being stuck here to question Weathers again. He ought to be home, fighting for Marge. Fighting for his marriage.

Fighting for his life.

Instead he was stuck here, fighting for everyone else. Well, that was typical. He'd been doing precisely that for a long time. It was his job. It was his duty. Ordinarily he never counted the cost, but right now it was all he could think of. Marge would be going out with Pete Little, and he damn well ought to be there to stop her.

Sandy Keller stepped into the office just ahead of Sam Haversham, and with them came an icy blast of winter air.

"It's snowing again," Sam announced. "Didn't mean to take so long, Nate, but the roads are getting slippery."

"No problem." Like hell. He rose to help Sandy with her coat.

"What exactly did you find?" she wanted to know.

"Ransom Laird found some cylinders dumped on his property." He turned and hung her coat on a peg. "He says they melted the snow around them, which means they're generating heat of some kind."

Sandy tilted her head back and looked straight up at him. "Radioactive waste?"

"That's what I'm worrying about. Anyway, it sure as hell wasn't on the list that Weathers gave us, so we need to know what else he omitted telling us. This is dangerous, Sandy."

She nodded but didn't address the issue directly. Instead she looked at Sam. "The plea bargain still holds—no new charges based on anything he says."

Sam nodded. "Absolutely. Same game, same rules. But I want to know why he lied the first time out. He wasn't keeping our agreement."

"Maybe he didn't dump this stuff."

And that thought chilled Nate to the bone.

Chapter 13

Upstairs, the three of them sat around the long table with Weathers again. He looked uneasy and kept shifting impatiently in his chair, as if he wanted to flee. Since the only exit was barred, Nate wasn't worried about him attempting anything.

"Okay," Sam said conversationally. "It seems you forgot about a dump when you gave us the information earlier. One was discovered this afternoon at the Laird place, and we're a little upset because it appears to be radioactive material."

Weathers blanched visibly. "I don't know nothing about it."

"You'd certainly remember this dump," Sam said firmly. "These weren't steel drums but cylinders. Round tubes. Do you remember them?"

Weathers shook his head quickly. Maybe too quickly. "I didn't dump anything like that. Not me."

Nate smothered a frustrated sigh and paced to the barred window. Snow fell gently, illuminated by the streetlights around the courthouse square. A car drove slowly down Front Street. Someone came hurrying out of a store across the square. Ordinary sights on a winter evening. The movie theater would be crowded: at least he could take solace in that.

And he didn't need to be thinking about Marge and her date. Like it or not, that person who had just come out of the store could eventually be harmed by what had been dumped around this county. He or his children might be seriously at risk. Marge was something he could deal with a little later. Right now he had to get to the bottom of this dumping.

He turned and looked at Weathers. "Kids play out in the gullies and draws all the time, Weathers. You know that. Especially in the late spring, when there's plenty of running water to fool around in. Benzene was found in one of those barrels you dumped. Are you aware that exposure to benzene is *known* to cause leukemia in children?"

Weathers looked away.

"Some of the stuff had a high lead content," Nate continued harshly. "You've certainly heard about the risks to children in that. And then there was mercury. Incredibly toxic stuff. And if you survive mercury poisoning, you have to live with aftereffects the rest of your life. Of course, a lot of the stuff is just carcinogenic. That's easy enough to ignore. After all, it doesn't show up for years and years. Hard for you to care if Conard County develops a higher-than-usual rate of cancer twenty or thirty years down the road.

"I won't even talk to you about the risk to the groundwater, and the cattle ranchers, and how tainted water could put them right out of business. How you could actually be wiping out people's livelihoods by concealing the whereabouts of this stuff.

"But I *am* going to talk to you about radioactive waste. About kids who play out in those gullies and would probably want to open those canisters. Have you ever seen a radiation burn? Do you know just how awful radiation sickness is? It can take up to two weeks to die, and it's not an easy way to go. Not an easy way at all. I can describe it to you—"

"Never mind," Weathers said sharply. "Never mind. I'm telling you, I didn't dump any canisters! It wasn't me!"

Nate stared at him for a long silent moment, as he began to understand. "Why don't you tell us who *did* dump them?"

Weathers paled visibly and jerked his head in a sharp, instinctive negative, but he didn't speak.

Nate crossed the room and half sat on the edge of the table so that he could look straight at Weathers. "There's someone else, isn't there? You're protecting someone."

Weathers shook his head again and looked away.

"Then you're protecting yourself," Nate said forcefully. "A mob connection?"

Still no answer.

Sam spoke. "The deal is off, Sandy. I'm pushing for aggravated battery."

"Now wait a minute, Sam. My client told you about all the places he dumped the waste. You can't renege—"

"I'm not reneging," Sam said sharply. "The deal was he would tell us everything he knows about the dumping. It's as obvious as the nose on my face that he knows something he's not telling. The deal's off."

"You can't be sure of that!"

Sam stood and leaned across the table to glare at Sandy. "What I can be sure of is that a dump was found this afternoon. A dump that wasn't mentioned by your client. That's all I need to hear."

"He said someone else did it."

Sam straightened. "Right. Well, let him prove it. Otherwise I have to believe he did it, and that he's trying to conceal the fact. And *that's* enough to negate the deal."

Sam turned toward the door. Nate hesitated only a fraction longer, reluctant to end the questioning if there was any hope of finding out more. Suddenly Weathers spoke.

"If I tell you everything, I walk?"

Sam turned around and faced him. "You walk, as soon as we substantiate what you say."

"Nothing will keep me here? I can just disappear?"

"That's right. Leave for Rio or run to Alaska. It's up to you."

Weathers looked at Sandy. "You believe him?"

Sandy scowled at Sam but nodded. "Yes, I believe him. The question here is what he means by 'everything.'"

Sam sat. "All the dump sites. And if there's something out there that he didn't dump, I want to know who dumped it."

"Maybe he doesn't know who else—"

"He knows," Nate interjected. "He knows. Don't you, Weathers?"

Weathers stared at him while long seconds ticked by, and then he looked at Sam. "I walk?"

Sam nodded. "When I'm convinced you've told me all you know, you walk."

More seconds ticked by, and then Weathers nodded. "Okay. But if he finds out I told you, I'm dead meat."

That immediately brought a new concern. Sam held up a hand. "We may need your testimony."

Weathers shook his head. "No. No. I'll tell you, and then I'm outta here. You get the evidence you need some other way. They'll kill me."

Sam looked at Nate. Nate nodded. "If we know where to start looking, we can probably get anything we need. Go for it."

"Okay," Sam said. "That's the deal. You walk. Scot-free."

"Okay. Okay. The guy who hired me to do the dumping is Pete Little from the railroad."

Nate swore explosively. Every instinct in him screamed for him to go get Little right now, to wrest Marge away from that snake and put him behind bars. But he couldn't do that, not without something more to go on than one man's statement.

Sam looked at him, almost seemed to read his mind, then turned back to Weathers. "We need more, Gary. We can't go after Little based on that—unless you want to swear a statement."

Weathers shook his head. "No way. I'd be safer going to jail. I met Pete Little when I was enforcing for Joe Corelli. Pete's married to Joe's daughter. Anyway, Joe had this operation for handling all that toxic stuff, but things were getting hot on the coast, I guess. At least, that's what I was told. People didn't want to have processing plants in their towns. Regulations started getting really tough. It was starting to cost money. So Joe put the screws to Pete, to get him to figure out how to move the stuff by railroad so he could just get rid of it cheaply and close down his operations."

Nate nodded. "How did he put the screws on Pete?"

Weathers gave a little shrug. "Pete's a high roller. I guess he owed some nasty people some money. Joe made helping with the waste a condition of paying Pete's debts. Anyway, Pete figured out how to ship the stuff to the middle of nowhere, and then he put the screws to me to get me to help."

"Why you?"

"Because I used to be a cowpoke before I wised up and figured out you don't get rich herding cattle. Pete knew about it, and figured it'd make a good cover for me to be out here while I was stashing the stuff." He shrugged again. "It did, too."

"And what about after the derailment?" Nate asked. "Why didn't you guys just clear out?"

"Because Joe wouldn't let us. He wanted Pete to stay right on top of it so he could know what the feds figured out. And Pete wanted me to lie low, but right where he could keep an eye on me. Said we might have to move some of the stuff quick, and he couldn't do it alone. So I hung out at the shack. Then I remembered about those damn shipping papers and I went out there to get them back, only you were already there, and I...well, I got scared. I wanted to get you away so I could get down there to get the papers. They've got the name of Corelli's company on them, and I knew you'd figure it all out. So I...tried to scare you, only those other guys started driving up, so I had to clear out." He shook his head.

"The shipping papers." Nate looked at Sam. "They'll nail Corelli, all right, if they really do have his company name on them. I need to call the feds to find out if they've deciphered them yet." He looked at Weathers again. "What about the steel cylinders? What do you know about them?"

Weathers shook his head. "Not a whole lot. There was some stuff in one of the shipments that Pete said he'd take care of. I didn't ask. I'd guess that was the cylinders, though. And that's all I know."

Sam looked at Nate. "Well?"

"I can work with this. In fact, I think I'll go question Little right now. I'll just let him think the shipping papers have given away the scam and that we're questioning him because he's married to Corelli's daughter. Maybe he'll talk, maybe he won't. I can hold him for up to seventy-two hours for questioning, though."

Sam nodded. "Do it."

Nate shook his head. "And just think of that snake dating my wife while he's married."

"He's not dating your wife, Sheriff," Weathers said. "He's using her to make sure nothing is going on that you're not telling him about. He figures you talk to her about your work."

"Son of a bitch," Nate said. "Son of a bitch."

Without another word, he turned and stalked out.

Marge and Pete had gone to the early show, Krissie said. In fact, Marge had made a point of telling the girls she was coming straight home, and so she wouldn't be any later than nine-thirty.

The theater was on the edge of town in a big steel building with a large, rutted parking lot. By the time the first show let out, Nate had four deputies out there with him. And Seth, who stood to one side near the entrance, observing.

He really wasn't expecting any trouble; after all, he only wanted to question Little, and all Little had to do was refuse to answer any questions. But legally he could hold the man for seventy-two hours without charging him, and it seemed like time to do that. Time to detain him while everybody scrambled to get to the bottom of it. And maybe, in the process, find out just where he'd dumped all that other stuff.

As usual, when the movie was over, there was a double crowd—the people lined up for the late show at one entrance, and the group departing from the early show surging out the other. Marge always liked to wait until most of the crowd was gone, and tonight appeared to be no exception. By the time she appeared inside the lobby, walking with Little, almost all the people who'd come out first were in their cars and pulling away. Which suited Nate just fine. With a nod, he signaled his deputies into place.

As soon as Marge and Pete stepped through the door into the cold night air, Nate accosted them.

"Pete, I need you to come with me to the office."

The other man's expression immediately grew tense. "Is something wrong?"

Nate cocked his head. "We just need to talk to you. Ask you a few questions."

"Am I being arrested?"

Nate shook his head. "Nope. Like I said, we just need to ask you a few things."

"Well, why don't I take Marge home first and then come by?"

Nate shook his head, never letting his gaze wander from Little's face. "No, I need you to come right now, please. One of my men will take Marge home. Marge, Charlie will take you."

He saw the instant Little realized for certain that he had been found out. It suddenly flickered across his face. Instinctively, Nate reached out to tug Marge to his side, but it was too late. To his horror, Little was armed, and in one swift movement he had his arm around Marge's throat and a gun to her head.

"You'd better move everybody back, Sheriff," Little said harshly. "Everybody. I'm going to get in my car and drive away, and if you don't bother me I'll leave your wife someplace safe."

"Don't be a fool," Nate said hoarsely. "Damn it, now you're in serious trouble. Taking a hostage— Damn it, man! Let her go! Dumping isn't even a serious crime!"

Little shook his head. "Get everybody back, Sheriff. Everybody."

Nate glanced at Marge, looked deep into her frightened green eyes and knew he had been the world's biggest fool. "I love you," he said.

"Get back now!" Little demanded, his voice strained. "Now!"

Nate held up his hands and began backing up. "Everybody stand back. Move back. Give the man some room."

And everybody, deputies and the handful of civilians alike, eased back, opening a huge circle around Little and his hostage. Only Seth didn't move. In his dark clothing, he nearly blended into the shadows to the right and behind Little.

"I need to send someone into the theater," Nate told the man as he backed up another step. "To make sure nobody comes out behind you."

"I don't want a deputy behind me!"

"What'll happen if somebody comes out that door? Are you going to kill my wife because some kid decides he doesn't like the movie?"

Little hesitated visibly, then began easing sideways, bringing Marge along with him, her feet stumbling as she struggled for balance. Seth, Nate noticed, edged in the same direction, keeping himself right behind Little. It was going to be all right. There wasn't a man in the world other than Micah Parish that Nate would rather have relied on right now. He knew Seth's training, knew Seth was capable of taking Little while protecting Marge. No, he couldn't have asked for a better man.

He looked at Marge again, trying to tell her with his expression that she was going to be all right. Her gaze clung to him, and while fear pinched her face, her expression was one of utter trust. Marge didn't doubt that he would get her out of this. His heart squeezed painfully and he wanted to look at Seth, to see surety reflected in his son's face. But he didn't dare, for fear Little would realize that there was someone behind him.

Dragging his eyes from Marge's face, he focused on the man who held her life in his hands. "Taking a hostage is a big mistake, Little. Violation of ICC regulations would have got you nothing but a fine. Yeah, you'd have lost your job, but you could find another one. Now you're looking at criminal charges."

"I was looking at them, anyway. You think I don't know Weathers spilled the beans and told you I was with him when he shot at you?"

"What makes you think Weathers said anything at all?"

"What makes you think you can keep a secret in this one-horse town? What do you think the first words Marge said to me tonight were? 'Isn't it wonderful that the dumper is cutting a deal with the D.A.?'"

Nate glanced at Marge, astounded. "I never told her that."

Little laughed harshly. "You didn't have to. That dispatcher of yours tells her everything."

Velma! So help him, he was going to roast that woman over hot coals... just as soon as he got Marge out of this mess. "You being there doesn't mean you were part of the crime."

"Right." Little shook his head and inched to the side some more. "Let me get to my car, Sheriff. Let me leave. If you don't follow me, I'll drop your wife off someplace safe with a quarter to call home."

The thought of this man driving off with his wife left Nate chilled to the very bone. No way. Absolutely no way.

"Look, Little, we can talk this out. We can work something out so that nobody gets hurt and you don't have to run."

"Don't have to run?" Little shook his head and laughed wildly. "Man, you don't know who my father-in-law is. When he hears about this—"

"Corelli is already talking to the feds," Nate said on impulse. "Right now. You might as well give up."

Little seemed to freeze. And in that instant, Seth sprang.

Nate's heart slammed into his throat as Seth leapt out of the shadows in one smooth movement and with all the speed and agility of a striking snake managed to lock one arm around Little's throat and grab the gun with his other hand.

Nate leapt forward in the same instant, catching Marge right up off her feet and running with her just as fast as he could go. Not until he had her around the corner of the building did he stop.

"Stay here," he whispered sharply as he set her on her feet. Then, cautiously, he peered back around the corner and saw that Little was on the ground and one of his deputies was cuffing the man.

Then and only then did he turn and take Marge into his arms. Holding her just as tight as he could get her, he thanked God for giving him another chance.

It was almost dawn. The girls were sound asleep, unaware of all the excitement of the night before, when Nate at last brought Marge home. They moved quietly as they stepped in from the icy night. The warmth of the kitchen, the familiar sounds of the refrigerator and the aroma of Marge's potpourri wrapped around Nate, giving him a blessed sense of homecoming.

Turning, he helped Marge out of her jacket and hung it on a peg. His own hat and jacket went right beside it.

"Seth was really something tonight, wasn't he?" Marge asked.

Nate didn't begrudge any of the pride in her voice; he was proud as punch of his son, too. "Yes, he was."

She smiled up at him, but the shadows were still in her eyes, he realized. Shadows of the wounds he had dealt her. He still needed to deal with what he had done and, by God, he didn't know how he would ever manage to convince her that he had been a fool but had come to his senses at last.

"Coffee?" she asked.

He nodded because he didn't know what else to do. Coffee would give them a reason to sit at the table and talk. Would give him a reason to linger until he could find words to say what needed saying.

But as Marge brushed past him, he forgot everything except the need to hold her close. His arms wrapped around her snugly, and he held her to his chest.

"Marge . . . Marge, I love you. Oh God, I love you!"

And suddenly she was clinging to him as hard as she could, sobbing wild tears into his shirtfront. "Nate . . . Nate . . ."

She wasn't any more coherent than he, and several moments passed before he realized his own tears were falling to join hers on his chest.

Marge realized it at almost the same moment. Slowly she lifted her tear-streaked face and looked at him. And for the first time since Vietnam, Nathan Tate wept openly. "Marge," he whispered brokenly. "Oh God, sugar, I've been such a fool!"

Another sob escaped Marge as she lifted trembling fingers to his cheek and touched the wetness there. "Oh, Nate . . . oh, Nate, we've both been fools!"

He shook his head and drew a deep, steadying breath. "I was wrong. Honey, I was so wrong. I never stopped trusting you. I never thought you were a liar. I was just so hurt . . . I acted like an ass. I struck out at you."

"I know. I know. Oh, Nate, I know! I know you were hurt! I never should have kept it from you. It was so wrong! And then . . . oh, Nate, you weren't the only one who was striking out in anger. I went out with Pete just because I knew it made you mad. Just because I knew you'd be furious and maybe jealous, and I wanted to make you jealous. . . ."

She buried her face against him and he held her tightly, stroking her hair, whispering over and over that he loved her. And one after another, his tears fell into the soft waves of her red hair.

"I've been trying," he said roughly. "I've been trying for days to find a way to tell you what a fool I've been. To tell you how sorry I am. To ask you to forgive me. Will you take me back, Marge?"

Tears were still streaming down her cheeks when she tilted her head back again to look up at him. "Can you forgive me?"

"There's nothing to forgive," he told her. "Nothing at all. Damn it, Marge, despite all my ranting and raving, the truth is I know you damn well did your best. Hell, if you'd told me back then . . . well, I probably would have acted like a self-righteous prig, and I know it."

It seemed almost as if a corner of her mouth twitched with humor, and he definitely thought he saw the hint of an old familiar sparkle in her green eyes. "You're sure?" she asked.

"Nothing to forgive," he said. "Nothing at all to forgive, sugar."

"Then I have nothing to forgive, either. Nothing at all to forgive. Oh, Nate, I love you, and all I want in the world is for you to come home!"

"That's all I want, too, Marge. That's *everything* I want."

It would take time, he thought as he held her snugly to his chest, time to erase the shadows of all they had done to each other. Time to heal the hurts and mend the wounds. Forgiving and forgetting were two different things.

But they'd make the time, he knew. They'd make all the time they needed to heal because their love was worth the effort.

Worth rescuing.

* * * * *

Look for Rachel Lee's next Conard County book, *Thunder Mountain*—an August 1994 Shadows release.

INTIMATE MOMENTS® Silhouette™

It's those rambunctious Rawlings brothers again!
You met Gable and Cooper Rawlings in IM #523
and IM #553. Now meet their youngest brother,
Flynn Rawlings, in

THE WILD WEST

by Linda Turner

Fun-loving rodeo cowboy Flynn Rawlings
couldn't believe it. From the moment he'd
approached beautiful barrel racer Tate Baxter,
she'd been intent on freezing him out. But Tate
was the woman he'd been waiting for all his life,
and he wasn't about to take no for an answer!

Don't miss FLYNN (IM #572), available in June.
And look for his sister, Kat's, story as
Linda Turner's thrilling saga concludes in

THE WILD WEST

Coming to you throughout 1994...only from
Silhouette Intimate Moments.

IT'S OUR 1000TH SILHOUETTE ROMANCE,
AND WE'RE CELEBRATING!

JOIN US FOR A SPECIAL COLLECTION OF LOVE STORIES
BY AUTHORS YOU'VE LOVED FOR YEARS, AND
NEW FAVORITES YOU'VE JUST DISCOVERED.
JOIN THE CELEBRATION...

April
REGAN'S PRIDE by **Diana Palmer**
MARRY ME AGAIN by **Suzanne Carey**

May
THE BEST IS YET TO BE by **Tracy Sinclair**
CAUTION: BABY AHEAD by **Marie Ferrarella**

June
THE BACHELOR PRINCE by **Debbie Macomber**
A ROGUE'S HEART by **Laurie Paige**

July
IMPROMPTU BRIDE by **Annette Broadrick**
THE FORGOTTEN HUSBAND by **Elizabeth August**

SILHOUETTE ROMANCE...VIBRANT, FUN AND EMOTIONALLY
RICH! TAKE ANOTHER LOOK AT US! AND AS PART OF THE
CELEBRATION, READERS CAN RECEIVE A FREE GIFT!

YOU'LL FALL IN LOVE ALL OVER
AGAIN WITH
SILHOUETTE ROMANCE!

CEL1000

If you are looking for more titles by

RACHEL LEE

Don't miss these fabulous stories by one of
Silhouette's most renowned authors:

Silhouette Intimate Moments®

#07370	AN OFFICER AND A GENTLEMAN	$2.95	☐
#07394	SERIOUS RISKS	$3.25	☐
#07430	DEFYING GRAVITY	$3.39	☐
#07463	CHEROKEE THUNDER	$3.39	☐
#07482	MISS EMMALINE AND THE ARCHANGEL	$3.39	☐
#07494	IRONHEART	$3.39	☐
#07535	LOST WARRIORS	$3.50	☐

Silhouette Shadows®

#27010	IMMINENT THUNDER	$3.50	☐

(limited quantities available on certain titles)

TOTAL AMOUNT	$
POSTAGE & HANDLING	$
($1.00 for one book, 50¢ for each additional)	
APPLICABLE TAXES*	$_____
TOTAL PAYABLE	$_____
(check or money order—please do not send cash)	

To order, complete this form and send it, along with a check or money order
for the total above, payable to Silhouette Books, to: **In the U.S.:** 3010 Walden
Avenue, P.O. Box 9077, Buffalo, NY 14269-9077; **In Canada:** P.O. Box 636,
Fort Erie, Ontario, L2A 5X3.

Name:_____

Address:_____ City:_____

State/Prov.:_____ Zip/Postal Code:_____

*New York residents remit applicable sales taxes.
Canadian residents remit applicable GST and provincial taxes.   RLBACK1

Silhouette ®
TM